Advance Praise for The Bang Devils

"Pop violence, wild writing, electrifying scenes, and an in-your-face plot that keeps you bleeding from the eyes as you rip from page to page. . . . Patrick Foss knows how to grab the reader by the throat and keep him gasping until the last sentence crackles away. *The Bang Devils* is big, badass, relentless contempo-noir entertainment."

—Jerry Stahl, author of *Plainclothes Naked*
and *Permanent Midnight*

"Brash and devilishly entertaining."
—*Kirkus Reviews*

"*The Bang Devils* moves faster than a yakuza punk on speed. If post-bubble Japan has become the capital of Dystopia, then *The Bang Devils* may well become this wasted generation's user's manual."

—Karl Taro Greenfield,
author of *Speed Tribes*

About the Author

Patrick Foss lives and works in Japan. He is currently working on his second novel.

To receive notice of author events and new books by Patrick Foss, sign up at www.authortracker.com.

An Imprint of HarperCollins*Publishers*

THE Bang Devils

Patrick Foss

HarperCollins books may be purchased for educational, business, or sales promotional use. For information please write: Special Markets Department, HarperCollins Publishers Inc., 10 East 53rd Street, New York, NY 10022.

FIRST EDITION

Designed by Renato Stanisic

Library of Congress Cataloging-in-Publication Data

Foss, Patrick (Patrick W.)
    The bang devils / Patrick Foss.—1st ed.
      p. cm.
    ISBN 0-06-055477-0
     1. Americans—Japan—Fiction. 2. Kidnapping—Fiction.
3. Japan—Fiction. I. Title.

PS3606.O749B36 2003
813'.54—dc21   2003053168

---

03 04 05 06 07 JTC/RRD 10 9 8 7 6 5 4 3 2 1

For my brother

Acknowledgments

To everyone on the list that follows, thank you. You know why.

Lee Colglazier
Chris Foss
Tom & Rita Foss
Mutsuo Ishibe
Sean Kramer
David Langie
Yuri Sakamaki
Andrew Vienneau

Loren Soeiro
Sandy Blanton

Mike Shohl

And, of course, Nobuko

Plus a tip of the cap—and a wink—to the master, Elmore Leonard.

Tonma

1: (Japanese slang term, literally "bang devil") *n.* Brutal, reckless criminal
2: (Standard Japanese) *n.* Idiot

"Jesus, that's good."

"Isn't it?"

"Wow . . . you bring this from home?"

"No, right here in Japan. This farmer up in Shiga grows it."

"Mornings in the rice field, afternoons tending dope. How do you know him?"

"I don't. He's like the brother of a friend of a guy at the bar."

"A friend of a brother of a sister of a guy of a what?"

"That's enough of this for you."

"Gimme that . . . mmmmm. How do you do it? I've been in this country for, fuck, seven years, and I've never found weed this good. You've been here, what, six weeks?"

"Seven. Two months on Wednesday."

"Two months on Wednesday. How do you do it?"

"I'm talented."

"Are you selling again?"

"There are a few people who call me up, now and then."

"Jesus, be careful."

"That's what everybody tells me, but I can't figure out why. Seriously, Jessica, have you ever seen a Japanese cop actually doing anything? They sit in those storefront police stations with the red lights hanging outside—"

"The *koban*."

"—they look half asleep—"

"*KO-ban*."

"Japan may be the safest country in the world, but it's not because of the fucking cops."

"Fucking cops."

"Here, drink some more of this."

"What is it?"

"That stuff that tastes like Gatorade. With the funky name."

"Pocari Sweat."

"Pocari Sweat, right. I love the name."

"I loooovvvve Pocari Sweat."

"Listen to yourself. You need to smoke more. You're really out of practice."

"I'm not, really. This is just so much better than what I'm used to."

"You're welcome."

"Thank you."

"You're welcome."

"Are you laughing at me?"

"Yes."

"Bastard . . . What were we talking about?"

"You needing to smoke more."

"No, before that."

"Japanese cops?"

"Oh, yeah."

"You know what I think? It's the society that keeps the Japanese in line. The police are just for show."

"Interesting. What else have you noticed?"

"What, about Japan?"

"*NipPON.* I've been here so long all the weird stuff seems normal."

"Weird stuff. Shit, I don't know. It's a lot hotter than I expected. It's so humid. You go outside, it's like breathing through a sponge."

"Uh-huh."

"Weird stuff. I like all the vending machines. Cigarettes, CDs, magazines, rice . . . beer. I love that, you can buy beer from a vending machine. Drink it walking down the street if you want."

"Yeah, that is pretty cool."

"You'd never be able to get away with it back home."

"I think you could get *away* with it."

"Yeah, but it's not legal. Not in most places."

"That's true."

"Hey, you know what else? There are no fat people here."

"Don't be rude."

"What, I can't say 'fat'?"

"No, it's not PC. What's the word everybody's using now? I can't remember."

"How about 'obese'? There are no obese people. Nobody's overweight."

" 'Overweight' is probably okay."

"Anyway. It's amazing. And McDonald's is always packed."

"Hmmmm. How do you like your place?"

"I don't know. It's all right for now. It's a *gaijin* house. Six-*tatami* room, communal toilet. It's like college all over again."

"How much are you paying?"

"Thirty thousand. What's that, two hundred and fifty bucks?"

"A little less. The exchange rate's, like, really shitty recently."

"It ends up being more, anyway. I have to pay to use the shower, the stove, every fucking thing. They're all coin-operated. The air conditioner in my room's five hundred yen an hour."

"Christ, what do you make at the bar? A thousand an hour?"

"Yeah, roughly."

"How's that going? You still working the door?"

"Most nights."

"Chris Ryan, boy bouncer."

"What, I'm not intimidating enough?"

"I'm just kidding. Actually, you've filled out a bit since we were in school. You work out?"

"Sometimes."

"You look good. I like the goatee."

"Thanks. They're really not in style anymore back home, but I see them everywhere here. You know, you're looking pretty good, too."

"Really?"

"Really."

"Thanks."

"You're welcome."

"Thanks—stop laughing."

"Sorry."

"Hey, I've been meaning to ask you—how do they pay you?"

"What, the bar?"

"Yeah. I mean, you don't have a visa, right? You're working illegally. They pay you in cash?"

"Every two weeks. Fuckers always undercount my hours, too. I'm waiting for the day when they don't pay me altogether."

"What would you do if they didn't?"

"I don't know what I could do."

"Mmmmm. Hold that thought. Are you going to light up another one?"

"Sure, if you want one."

"Good. Let me put this one out, it's starting to burn the back of my throat."

"Here."

"Thanks . . . Oh, much better."

"You're welcome."

"Don't start. Let me ask you a question."

"Yeah?"

"A hypothetical question."

"Hypo-what?"

"Hypothetical. A hypothetical question. Let's say the bar didn't pay you. They tell you, you're fired, take a hike."

"Okay."

"They owe you, say, fifty thousand yen."

"That's, like, four hundred bucks, right?"

"Give or take."

"Okay."

"They owe you fifty thousand yen, and they refuse to pay you."

"Okay."

"Now, let's say . . . I don't know about your place, but most of these bars, every night the boss takes the cash from the register and does one of two things. He brings it to a night deposit box at a bank, or he brings it home. These guys never have any security; they carry the money in these pouches."

"You're asking me would I take it from him?"

"Yeah."

"How?"

"I don't know, sneak up behind him—"

"Knock him out and take the money?"

"Sure. Nobody would see you; everybody else has already gone home. Do it right, the guy wouldn't see you either. You'd get away scot-free. Would you do it?"

"How would I know that nobody's going to see me?"

"It's late. There's nobody around. You could wear a mask and gloves, if you thought it would help. Why are you looking at me like that?"

"I can't believe we're talking about this. Mask and gloves. It still sounds pretty risky. What if I can't knock him out? That stuff only works in the movies. Besides, hit somebody hard enough on the back of the head, you could kill him."

"You're making this too difficult. Here, forget hitting the guy. You approach him some other way. My *point* is, would you take the money if you could?"

"We're still talking about the fifty thousand he owes me, right?"

"Fuck, whichever. All of it, I don't care. It's up to you."

"Let's stick with the fifty thousand."

"Fine."

"Well, if there was a way to get what he owes me, without being caught—and that's a pretty tough hypothetical—then I think I'd do it."

"It wouldn't be stealing?"

"Not if I only take my money. The guy's a prick. He owes me."

"Interesting."

"What would you do?"

"Just a second. Let me give you another situation."

"Jesus."

"What if it wasn't fifty thousand yen? What if it was a lot more?"

"Like what?"

"How about a million dollars?"

"A million dollars."

"I just picked that out of a hat."

"Somebody owes me a million dollars."

"Yeah."

"Why?"

"Because you're so cute—I don't know. Don't worry about that. Let's just say that they do. What would you do to get it?"

"A million dollars. I don't think I can answer that question."

"Why not?"

"It's not realistic. I can't say what I would do, because I can't imagine being in that situation."

"What if I said that I was?"

"You were what?"

"In that situation."

"Somebody owes you a million dollars?"

"Give or take."

"Wait a minute. This is another hypothetical question, right?"

"Depends."

"On what?"

"On how you look at it."

PART 1

Sunday night, Jessica took Chris to the Hotel Happy Casanova in Minami-ku.

"This has to be the most private love hotel in Osaka," Jessica said, "which is exactly what we want. First, no windows. Those pink shutters you're looking at, they're just for effect. Second, you can't see the door or the steps leading up to the door—everything's hidden behind those tall hedges over there. Third, they've even got magnetized metal strips in the parking lot that you can put over your license plate so somebody's private detective won't be able to identify your car. And this is all just on the *outside*."

She took his hand, pulling him toward the entrance. "You ever see a pink-and-blue hotel before? With a neon sign fifteen feet high? Outside of Las Vegas? Wait, you're from Florida, forget I said that. Here, check this out."

She pushed open one of the heavy glass doors, and they stepped inside a tiny, L-shaped lobby with artificial trees lined up against the walls. Chris heard the door close behind him, then a sharp *click*. When he turned around and tried to open the door, he was surprised to find it locked.

"Doesn't that freak you out?" Jessica said. She pointed to a small sensor with a pulsing red light on the wall. "Once we walked in, that light came on, and the door locked itself. It'll stay locked for two minutes—I've timed it—giving us time to choose the room we want without meeting other customers. Then the red light goes off, the door unlocks, and it's back to the races. Cool, huh? First time I was here I was like, hey, what if the power goes out while the doors are locked? 'The Happy Casanova: Perverts check in, but they don't check out.' But no, there's a back door around that partition in front of us. The exit. When you leave, you're actually supposed to go out that door, and not the one we just came in."

Chris was looking at the surveillance cameras hanging from the ceiling. "What about those?" he asked.

Jessica put her hands on her hips and made a face, blowing loose strands of blond hair away from her eyes. She was about five-seven but looked taller, rocking back on her heels, a bundle of nervous energy tonight in stonewashed jeans and a T-shirt from the Hard Rock Café in Bangkok. She stared at the cameras as if they were a personal affront. "Yeah, those are a small problem. They keep a lookout for ratty-looking homeless guys or gays and lesbians in hotels like this. A middle-aged businessman and his junior-high-school sweetheart, no problem, but two guys or two girls, forget it. But don't worry, we can get around that. I've got it all taken care of."

Chris looked up at the cameras again. He was a shade over six-one, not big but not skinny either, preppy today in a black polo shirt and khaki shorts. He shook his head, thinking he should be hiding his face. Thinking he should actually turn around and go home. *I've got it all taken care of.* Jessica was leaving no cliché unturned. He wondered how many idiot bad guys in how many movies had said the same thing. Usually just before getting caught. It stopped him, and he thought, Jesus Christ. He wasn't watching this movie; he was *in* it. That stopped him a second time. How many idiot bad guys in how many movies had also said something like *that*?

The first time Chris Ryan met Jessica Romano was at a frathouse keg party in Bloomington, Indiana, when he tried to sell her a joint that was half cheap brown schwag and half dried weeds from the vacant lot behind his apartment. The frat brothers from Sigma Gamma had been snapping them up all night, taking turns buying rounds for their buddies and complimenting him on the "powerful shit" he always managed to get ahold of. Jessica, whose boyfriend Ed had already passed out under a table by the time she showed up, took one drag, coughed, said, "Holy Jesus," then said loudly, "This is the worst fucking dope I have ever had in my entire life. What, did you go out in a field and roll up anything you could find?"

Chris was feeling pretty mellow at the time, so rather than argue, he slipped her one of the joints he was saving for himself, this one a grade-A Gainesville Special, and the two of them sat down in a corner and got to know each other. Or rather, he got to know her; with Jessica it was hard to get a word in edgewise. She was a sophomore from Chicago, bored with school, thinking about dropping out and flying over to Japan to "work in TV or maybe model." Jessica had heard that blond, blue-eyed girls with nice tits were just rolling in yen. "Like this," she said, and she stretched out in front of him, gave him the joint, and rolled over from her back onto her stomach, then onto her back again, making sure Chris got a good look at all her job qualifications. Chris took a drag and said: "I'd hire you." Jessica sat up and took the joint back. "I hope that wasn't the best line you could come up with," she said. "You're lucky marijuana gets me all frisky." They ended up in Jessica's boyfriend's room down the hall. His roommate stumbled in sometime around three in the morning, took one unsteady look at Chris, and said, "Ed, fuck man, did you shave off all your chest hair?" Then: "Hey, get the Barbasol and do me." Chris got out of there.

True to her word, Jessica dropped out of school at the end of the semester. Chris didn't see her again for seven years. The next time they ran into each other was outside the Bar Rumble in America Mura, just a few minutes on foot from the Hotel Happy Casanova. America Mura was four city blocks of U.S. pop culture distilled through a Japanese filter. It was mostly sneaker stores and vintage clothing shops—*the* place to buy used Hawaiian shirts—plus a few bars and dance places where *gaijin* groupies hung out. Chris had been working the door at the Bar Rumble for three weeks when, he couldn't believe it, there was Jessica holding out her hand for him to stamp. "Jesus," he said. "How are you doing?" She looked at him and said, "You still haven't come up with any good lines, have you?"

Jessica was still loud and brassy, straightforward in a way that he liked. But there was something different about her now, something he couldn't put his finger on at first. A little harder, maybe. A little more impatient. And there was something about the impatience that seemed, well, almost desperate. Desperate wasn't Jessica. It didn't make any sense. Until suddenly it did, sitting on the straw *tatami* floor in a ramshackle old house that some friends of hers rented, smoking a little for old times' sake, when she told him the Idea. Her ridiculous, impossible, unbelievable Idea. The reason they were in this Japanese sex nest studying the selections on a wall-mounted computerized display.

"Mirrored ceilings, heart-shaped beds, hot tubs, theme rooms. This place has it all," Jessica said. "All the pictures that are lit up are available. The ones that are dark are already taken. You're lucky, today you've got your pick. Friday or Saturday night this whole screen might be black."

Chris was getting a kick out of all the different types of rooms. Some of the pictures on the display were labeled, most in Japanese but some in English. One of them read UFO, and the picture below it showed reflective wallpaper, a round bed with silver sheets, and an assortment of what looked like surgical instruments arranged neatly on a metal cart next to the bed. Another picture was labeled DUNGEON but was unfortunately blacked out. Chris said, "Which one are you and the guy usually in?"

Jessica pointed to one of the pictures without a label. "That one on the end. Room 301. It's pretty standard. No really kinky stuff. He doesn't go for anything too weird. What I'm thinking, if you finally agree to do this, you and Taro take a room on the same floor. Make things as simple as possible."

She showed him how it worked. Below each picture on the

display were two prices: one to "Rest" and one to "Stay." A "Rest" was two hours and cost thirty-five hundred yen. A "Stay" was all night, check out at ten the next morning, and cost ten thousand yen. Theme rooms were more expensive.

"The best thing about it," Jessica said, "is that you don't have to tell anybody which room you want. In most love hotels, you pay for your room and get your key from a clerk hidden behind a smoked-glass window. You can't see her face—it's always a woman, for whatever that means—and she can't see yours, but you've got to talk to her. That can get pretty embarrassing."

"Excuse me, the 'Dungeon' for two please."

"Totally. Here, all you have to do is decide 'Rest' or 'Stay,' push the button next to the price, and feed the bills into this slot over here on the right. Just like a vending machine. Once you've put in enough money, a key card pops out of another slot next to the picture of the room you chose, and that's it. You're on your way. When your time's up, you put the key card back in the slot."

Chris said, "What if you fall asleep and go over the time limit?"

Jessica blinked. "I don't know," she said. Staring at the display, she nibbled on her middle finger. Finally she said, "I guess they call you on the phone in the room."

"What if you walk out with the key card?"

Jessica looked at him. "Why would you want to do that?"

"No reason. Just what if we did? What would happen?"

"Fuck, I don't know," Jessica said. "An alarm goes off, maybe. Somebody on the staff comes running out. Who cares? Don't do it, then you won't have to worry about it. Okay?" She looked at her watch. "It's after nine. Can we get out of here, go talk about the details, or do you actually want to check out one of the rooms?"

Chris smiled.

"Gee," he said. "Only if it isn't too much trouble."

They paid for a "Rest" in the DISNY LAND (Chris checked the spelling twice, just to be sure) and took the two-person elevator up to the third floor. There were actually two elevators, Jessica explained, one for going up and *into* rooms, one for going down and *out* of rooms. The elevator going down opened facing the exit.

"Odds are," Jessica said, "the whole time you're in here, you won't see another human being. It's totally designed that way. And if you *do* run into somebody, they won't even give you a *first* glance. Forget about a second."

To prove her right, in the hallway on the third floor they passed a couple on their way out: an older man in a three-piece blue suit and a much younger woman with straight, jet-black hair that hit the top of her ass. They huddled close together as soon as they noticed Chris and Jessica and hurried past without making eye contact. Jessica looked at him as if to say: *See what I mean?*

"You could run naked down the hallway," Jessica said.

The DISNY LAND was Room 305. As one of the theme rooms, it was more expensive. As soon as he opened the door, Chris decided it was worth it. Maybe worth double. "This kind of thing," he said, "is why I came to Japan."

It was DISNY LAND all right. Chris wondered how long it would take to walk around the room, count all the copyright infringements. There were at least four on the pink, queen-size bed: knockoffs of Mickey, Minnie, Pluto, and the Little Mermaid, neatly arranged between the candy-striped pillows. One of the end tables had a Mickey Mouse phone, the other had two Mouseketeer caps on a small hat stand. Other knickknacks were scattered about the room: a throw rug with scenes from *The Lion King*, a life-size Bambi doll next to the leather sofa, a chintzy plastic tiara on the vanity in case someone didn't want to wear a Mouseketeer cap. Surrounding everything was glossy red-and-white wallpaper imprinted with Mickey and Minnie in various states of romantic bliss: Mickey giving Minnie flowers, holding her hand inside a giant heart, dancing cheek to cheek.

Jessica threw her purse on the bed and sat down, crossing her legs. She took out a cigarette. "This country," she said, lighting up, "has a terminal case of the cutes."

"Don't be so elitist," Chris said. There was a package of GENUINE DISNY CONDOMS in a white plastic tray on the end table with the Mouseketeer caps. He showed them to her. "How can you mock such careful attention to detail? They're ribbed, even."

"Put one on. This Australian guy I know says Japanese condoms are so small, when he wears one it's like a vise down there." She looked at his crotch and grinned. "Of course, you might not have any problem."

"Let's find out." Chris picked up one of the Mouseketeer caps and put it on her head. "M-I-C-K-E-Y, give-me-some-pussy."

Jessica blew smoke in his face. "You wish." Gesturing with her cigarette at the TV, she said, "Hand me the remote, will you? While you look around?"

Chris had never been to a motel in the States where you paid by the hour, but he could imagine one: cigarette burns in the carpet, dirty sheets, grunts and moans through the paper-thin walls from the room next door. The Hotel Happy Casanova was different. It was immaculate, the walls were solid, and it had everything. The wide-screen TV was a Sony, with a DVD player, PlayStation, and karaoke machine hooked up to it. Adult DVDs and computer games were stacked neatly inside a small cabinet. Chris looked through the DVDs and found an X-rated, Japanese version of *Snow White and the Seven Dwarfs*, which he thought was a nice touch. A video camera was on hand, mounted on a tripod, in case you wanted a record of the evening's action. There was a minibar stocked with soda and beer and those miniature bottles of liquor you get on airplanes. There was even a small vending machine full of sex toys. No DISNY merchandise. Chris said, over his shoulder, "I always thought Mickey would make a nice dildo. Those ears, you know? What do you think?" but Jessica was ignoring him.

Dumbo was smiling up from the rug on the lid of the toilet seat.

The bath and shower were separated from the rest of the bathroom. Chris opened the door and turned on the light, grinning as the room glowed red. A sunken, heart-shaped Jacuzzi sat amid black tile, surrounded by mirrors. Some of the mirrors had foot-long metal bars arranged at various levels. Chris couldn't figure out what they were for until it suddenly came to him, yeaaahhh, just the right gripping height for some backdoor action. He wondered how many couples had done it right there, just like that.

When he walked back into the room, Jessica had found the porno channel. "Hey, leave it there," Chris said.

"I don't get it," Jessica said. She pointed at the screen with the remote. "That guy with the microphone, the one who looks like a reporter? He's interviewing those three naked guys and their girlfriends in that hotel room. Maybe. Actually, I'm not sure what they're doing."

Chris thought it was pretty funny, the guys standing there naked, answering questions, their girlfriends sitting on the bed watching them. Some kind of computer-generated mosaic was blurring the guys' privates and pubic hair, but it was easy to see what was what. "No Long Dong Silvers in this bunch," Chris said.

"Not in all of Japan, Chris-*san*."

They waited for something to happen, but the story didn't get any better. Every once in a while one of the guys would say something that one of the girls thought was funny, and the camera would pan over to her covering her mouth as she giggled. Sometimes a second camera, this one set on the floor, would zoom in on one of the girls when she crossed her legs, maybe get a panty shot. Chris wondered if that was some kind of Japanese turn-on. Otherwise, why not just get to it?

Jessica was looking at him over her shoulder, biting her nails again. "So what do you think?"

"About what?" Chris was still hoping that one of the girls would at least take off her top. "I think this is the worst porno I've ever seen," he said.

Jessica took his chin in her hand and turned his head toward her. "Not about that," she said, serious now, "about *this*. It'll work, don't you think? You and Taro come in when the guy's asleep, we dress him up, walk him out of here, and nobody will know the difference. Assuming everything else goes right, we're home free." She shook his chin playfully. "Say something."

He took her hand and put it in her lap. Then he got up off the bed and walked over to the video camera. Bending down, he peered at Jessica through the viewfinder. She looked nervous.

"Well?" She was also getting impatient.

Chris wasn't sure how to put it. He leaned back against the wall. "I agree this place is as private as you said it was. If the cameras downstairs can actually be avoided, and you think they can, you could probably kill someone in here and get away with it."

"Exactly."

"Yeah, but the problem is, you don't want to kill anyone. You're—" And he had to stop for a second, realizing what he had just said. She didn't want to kill anyone and that was a *problem*. Good Christ. He started again. "Jessica, unbelievable as this sounds, you're talking about something a lot more difficult than murder. People get away with murder all the time, but this," he said, voice dropping, thinking one thing and finally saying another, "Jessica, nobody gets away with kidnapping."

Kidnapping. Jesus. Chris couldn't believe he was in Japan, in this hotel room, talking about kidnapping someone. Talking *seriously* about it. He saw Jessica roll her tongue around the inside of her mouth, staring at the floor, thinking it over. It reminded him of something, the tense way she was sitting. A movie, maybe. An actress. He grinned, realizing it. It was *The Getaway*, and he was Steve McQueen and Jessica was Ali MacGraw, sitting on a bed in a cheap motel room and working out the details of their next job. It made him giggle, the scene playing out in his head. That was exactly what he and Jessica were doing, working out the details of their next *job*. Their next *caper*. Their next *score*. It made him giggle even harder, and now Jessica was staring at him, looking a little pissed.

"What is so funny?" she asked.

Chris had tears in his eyes. Taking a few deep breaths, trying to control himself, he said, "Jessica, what the fuck are we doing here?"

"What are you talking about?"

"I'm talking about this scene from a B movie. We're in a room with Mickey Mouse wallpaper in a sex hotel researching a *kidnapping*. Don't you find this all just a little surreal?"

Jessica said, "It's not a kidnapping."

"What?"

"We're not kidnapping anyone. It's not a kidnapping."

"It's not? What is it? Jessica, you want me and your fucked-up half-Filipino boyfriend to help you grab some guy, take him out of this hotel against his will, so you can extort money from his loving family. That's kidnapping. What the fuck else do you want to call it?"

Jessica paused. "Maybe technically it's kidnapping," she said.

"Technically?"

"Legally. Whatever." She stood up, her eyes bright again, and Chris could almost see the wheels turning inside her head.

"What I'm trying to say is, it won't look like a kidnapping. It won't feel like one. I know what you're talking about, the movie thing. What was that one with Mel Gibson and the other guy? He was in *Apollo 13* and that really bad clone movie with Madeleine Stowe. You know who I'm talking about." She snapped her fingers. "Gary Sinise."

"*Ransom*, yeah. I saw it."

"*Ransom*, right. That's your classic kidnapping. Gary Sinise grabs Mel Gibson's kid, tells Mel to pay up or else, and then everything goes wrong."

"Only if you look at it from the bad guy's point of view. Which is exactly my point. We're not bad guys." Chris wasn't sure why he couldn't convince her of this.

"Just wait a minute, okay? Now, why does everything go wrong?" Head cocked like she was the teacher, waiting for him to raise his hand.

"I give up."

"Everything goes wrong," Jessica said, enunciating every word, "because Gary Sinise isn't in control of the situation. He *thinks* he is. He's got the kid tied up in a room, music blasting so the kid can't hear anything, he sends Mel an e-mail that can't be traced, he alters his voice on the phone, but he's still screwed, because he has to rely on Mel to do all the work. Mel has to come up with the money, bring it to a designated place, not call the police, not do something stupid . . . Fuck *that*."

She was standing close to him now, biting her lower lip, moving her shoulders slightly from side to side like she was dancing. She put her arms around his neck. "Once we leave this hotel and get that old fuck inside Taro's van, we will be totally in control. Then, in three hours, in *two*, we'll either be rich or we won't. Nobody is going to have any time to call the police, or mark the money, or do anything. Even if something happens and we *don't* get the money, nobody will be able to prove we had anything to do with it, not the way I've set it up. I'm the only one anybody could even *suspect*. You have got absolutely nothing to worry about."

Chris could feel her breath against his face. He liked it. "This is good," he said, grinning. "I was comparing you before with Ali MacGraw, but now I'm thinking Kathleen Turner." When Jessica looked at him blankly, he said, "You know, *Body Heat*? Kathleen Turner spends the whole movie messing around with William Hurt's mind, trying to get him to kill her husband for her. He does, too." Jessica made a face. She took her hands away from his neck and pushed him away. "Hey," he said, "don't get mad. I like your plan, I really do. That's not the problem. We're the problem. We're not criminals. We don't think like criminals. Fuck, you're the one who dreamed up this bright idea, and you haven't even thought it through."

She sat back down on the bed and dug another cigarette out of her purse. "What do you mean?" she said.

He reminded her of all the things she didn't know about the hotel—like what happened if you walked out with your key—the questions he'd started asking her downstairs before she got irritated and cut him off. "I wasn't trying to piss you off," he said. "I read somewhere once, for every criminal plan, there's a hundred things that can go wrong, and a good criminal is lucky if he can think of fifty. How many do you think we're going to catch? Ten? Twenty? We don't know enough to know what we don't know."

Jessica motioned for him to sit down next to her. On the TV, the three girls finally had their clothes off and were giving their boyfriends blow jobs. The reporter was counting off from a stopwatch, an amazed look on his face. Jessica lit a cigarette for Chris and handed it to him. "How many times have you sold weed?" she asked, blowing smoke at the TV screen. "Like, in your life?"

It stopped him. "I don't know," he said. He lay down on the bed, looking up at the ceiling. "Shit. A lot."

"How about since you came to Japan?"

"A few times, maybe."

"Do you always know the people you sell to?"

Knowing where she was going now. "More or less."

"More or less." She laughed and fell back on the bed next to him. Flakes of ash from her cigarette swirled through the air. "What if one of them turned out to be an undercover cop?"

He looked at her. "Kidnapping a guy is not the same as selling somebody a joint."

"The Japanese police would disagree." She put out her cigarette and turned on her side, propping her head up on her elbow. "You could go to jail for twenty years. You know about the drug laws over here; they're draconian. So what do you keep doing it for? Do you have criminal tendencies? Can't help yourself?"

"Maybe I'm just stupid."

"There's a thought," she said. "But no, I think you do it because it's profitable, it doesn't hurt anybody, and the risk of getting caught is minimal. Some people would say it isn't even a crime. Which is exactly the kind of thing I have in mind."

Chris laughed. "Maybe not 'exactly.' "

On the TV screen, the reporter was shouting encouragement at the girls, who had been at it now for fifteen minutes. Two of the guys seemed ready to pass out. Jessica reached over and found Chris's growing hard-on. "This is my money," she said, gently stroking him up and down. "He promised it to me, and I just want him to pay up. Where's the crime in that?"

At the sixteen-minute mark, one of the guys finally lost it and came all over his girlfriend's face. It was shown again in slow motion, the time elapsed blinking in bright red in the top left-hand corner of the screen.

"Think of it another way," Jessica said, unbuttoning the top of his shorts. "What's being good ever gotten you?"

When Tamotsu Zeniya brought Jessica to see his house, she never imagined he'd offer her a million dollars to be his mistress. But that's exactly what happened.

The two of them had just finished a late supper in Esaka, at an *unagi* restaurant that Zeniya liked. Jessica wasn't particularly fond of *unagi*—eel never failing to remind her of snake—but they'd had excellent sushi and steamed vegetables as well; and besides, Zeniya had paid for it. While they were standing in front of the restaurant, waiting for Zeniya's driver, Nishida, to swing around and pick them up, Zeniya had looked over at her and grinned.

"I have surprise," he said.

He always said this when he was about to give her a present. His eyes, little black beads stuck deep in the wrinkled folds of his skin, would open up and shine like twin oil slicks.

Jessica, who had her arm in his, squeezed him gently. "Tell me, tell me," she said.

He grinned again, showing straight but discolored teeth. Sometimes Jessica found it hard to look at him; the man was repulsive. Turning away, she caught the eye of a middle-aged woman in a kimono leaving the restaurant. The woman was glancing over at Jessica with obvious distaste. Jessica didn't blame her. A young blonde in a slinky Louis Vuitton arm in arm with an old, bald Japanese man . . . Jessica was used to getting the evil eye.

When the car, a black Nissan President, pulled up to the curb, Zeniya made a fuss about showing her into the backseat, then stumbled on the way over to his side. He had been edgy all evening, drinking much more beer and *sake* than usual, and Jessica had been constantly looking out for his hands. He'd take a drink, and she'd feel his fingers crawling up her knee like a spider. Then she'd have to say, demurely, "Zeniya-*san*, what are you looking for?"

His hand would stop about halfway up her thigh. "I am looking for black cat," he would say, grinning, and she'd have to look at those teeth again.

"No *black* cat down there," she'd say, and then she'd take his hand away and bring it up to her blond curls, let him run his fingers through them. Give him something to think about.

She'd done this at least half a dozen times tonight.

Nishida drove north on Highway 423, past Ryokuchi Park, and turned off at Senri New Town, the tony suburb at the end of the Midosuji subway line. Senri reminded Jessica of America: wide streets, saplings scattered around glass office buildings, everything spread out so you had to drive to get anywhere. Zeniya had told her before that he lived out here.

"*Hidari ni magatte,*" Zeniya said.

Nishida turned left into a residential area built into the side of a hill. It was a nice neighborhood. You could tell because only the second floors or the roofs of the houses were visible; stone walls and thick bushes kept everything else hidden. Jessica thought of her parents' place in Willimete, Illinois, a big English Tudor with a landscaped yard in the front, the whole place screaming: *Look at me!* You had to show how rich you were in American suburbia. In Japan you had to hide it.

Nishida stopped the car in front of one of the walls, this one with a wooden gate on the end.

"My house, my house," Zeniya said, pointing at the property, as if Jessica might think he would bring her to someone else's house at one o'clock in the morning. He said something to Nishida, who got out and opened Jessica's door for her. "I want to show you inside," Zeniya said.

The wooden gate was locked, and he had to fumble through his pockets searching for the key. The gate had a slot for mail at one end, and was big enough for a medium-size car to fit through. Jessica wondered what Zeniya was doing with a monster like the President; it was too long to even turn into the drive. Maybe an ego thing. Have to park your car on the street because it won't fit in the driveway.

Zeniya was still looking for the key, the old man drunk as a skunk. What was she was doing here? Hadn't he said he was married?

"Where's your wife?" Jessica asked.

"*Kore* . . ." Zeniya said. He turned the key in the lock and began sliding the gate into a recess behind the wall. He looked back at Jessica, smirking. "She taking a trip," he said. "Her sister live in Shikoku." Whispering it, like she was a partner in whatever plan he had cooked up.

Jessica looked up at the dark house. She didn't want to go in there with him alone. "Zeniya-*san*," she said, "I don't really think—"

"Five minutes!" He was already walking up the steps through the garden to the front door, waving his arms, motioning for her to follow. "I have big surprise."

If the surprise was his little dick popping out of his pants . . . It crossed her mind that this was a setup: get her into the house, have Nishida stand guard at the door—she looked back to see if he was coming in, but he was already back behind the wheel, hat cocked over his eyes like he was sleeping. Maybe he was going to stay right there. If it was only the old man she had to deal with, Jessica thought she could handle it. It wasn't like he was all that big, and she had a little can of pepper spray in her purse if worse came to worst.

Zeniya had the front door open. Hesitating, she watched the downstairs lights come on one by one.

He was at least sixty-five years old.

What could he realistically do?

The house had an old-fashioned feel to it: lots of wood, *tatami* floors, little alcoves in some of the rooms with wall hangings and flowers carefully arranged in ceramic pots.

Zeniya was in the back, in a small room that looked like a study. He already had a drink in his hands and was swaying slightly back and forth, occasionally brushing against a rolltop wooden desk. His suit coat was thrown over the back of a stiff leather chair. When he saw Jessica he put a finger to his lips, hitting his nose in the process.

"You see this room?" he said. Whispering again.

Jessica looked around, wondering if it was a trick question. "What about it?"

He leaned forward, putting his hand on her shoulder. "It's my bank."

"Your bank?" Jessica asked.

Zeniya put his finger to his lips again. He put his drink on the desk and walked over to a small bookcase set against the opposite wall. Grunting, he pushed the bookcase a few feet to the left, then turned back to Jessica, grinning. "Zeniya bank," he said.

There was a safe built into the wall.

Now *this* was more like it. "Zeniya-*san*!" Jessica clapped her hands together. "Just like James Bond!"

"Zero-zero-seven!" he exclaimed, and he made his fingers into pistols. "Bang! Bang! Pow! Pow!" Then he looked down at his fingers and started to tremble. Quickly he walked over to the desk and picked up what was left of his drink. He drank it like a shot, his back to Jessica. When he turned around, his eyes were watery. Jessica thought she had never seen anyone look so old.

"I love you, Jessie-*chan*," he said, using his nickname for her.

"Oh, Tamotsu . . ." She walked over and put her arm around

him, almost kissing the top of his bald head before deciding no, not to overdo it.

"I am so lonely, you don't know," he said, his voice choking, really getting maudlin now. Not able to look at her. "Only you are important for me."

What could she say to that? "Tamotsu, you know I'm always here." Yes, that was good. Keeping her in the game, but not clear enough to mean anything specific.

He patted the top of her hand on his shoulder. "Yes, I know." He tried a smile, pointing at the safe. "That's why I show you this!"

He put his hand up, signaling her to wait. Getting some of his energy back. In front of the safe, he crouched over and began spinning the steel dial. After the first two numbers, he looked back craftily. "Can you guess?" he asked.

"The combination?"

The word seemed to confuse him. "Secret number," he said.

Jessica thought for a minute. "Your birthday?"

Zeniya started laughing, then coughed once violently. He put a finger to his lips. "*Wife's* birthday," he said.

"Really." Jessica smiled. She needed something lighthearted here, the gold digger's obvious question. "When is your wife's birthday, Zeniya-*san*?" she said, putting something into it. "April? May?"

He put the finger to his lips again. "Shhhh," he said.

When he had the safe open, he said, "Look, look," and Jessica crouched down next to him, her arms hugging her bare knees. She was excited, sure now that the old guy was going to slip her some cash, maybe a few hundred thousand yen, tell her to go out and buy something nice for herself. It was about *time*. She was so tired of earrings and bracelets. Five hundred thousand yen, say, would be a start . . .

Instead, he started pulling out packets of hundred-dollar bills. Lots of them.

Thick packets.

When he was through, there was a small mountain of hundred-dollar bills on the *tatami* floor. All of them new and crisp, like they were straight off the press, big pictures of Ben Franklin everywhere. Jessica was afraid to blink, thinking if she did the money would disappear.

Zeniya couldn't possibly be thinking of . . .

Could he?

"One million dollar," Zeniya said. He picked up one of the packets and riffled through it. "Plus *alpha*. One million, one hundred thousand? Two hundred thousand? *Wasureta*. I forget."

"You forget." Jessica had to sit down.

"In real bank there is more."

"More in the bank." She laughed then, *had* to, her voice shaky. "I understand, this is the petty cash."

His brow furrowed. "Yes, pretty." He took her hands in his. "Jessie-*chan*, you are young and beautiful girl. I am ugly old man."

"No, Tamotsu, don't—"

"It is true. Ugly old man can give young beautiful girl one thing only." He put her hands on the mountain of hundred-dollar bills. "This money, I give you."

"Tamotsu—"

"You become my *aijin*."

Jessica stared at him, seeing the determination in his eyes, feeling the money beneath her fingertips. One million dollars.

Plus *alpha*.

He wrapped her hands around one of the packets, and said, "This one for now. Okay?"

Aijin.

Mistress.

When Jessica first started working in the Japanese hostessing industry, she made herself promise to follow one rule. She even wrote it down on a piece of paper. It read: I WILL NOT, UNDER ANY CIRCUMSTANCES, SLEEP WITH A CUSTOMER FOR MONEY.

One day a friend of hers saw it and said, "What, you can't remember that?"

Jessica worked at a members-only club called the Pony Tail, in the upscale Kita Shinchi district downtown. Kita Shinchi was where the executives went to play, its tall, narrow buildings honeycombed with private and highly exclusive bars. The membership fee at the Pony Tail was supposed to be a secret, but one of Jessica's customers had told her it was close to ten million yen. In dollars, that was twice what Jessica's father, a high-school principal, made in a year. The owner of the club, an elegant, fiftyish woman called "Mama" by the patrons and staff, fancied antique silk kimonos and gold jewelry, and tooled around town in a green Mercedes 380SL. She was rumored to be the mistress of a local construction king or a high-ranking politician. Either way, Jessica thought she had a nice racket going. Each one of Mama's kimonos cost more than the Mercedes.

For their money, the patrons of the Pony Tail expected certain refinements. It was decorated in a style Jessica called Gaudy Isn't Enough; she always got a kick walking inside. The front doors were carved from solid oak and had been imported from Italy at great expense. The main room had booths with low mahogany tables, plush velour sofas, and leather wingback chairs. Impressionist paintings in gilt-edged frames hung from the walls. A gold fountain in one corner featured perfumed water and a rendition of the *Venus de Milo,* and the baby grand piano in the opposing corner was set in polished red lacquer. Mama liked to play "As Time Goes By" and selections from Gershwin. Behind the bar was a locked glass cabinet where bottles of liquor and crystal decanters and tumblers were reserved, marked with members' names on thin gold plaques.

The manager and the waiters were always dressed in black tuxedos.

Sometimes Jessica tried to explain what she did in Japan to people back in the States.

"Imagine going to a cocktail party every night," she would say, "and that's your job." It wasn't far from the truth. Jessica's day typically started at five P.M., when she opened her closet to pick out something to wear. Getting dressed was the trickiest part of hostessing. You needed something classy and expensive looking but not formal; suggestive and sexy but not slutty. Jessica preferred black Chanel skirts that stopped just a few centimeters short of proper, and low-cut silk blouses from Prada or Valentino that she wouldn't wear during the day but looked great in semidark rooms. You had to get the effect just right. Every evening after getting ready, Jessica would look in the mirror and say: "Michelle Pfeiffer in *The Fabulous Baker Boys* or Glenn Close in *Fatal Attraction*?" If it was *Fatal Attraction* she had to change.

She had to be at work at eight-thirty, and the manager pushed the doors open at nine. Jessica and the Japanese and Filipino hostesses would wait by the bar as men in groups of threes or fours trickled in. Most of them were company guys: executives or middle managers on the way up. They were usually well-off but not rich; their companies owned the membership at the Pony Tail. Some of the customers, though, Jessica knew were loaded. They owned shipping companies and restaurant chains and who knew what else. They came with bodyguards. Whatever they did for a living, all of them were at the Pony Tail to relax. A hostess made sure they did.

What happened was, Jessica's manager would direct her to a particular table, tell her to liven things up. If she didn't know the customers, she would introduce herself, see how much English they knew. Even after seven years, Jessica didn't speak much Japanese. She would play card tricks, light cigarettes, and pour drinks, getting the boys tight enough that they would sing a few karaoke songs and order ten-thousand-yen bowls of mixed nuts. Making sure everybody had a good time. It wasn't hard work. It was even fun, sometimes, if you could find a vice-president who was good at telling jokes or an accountant who knew the theme song from *Laverne & Shirley*. Yes, it was true, some of the guys liked to flirt a little. What was wrong with that? "Guys flirt," Jessica would say to people back home. "It's just them being guys. Why make a federal case about it? I just play along, let them think they're going to get somewhere. It's not like I'm going to go home with them. Honestly. Hey, you should see some of these guys. I'd have to be out of my mind."

The reactions she got varied. Most people got the wrong idea, thinking there had to be more to it than drinking and flirting. Her friend Amber wanted to know if it was true that Japanese cocks were smaller but harder, and were the guys real samurai warriors in bed, or what. Her older sister Barbara, who had a husband and two kids, wanted to know if the men were married, did Jessica even care. Hinting around, not willing to say it. Her mother was more direct. "It sounds like you're a call girl, Jessica. That is what you're trying to tell me, isn't it? That you're a call girl? I mean, I might as well lay my cards out on the table."

Jessica admitted that hostessing wasn't a very orthodox profession. She had been groped more than once in the line of duty, and had been propositioned more times than she could count. Japanese men all seemed to have sex on the brain. She was asked the same questions so often, she developed a list of stock replies. When things were slow, she would write them down on cocktail napkins and show them to the Japanese hostesses, who were always asking her to teach them English. Jessica would say: "Here's the answer. What's the question?" to something like:

NO, I'VE BEEN WAITING FOR YOU TO ASK ME OUT.

or

WHY, I ALWAYS SLEEP THAT WAY. DON'T YOU?

or

I'M WORRIED IT WOULD BE MUCH TOO BIG FOR ME.

and the other women would laugh until they cried, because they were always saying the same things in Japanese.

Jessica never took things personally. It took a lot to get her upset. One time, when she was living in Tokyo and working at a bar called the Pink Lady, the president of a small semiconductor company had invited her over to meet a few of his staff. All of them were already half in the bag, red-faced, neckties crumpled against their chests like wet rags. When Jessica sat down, the president, whose name was Nakano, announced that he wanted to give her a present. Please would she to close her eyes. Jessica did, and the table erupted in nervous giggles. She sensed Nakano squirming in his seat beside her. "Now hold out hand," he said, and when she did, he took it and wrapped her fingers around something short and rubbery. And warm. Jessica was ready to slap him, hard, but when he said, "Open your eyes," drawing out every word, the rest of the group giggling like mad, she got another idea. Eyes still closed, she said, "Wait, *chotto matte*, can I guess? Is it a cigarette? No? *Ebi?*"— using the word for shrimp—"No, it's lipstick!" Nakano took her hand away, and when she opened her eyes he had zipped up and was glaring at her. Jessica smiled at him sweetly. "Nakano-*san*," she said, "what happened to my present?" Later that night, the manager of the club called her into his office, told her she was not living up to the standards of the Pink Lady, and fired her.

Her sister told her she should be ashamed of herself, and that by allowing such offensive behavior, Jessica was setting the women's movement back a hundred years. Her sister, who sat at home watching *General Hospital* while she ironed her husband's shirts. Jessica couldn't have cared less.

"Most of these guys," she told her sister, "are so clueless, you can't help but laugh. I actually feel sorry for them. I mean, Jesus, take this one customer that I know. He's a regular, an up-and-coming executive at one of the big Japanese banks. When this guy was in *preschool*, his mother was making him go to prep classes so he could pass the entrance test for a top kindergarten. All he did, his whole childhood, was study. He went to an all-boys' high school, he never dated in college, and then he got married to this girl his parents picked out. I mean, give me a break. This guy is emotionally, like, thirteen years old. How can you get offended at a thirteen-year-old?" Jessica loved the books from the mideighties about the all-knowing Japanese businessmen who were taking over the world, since many of them were the same guys that giggled when they asked her if she was wearing underpants.

Because she was flexible and outgoing, Jessica was good at her job. That and her *Charlie's Angels* look—lightly curled blond hair, violet-blue eyes, athletic build—had kept her in high demand throughout the seven years she had been in Japan. She had worked in some of the most exclusive clubs in Tokyo and Osaka, and usually commanded the top rates. Even now, the Japanese economy deep in a recession, Jessica was still paid a minimum of five thousand yen per hour, and most clubs had bonus systems that bumped her salary up even further. At the Pony Tail, every time a customer asked for her by name, it was an extra two thousand. Every time a customer called the club and asked to take her to dinner, it was an extra seven thousand. In an average month, she earned just over five hundred thousand yen, which was in the neighborhood of four thousand dollars. Not bad, considering her official duties were mainly talking and drinking.

What's more, Jessica's salary was only the beginning. Her customers also tipped her, and tips could really push a hostess's salary into the stratosphere. Sometimes Jessica's regulars gave her money, usually twenty or thirty thousand yen in a glossy envelope with red and gold ribbons. More often they gave her presents. In her apartment, Jessica had four sets of pearl earrings from Tiffany's; a gold Jaeger-LeCoultre watch; three Prada handbags and six backpacks, all black; dresses from Chanel, Donna Karan, and Christian Dior, plus a number of expensive Japanese knockoffs; a cellular phone that worked anywhere, even five floors below a train station; and a laptop computer. And these were just the more recent gifts; whenever Jessica stopped working at a club, she would take boxes of stuff to pawnshops. It wasn't only a matter of money. She said to her friend Amber once: "You know Richie Rich? That twelve-year-old kid in the comics who's got more money than God? Imagine if Richie Rich wanted to be your boyfriend and was sending you presents. Imagine all the expensive, tacky crap he'd probably pick out. That's the kind of stuff I get." Still, sometimes it was hard, getting rid of things. Once, when she was offered the equivalent of two thousand dollars for a diamond brooch worth twenty thousand, she almost cried. But the brooch was set in the shape of a butterfly, with a giant ruby for a body and two tiny emeralds for eyes. What else was she going to do with it?

Jessica lived in a rooftop, two-bedroom apartment in a fashionable part of neighboring Kobe, with a model who was always out on assignment. Jessica was single; being a hostess was hard on your love life. The hours were late, and most men, though they might try at first, eventually couldn't accept what she did for a living. Jessica understood. She tried to stay away from serious relationships, making it a rule never to go out with any one man more than three times. Jessica was superstitious about the number three. She had broken this rule only once in seven years, with an investment broker named Brad. She had met him at an English-style pub in Roppongi, when she was still living in Tokyo. With his red suspenders and boyish face, Brad looked just like Charlie Sheen in *Wall Street*, and Jessica spent the evening getting him to buy her drinks while she kidded around, calling him the Wham Bam Stock Man. But Brad surprised her; he was soft-spoken behind his power tie, and unlike Charlie Sheen, there were cute crooked teeth behind his smile. Brad said he didn't care what she did for a living. If Jessica said she wasn't sleeping around, that was good enough for him.

They dated for six months. Brad worked late, trying to make trades during business hours in New York, so he didn't mind meeting her at two o'clock in the morning to have dinner. She would talk to him for hours—about work, customers, life in Japan, life in general—racing along at what he called "Jessica speed," hardly letting him into the conversation. He always paid attention, slipping in a question every now and then to challenge her, get her to look at what she was saying in a different light. Brad was smart. He was funny, too, in a dry sort of way; he'd say something, not putting a lot into it, and thirty seconds later Jessica would catch on and see the sly grin on his face.

The only place their relationship didn't seem to click just right was in bed. At first, Jessica thought it was a problem of different styles. She liked to roll around, get into it, but Brad was more straightforward. "I swear," she told Amber, "his hips are the only part of him that moves." Amber said Jessica had to look at the total picture, not just the stud aspect. Eighty percent perfect was still pretty damn good. But as time went on, Brad seemed to get even less interested in sex, and they sometimes went for a week or two without doing it. Finally, one night at her place, when he was inside her, she felt his penis go limp, and he rolled off her. For a while, they lay next to each other, quiet, Jessica wondering what she should say. She couldn't think of anything good, so she finally told him not to worry about it, that it happened sometimes, that he must be tired. Or maybe stressed-out, the Wham Bam Stock Man busy all day keeping the world economy going.

In the dark, she heard his voice say: "Maybe I just can't get it up with a whore."

Jessica couldn't move. She wanted to ask, *What? What did you say?* like they did in the movies, but she was too afraid that she would hear it again, hear that word: *whore.* She wanted to turn on the light so she could look at his face and see that sly grin, listen to him say, "What? Did you think I was serious?" But she was too afraid that it wouldn't be there, that he wouldn't say anything. She lay there, not moving, until he got up and got dressed and walked out.

That had been almost two years ago. She hadn't wanted to take the chance of running into Brad somewhere in Tokyo—with only twenty-nine million people in the greater metropolitan area, the odds were too high—so she sold off everything she owned and moved to Osaka. Osaka was Jessica's native Chicago all over again, a workers' town, with none of the style and glamour of Tokyo. People shouted at one another across the street in Osaka. They walked outside in their pajamas or in loud cheap clothes. The air always had a vaguely toxic smell. It was ugly. It made her feel ugly. She lasted there only three months before moving over to the more elegant Kobe. Kobe was better than Osaka, but she still felt as if she had fallen off the edge of the earth.

Lately, she had been thinking more and more about her future. One day, she sat down with a calculator and estimated she'd earned approximately eight hundred and fifty thousand dollars in seven years of hostessing. Yet there she was, still living with roommates and getting by from month to month. The money came so easily, she couldn't hold on to it. The rent for her apartment, even the half that she paid, was more than the mortgage on her parents' house. She vacationed at resorts in Thailand and Micronesia for months at a time. She never cooked, she made it a point never to walk when she could take a cab instead, and she went clubbing three times a week. There was always pot somewhere inside the apartment, despite the fact that strict Japanese laws kept it pricey, and every so often she liked to expand her perceptions with a hit or two of Ecstasy. About the only thing she could point to in her favor was that she didn't do coke and heroin; hard drugs made her think of that old TV commercial with the egg in the frying pan and freaked her out.

Eight hundred and fifty thousand dollars. And the time she had left for making more was quickly disappearing. Hostessing was a young woman's game, and at twenty-seven . . . she wasn't *old,* certainly not, but this was Japan, where you could buy schoolgirls' used panties from vending machines and men proudly admitted having *roricon*—Lolita complexes. Just a year ago, Jessica had showed up at a club near her apartment to interview for a job and got stopped at the door. The manager asked to see her passport. When she gave it to him, he opened it up to the first page and shook his head. He told her he was sorry, but she wasn't what they were looking for. The manager said: "You know in Japanese, *Onna no ko wa Kurisumasu keki to onaji . . . ?*" Jessica said she didn't. The manager translated: " 'Girl is like Christmas cake. After twenty-five, no good.' "

She needed to do something fast. Otherwise she was going to end up in her thirties with nothing. Jessica had no college degree and no skills beyond dodging crude advances. What else could she do?

What else did she *want* to do?

She knew what she didn't want. She didn't want to get married, not yet anyway, do the daytime-TV-and-rugrat race like her sister. She didn't want to go back to school. If truth be told, she didn't want to get a real job either, even if she could, some living hell where she sat around in an office and pretended to be doing something important for forty years, just so she could retire and go play shuffleboard all day in Phoenix or Tampa.

What she wanted, she finally decided, was just to be. The last time she was in Thailand, she'd spent a week in a guest house on the beach thirty miles north of Phuket. While she was there, she met a woman from Norway named Brigit. Brigit was thirty-five and the most relaxed person Jessica had ever met. Two years ago, Brigit said, she had sold everything she owned back in Norway and moved to Southeast Asia. She did nothing now but lie on the beach and read and take long walks. One evening, sitting on the balcony of the guest house, watching the sunset over the ocean, Jessica asked her what she was planning to do when her money ran out. Brigit said that wouldn't be for at least another two years, which was much too far ahead to plan. Jessica asked what her goals were. Brigit pointed to the sun, just beginning to sink beneath the waves, forcing streaks of pink and yellow across the sky. She said: "To see that. To be. What else is there?"

Just to be. Now, *that* was a worthwhile ambition. But unfortunately, even doing nothing took money. She had to do things differently from Brigit, that was for sure. If Jessica was going to be a bum, she was going to be a financially secure bum. She spent a few weeks researching offshore banks and the costs of living in Thailand and Malaysia. She figured with about three hundred thousand dollars, she could live forever on the interest. Sitting down with her calculator, she worked out how long it would take her to save that kind of money, assuming she cut back on expenses and maintained her current level of income.

Estimated, she was looking at ten years, minimum.

Ten more years of pouring drinks and batting her eyelashes at short, shriveled lechers.

Jesus wept.

Of course, there was another, faster way of getting that kind of money.

Jessica had heard the stories of hostesses who struck it rich. They were part of the lore, the women who'd found the Holy Grail. There was the one from Yokohama who now lived on a yacht off the coast of Greece. Another one owned a small inn in Karuizawa and favored gold-tipped English cigarettes. Jessica had assumed the stories were just that—stories—but then one of her friends, Michelle, turned up with a controlling interest in an exclusive cosmetics boutique off the Ginza in Tokyo. True, that had been six years ago. The economy hadn't been great then, and it was a lot worse now. Still, anything was possible.

She just had to adjust her perspective a little.

Jessica still had the piece of paper with her rule about never sleeping with a customer for money; she kept it in her wallet where her American driver's license used to be. One day she opened it up and read it aloud:

"I will not, under any circumstances, sleep with a customer for money."

It was strange, hearing it. It seemed silly now, like something a kid would write. It didn't give her the same kick that it once had. That surprised her, that she wasn't still totally repulsed by the idea. She was physically repulsed, certainly; just thinking about one of those drunken, middle-aged assholes touching her, *inside* her, sent shivers up the back of her spine. But then, lying down in shit or eating a bug would be just as repulsive, and she'd do either one of those for three hundred grand. Mentally, it didn't seem to bother her at all.

All she needed was to find the right guy.

Six months later she met Tamotsu Zeniya.

The first time was disgusting.

She had expected the Hilton, not the Hotel Happy Casanova, and when Nishida turned into the parking lot, she looked over at Zeniya and asked, "Are you serious?"

Inside the room he had her bend over the vanity.

"It is better for me to stand up," he said.

So for the next five minutes she had to watch herself in the mirror of the vanity, her clothes on the bed, Zeniya behind her holding on to her ass while they did it. His skin was patched and scarred like he'd been in a fire; she had to concentrate on her face or close her eyes to keep from throwing up. Then suddenly it was over, and Zeniya slumped down onto the bed, breathing hard.

"Make us some drinks," he said.

Then he got up and went to the bathroom.

Jessica looked at herself in the mirror and wondered if the million dollars he'd shown her was going to be enough.

Zeniya didn't mention the money the first time. After he came back from the bathroom, he gulped down a glassful of Johnnie Walker and collapsed on the bed, right on top of Jessica's Issey Miyake blouse. Within minutes, she could hear him snoring. The next morning, when they got in the car, he kissed her lightly on the hand and had Nishida take them back to her apartment. As she was getting out in front of her building, he patted her on the behind and said, "Next month."

The next month, they did it on the bed.

After the third time, an afternooner, they stopped off at a coffee shop on the way back to Kobe. Zeniya gave her a present, a picture of the two of them in a diamond-studded silver frame. Jessica, appalled, brought up the money in the safe. Not that she didn't trust him, she said, of course not that, but how was he planning on giving it to her? Should she set up an offshore account? Open up a safe-deposit box? What exactly did he have in mind? He took her hand and kissed it.

"Jessie-*chan*, Jessie-*chan*. If you want to, we can look for new *mansion* next week."

"A new *mansion*?" *Mansion* was Japanese-English for "condominium."

Zeniya nodded. "For us. There is one new building in Kobe, I think you will like it. We can be happy there."

"We."

He picked up the picture and smiled, looking at it. "Isn't that beautiful?"

Just before the fourth time, one of the other hostesses at the Pony Tail asked Jessica how things were going with Zeniya. Suu Yi was from Vietnam. She was thirty-five, with the most beautiful skin Jessica had ever seen, and had worked at most of the top clubs in Osaka.

"I ask you, you know," Suu Yi said, "because he is one foolish man. He use to go to another club in Sinsaibashi. Go out with my friend Rina."

"Really," Jessica said.

"Really. You know what he did?" Suu Yi rested her elbow against the bar and wagged a finger at Jessica. "He take Rina back to his house, show her this money he got. He say, if Rina be his lover, he give all the money."

Jessica felt as if she were outside herself, looking down. "How much money?"

"Million dollar. You believe that?" She laughed. "Plus *alpha*, Rina say."

"What did she do?"

Suu Yi shrugged. "Hey, Rina no whore. She say, 'No thank you. We go home now.' But I hear other girls, some of them say yes. Get a little money, maybe ring or necklace. Get fucked for nothing." She put her hand on Jessica's shoulder. "You be careful around foolish man like that."

That night Zeniya asked her to be on top. Jessica said, Sure, why not.

She already had a plan in mind.

The girl Chris was dancing with giggled and said, "Your nose is very high."

He wondered if he had heard her right, hip-hop pounding from the big overhead speakers. "High?" he asked.

She nodded, putting her hand to her nose and gesturing outward.

"Oh, you mean *long*," he said. "Yeah, I know. It's my worst feature." Saw her wrinkle her brow, puzzled, and said: "Worst. Most bad. I don't like my nose either."

Her eyes widened and she took his arm, shaking it lightly. "No, no," she said. "It's so handsome. You have beautiful nose."

Oh. He said, "Well, thank you," and moved in closer, putting his arm around her waist, brushing against her with his lower body as they swayed back and forth to the beat. She didn't seem to mind, reaching up and wrapping her arms around his neck. She was something, Chris guessed twenty-one or twenty-two, with traces of glitter around her eyes and wearing a tight-fitting black dress that hugged the top of her thighs. He said, "I think you're very beautiful, too." He let his gaze fall to her breasts, not even trying to hide it, then back up to meet her eyes. "Very beautiful." When she giggled again, he added, "How do you say 'beautiful' in Japanese?"

"*Kirei*," she said.

"*Kirei*," he said. He moved in closer, feeling her pelvis rubbing against him, starting to get a hard-on. "You are very very *kirei*, Tomiko."

"Tomoko," she said.

When the song was over, Chris went to the bar to get her a drink. He watched her sitting down at the table with her friends, saying something, the four of them giggling now in unison, looking over at him and waving. He waved back. Unreal, each one of them stunning, long bare legs and hot pants poking out everywhere he looked.

Grant, from South Carolina, was leaning on the bar with his elbows, dishtowel slung over his black Bar Rumble T-shirt. He said, "The one with her hair cut short, sitting on the end? That's where you need to be making your move."

Chris said, "I'm thinking about making a move on all of them. Four Tom Collins and a tequila shot."

"That's the spirit," Grant said. He began turning over glasses and lining them up on the bar. "You off tonight?"

"Start at ten-thirty."

"Not much time."

"Yeah, I know."

Waiting for Grant to finish up, Chris turned around, back against the bar, letting his eyes roam. The Bar Rumble was like a small cave: black walls, blue ceiling, white pillars covered in graffiti. It was stark, too, nothing in the place but a few tables and chairs, the bar against one wall, a roped-off section for the DJs against another. No frills, but it was packed, tonight and every night since Chris had started working there. The crowd was usually forty percent *gaijin*, most of them men, and sixty percent Japanese, most of them women. *Beautiful* women: great skin, hair, bodies. Sometimes their teeth were a little fucked up—the Japanese were not big on orthodontics—and most of them weren't much in the ass department, but Chris had yet to see a real bowser. And they'd let pure geeks come on to them: skinny guys in raggedy ponytails and glasses, guys with beer guts and belts that had big initials on the buckles. Anybody, so long as he was white. Chris felt like he was constantly being stared at, like he was Tom Cruise or Brad Pitt, some kind of movie star. College girls would walk over with disposable cameras, ask if they could take a picture with him. Sometimes, back at his place, he'd look at himself in the mirror, wonder who the girls were seeing. Sure, he was good-looking, but *come on* . . .

Turning back to face the bar, he said, "Grant, how long have you been here?"

"In Japan? Five years this fall."

"Still like it?"

"It's all right." He spritzed tonic into glasses one by one. "I like working at the bar. I was at one of the big conversation schools for a while, but that really sucked. I just stayed there long enough to pick up some privates. Thinking about opening up my own school, actually."

"English school."

"What else? The *eikaiwa* boom is over, but you can still make a living at it. And I'm probably going to get married next year, so . . ."

"Japanese girl?"

Grant nodded. He stopped, holding the spritzer in his hand like a gun. "You know what she said to me the other day? She said, 'If you meet other girls after we get married, don't tell me about it.' "

"Seriously?"

"Dead serious. I said, 'What are you talking about?' And she said, 'Men sometimes want to meet other girls. I don't want to know about it.' Like she's expecting me to play around."

"Think you will?" Chris asked.

Grant put the drinks on a tray and handed the tray to Chris. "Fuck yes I will. With that kind of invitation?"

The girls squealed when he brought the drinks, tittered among themselves, and pulled out their wallets. No, no, Chris said, they were on the house. As an employee he could get free drinks. The girls clapped, saying *"Sugoi! Sugoi!,"* which he assumed was something like "Fabulous!" They toasted him, clinking their glasses together, saying *"Sugoi! Sugoi!"* again when he downed the shot of tequila.

Their names were Tomoko, Mari, Yuko, and Ayumi. All of them were twenty-two, seniors at Osaka something something

University. Tomoko, his dance partner, had the best English; her friends would ask him a question and she would translate. Where was he from? America, he said. Then: Florida? Near Disney World? "*Sugoi!*" they said in chorus. Mari, navel showing under a T-shirt that read NUDES! ALL NUDES! TWENTY-FOUR HOURS! said excitedly that she had been to Holland last year. Really? Chris asked. He asked her where else she had been in Europe. Mari said, Europe? After a few minutes of confusion he figured out that she wasn't saying "Holland"; she was trying to say "Orlando."

Did he have any brothers and sisters? No, he didn't. Could he eat Japanese food? Yes, but he didn't like the little pickles that seemed to be served with everything. The girls nodded, like this was to be expected. How tall was he? He started to say six-one, realized they wouldn't have any idea what he was talking about, and tried to figure it out in centimeters. Grant's favorite, Ayumi, told him to stand up. They got back-to-back, Ayumi kicking off her heels and measuring with her hand. One hundred and eighty-four, she said. The others clapped. "*Sugoi! Sugoi!*"

Did he like Japan? Yes, he did. Why? All the beautiful women, he said, prompting another round of giggles. Yuko marveled at the length of his eyelashes. She asked if she could touch them. Sure, he said, and she reached across the table, brushing her slender fingers across the tips of them. He caught a whiff of her perfume and suddenly got goose bumps.

He was starting to wonder seriously how he could get two of the girls to go back home with him. Or three of them. Fuck, all four. He wasn't sure what he could do with four at one time, but he could cross that bridge when he came to it. The important thing was, the idea didn't seem that far-fetched. Chris had been in Japan now two months and had slept with a dozen different women. He felt the total could just have easily been a hundred; he had yet to experience even the slightest rejection. It was like going to the store: pick out the girl you like and bring her home.

It was almost ten-thirty. Chris wanted to buy cigarettes before going out to work the door, so he ordered another round of drinks for the girls and told them not to go anywhere. Bye, they said, giggling. Don't go anywhere, he said again.

Outside, America Mura was alive with kids, packs of them roaming the narrow streets, trying to look cool in their floppy hats and dyed hair and baggy jeans. Plaid was in, so were eyebrow rings and Nikes. It was America rewound five, ten years. A trio of girls in miniskirts and oversize sweaters giggled nervously as they passed him, one of them saying "Hello!"—her ls sounding like rs. "Hello!" he called back. Behind him, he heard another eruption of giggles, a different girl yelling now: "I love you!"

It was almost too much. Chris had never felt more confident in his life. His senses had never felt more acute. He was picking up everything, on top of everything. He felt bigger, stronger, and smarter than everyone around him. Japanese men got out of his way when they saw him coming. Japanese women looked at him with frank invitation. He was like a king. He could do anything and everything he wanted. That was how it seemed, anyway, and wasn't that what was most important? The only thing he lacked, he thought, was a sound track pulsing around him—the theme from *Rocky*, maybe, or something from a James Bond flick.

Thinking about movies made him think about Jessica and her Idea. God help him, but he was beginning to consider it. He would have rejected it out of hand at home, but then, would Jessica have brought it up at home? Chris didn't think so. It was Japan that made it seem possible, Japan where *everything* seemed possible.

He found a cigarette machine next to a bus stop and fed it coins. Two hundred eighty yen a pack, but Chris had seen worse prices in Europe. He found the button for Marlboro Lights and pressed it. Waited for the box to fall into the tray at the bottom, whistling, hands in his pockets. He was unwrapping the plastic from around the box when he noticed the salaryman.

The salaryman was sitting alone on a bench in the dark, wearing a wrinkled blue suit. He looked like he was waiting for a bus, but the lights around the timetable had gone out; there would be no more buses tonight. Lighting up, Chris walked over to take a look at him. Realized the guy was asleep, head lolled to the side.

Next to him was a man's carryall.

Unthinkable at home . . .

Chris sat down on the bench. Took a drag on the cigarette, let it rest between his lips. His heart started to beat a little faster. Reaching out casually with his left hand, he took the carryall and put it in his lap. The salaryman didn't move. Chris found the zipper and slid it open as quietly as he could. Let his fingers dig through the carryall.

There was seventy thousand yen in the billfold.

Chris put the cash in his pocket and put the billfold back in the carryall. Zipped it closed. Then he put it back next to the salaryman and stood up.

Finished his cigarette.

Absolutely *anything*.

Walked back to the bar, hearing the "Imperial March" from *Star Wars* pounding in his head.

Jessica was waiting for him at the door.

"Where have *you* been?" she asked.

He held up the pack of Marlboro Lights. "Cigarettes."

"They're bad for you. Listen, take the night off."

"What for?" He was looking over her shoulder, trying to see if the girls were still there.

"There's somebody I want you to meet."

There. At a different table now, a couple of Australian guys Chris knew hitting on them.

Fuck.

He looked at Jessica.

"Meet who?" he asked.

Legally speaking, Taro Shimada lived with his mother in a two-bedroom apartment above a cute little Filipino restaurant called the Manila Grilla. Practically speaking, Taro lived in his van. More precisely, his customized Super V8 1997 Chevy Astro Galaxy Lowrider.

When Taro bought the Astro it had all the pizzazz of a refrigerator on wheels: white, boxy, power-nothing. He added running boards and body skirts, and raised the roof for a more streamlined look. He installed fog lights (why not?) and Super Chrome Hellcat hubcaps. When he had the sort of look he wanted, he drove it in to a body shop and had the van painted black with orange flames raging along the sides. Finally, he tinted the windows. Now every night he cruised up and down the streets of Osaka and watched people trying to look in, figure out who the bad motherfucker was behind the wheel.

There was a report on Taro at the Osaka Central Police Station in Sonezaki. The first part of the report read:

Name: Taro Shimada. *Aliases:* None. *Address:* 6-2-5 Furuichi, Hirakata. *Date of Birth:* March 13, 1978. *Nationality:* Filipino/Japanese (Japanese father—identity unknown). *Residency Status:* Japanese citizen. *Occupation:* Waiter. *Marital Status:* Single.

The next part of the report was titled "Criminal History/Previous Arrests or Convictions," and included juvenile offenses. The first one was for substance abuse: sniffing paint thinner under a bridge when he was twelve. Released into the care of his mother. The second one was two years later, this time for "assault on an educational authority": ordered to spend two weeks under observation, pending trial, at the Neyagawa Juvenile Detention Center. His "violent tendencies" led the family-court judge to sentence him to the Osaka Boys Correctional Facility. Released after six months. Was back the next year, this time for grand larceny. Released after nine months. The fourth and final arrest was also for grand larceny, this time as an adult. Did just under a year at the Danjiri Sowa Prison out in the country, in Kurashki, Okayama.

Taro knew all about his police report. He had read it. The last time he was in police custody, under suspicion of drug trafficking, one of the cops had thrown it at him. The cop asked if everything was in order, and was it fair to say that Taro was a no-good, degenerate, half-breed piece of human shit. Take your time, the cop said.

Taro couldn't argue with the facts. He didn't like the language. All those legal terms, making him sound like a hardened criminal. *Grand larceny,* for example. What was that? Certainly not stealing 50cc Honda scooters that started to shake at fifty kilometers an hour. And *assault on an educational authority,* that was really unfair. If anything, his eighth grade teacher had assaulted *him,* the skinny, prissy bitch in her wire-rim glasses, accusing him of cheating when he hadn't, then telling the class that "people like Taro" should go to their own schools and stay away from decent Japanese children. Who wouldn't get mad, having to listen to something like that? Even then, all he did, he grabbed her glasses off her face and stomped them to bits on the floor. That was it. He hadn't *assaulted* the woman.

Still, try and tell the police something like that. The cops never wanted to hear your side of the story; they just wanted you to repeat *their* side. They had ways of making you do it, too. Slapping you around until you couldn't tell right from left, or making you sit on your heels on top of rows of knobby bamboo sticks until your legs practically fell off. They could hold you for twenty-three days before they even had to declare a charge, and nobody lasted that long. Taro's first arrest for grand larceny, he had lasted only three days. By the time it was all over, he had given up his partner, his fence, and just about anyone else who came to mind. He even told the police about his dead grandmother's illegal distillery on Laguhana Island back in the Philippines.

He was doing his best to stay away from the police these days. Stealing scooters was too high risk. You had to break them open without damaging the shells, keep someone from seeing you, stash the bikes somewhere while you waited for your fence, hope that your fence wasn't being leaned on by the cops ... At fifteen thousand yen a scooter, it wasn't worth the stress.

No, Taro had decided the secret to being a successful criminal was being part of a group. Sharing the workload. Recently he had hooked up with a gang of Iranians who had a novel way of breaking into warehouses. The Iranians worked on construction sites during the day, and they knew how their Japanese bosses cut corners by using quality materials on only certain parts of a building. The Iranians would scout out a promising location, then late on a rainy night would have Taro drive them out there in a borrowed truck. (Taro was the only one who looked Japanese enough not to get stopped driving around a warehouse at midnight; the police were always on the prowl for suspicious-looking Arabs.) At the warehouse, the Iranians would show him just where to line up the truck, then Taro would gun the engine and back the truck right through the weak part of the wall.

It worked like a charm. The rain covered the sound of the truck smashing into the wall. No alarms went off—they were connected to the doors. And the Iranians always knew what was inside that was worth stealing, so they were usually in and out in ten or fifteen minutes. Taro had made more money in the past six months working with the Iranians than he had in six years stealing scooters. He had bought a top-of-the-line Do-CoMo cellular phone, a three-hundred-thousand-yen stereo system that played minidiscs, and had paid for the Astro in cash. Taro was having a good time.

And, as if that wasn't enough, he was in love. She was an American, a hostess like Taro's mother had once been. She was so beautiful, the American, with her blond curls and violet eyes. Taro got an erection every time he saw her. He had gotten one the first time, right after she walked into his mother's restaurant with some of her foreign friends. He had to hold a menu over his pants when he walked over to take their order. The American girl asked whose cool van was parked outside, and when he said it was his, she looked right at him, smiling just a little, and said: "I knew it." Later that evening her friends left, but she stayed, and when it was time to close up the restaurant, Taro drove her home. Her name was Jessica.

Taro had told Jessica everything: about his childhood, his trouble with the police, what he was doing with the Iranians. Jessica wanted to know if he was happy. She asked him one night in the Astro, condensation dripping from the windows, the two of them naked on the single bed in the back. Are you happy? He said he was doing all right. Yeah, she said, but are you happy?

He asked her what she meant.

"Well," she said, "look at the life you have. You're half Filipino, so you're a second-class citizen, I don't care what your passport says. People look at you funny when you walk down the street. The police hassle you all the time. You have to break into warehouses and steal stuff to make a living." She rested her chin against his chest. "Are you happy?"

He had to think about that one.

What if, Jessica said, what if the two of them could go somewhere else, somewhere warm and friendly, where they wouldn't have to worry about money, where nobody would stare or make faces when they saw them, where they could start feeling good about themselves for a change. Wouldn't that be nice?

Taro admitted it would.

Jessica said, "I've got this idea . . ."

"Taro is a total pussycat," Jessica had said to Chris on the way over, "you're going to love him. He is so whipped. If I asked him to be my kitchen mat, he would lay down in front of the sink."

Taro's Astro was parked along Midosuji Boulevard, in sight of the European contours of Namba Station. Other lowriders idled nearby under the swaying ginkgo trees. Chris thought some of the custom jobs were pretty good. One El Camino had a girl in a bikini painted on one side, her head resting on top of the rear wheelwell, her toes just touching the edge of the front blinker. A black Nissan Skylark had the Grim Reaper sprawled across the hood. Hip-hop music, heavy on bass, was pouring out of most of the cars, the vibrations from the amplifiers making the lowriders bounce up and down. A few high-school girls in their school uniforms, skirts hiked up, wearing tall baggy socks, were running between the cars, trying to peer inside the tinted windows. The drivers, some in T-shirts, some in black leather jackets, all wearing wraparound sunglasses despite the fact that it was close to midnight, ignored the girls. The drivers tinkered with their engines or slurped noodles bought from street peddlers pushing their carts along the sidewalk or just sat behind the wheels of their cars, smoking and looking bored.

Taro was showing Chris and Jessica what he had done to the inside of the Astro.

"I soundproof the walls just before," Taro said. He rapped on the white carpeting that seemed to cover everything, making a dull, thudding sound. "Well, it's not soundproof one hundred percent, but almost. Windows are really thick, see? And there are double locks for doors."

"You torture small animals in here on the weekends, don't you?" Chris said.

Taro looked at him quizzically, Taro about what Chris had expected: not too tall, wiry, maybe a hundred and fifty pounds in his Doc Martens and black jeans. He looked Japanese except for his nose, which was a little too pointed, and his round, almost girlish eyes, squinting at Chris now as he said: "What is 'torture'?"

"Watching Japanese TV," Jessica said. "Show Chris all your toys, Taro. Let's start up front."

Taro stared at Chris for a minute, then climbed up into the driver's seat, one of a pair of matching captain's chairs up front. There were no chairs in the back, only a single bed against one wall and boxes of stuff—clothes, baseball bats, Styrofoam packages of instant ramen—against the other. Chris had been sitting on the floor, but when Taro moved up to the front, Chris got up and sat next to Jessica on the bed. Taro didn't look happy.

Chris was beginning to think this would be fun.

Taro pointed at a black box with flashing red lights under the radio. "This is Aiwa 437 police scanner. I bought it from some Vietnam guys in Den Den town. It's strong. I can catch many signals." He turned on the power and the box began squawking in rough-sounding Japanese. Taro said: "The cop talking now says a drunk guy just, how can I say, Jessica?" He gestured with his right hand moving quickly away from his mouth. "*Hakushi-mashita?*"

"Threw up?" Jessica made a face.

Taro smirked. "Threw up in his police car."

"Take him out back and shoot him," Chris said. He put his hand on Jessica's knee and starting massaging it gently, watching Taro's eyes and teeth and fists clench. "What else you got?"

Taro bent over to look under his seat, moving too fast, and hit his head on the steering wheel. He swore something in Japanese but didn't look back at Chris and Jessica. Jessica asked if he was all right, but Taro waved her off. "*Et to . . .*" he said in a strained voice, digging underneath the seat, "I got radar detector." He showed it to them over his shoulder. "There's a voice changer under here, too."

Chris said, "A what?"

"You know," Jessica said, "one of those little gizmos, you hook it up to your phone and it electronically disguises your voice? Like in the movies. It's totally cool. "

"Where did you get it?" Chris asked.

"Tokyo," Taro said. He was rubbing his head.

"God, I miss Tokyo," Jessica said. "Taro, can we try it out?"

The device was about the size of a Walkman, with two long cords snaking out from either side. One of the cords had a large jack on the end; the other was connected to a foam-covered pad. Taro plugged the end with the jack into the Astro's cigarette lighter, and attached the pad to the mouthpiece of his cellular phone. They took turns calling one other. Jessica thought the scrambler made each of them sound like Chewbacca.

Taro had more interesting stuff. He had crowbars and heavy-duty metal cutters, the kind that could snap through barbed wire or steel chains. He had a ring of skeleton keys. He had a collection of stolen license plates.

There was even a hidden compartment under the bed.

Taro said, "If you take off mattress and top board, there is big space here." He showed them. He had futons and blankets in there. "But under there is more. You can take out this board"—he did—"and there is another big space."

"Just enough for one small asshole," Jessica said.

"Or maybe a cozy hiding place for two," Chris said. He wrapped his arms around Jessica's waist from behind and put his lips close to her ear. "What do you say?"

She pulled his hands away. "You're not getting me in there," she said.

Taro let the top board fall with a bang.

"That's all I got," he said.

Watching Taro burn rubber as the van peeled away, Jessica said: "Do you practice being an asshole or does it just come naturally?"

"I practice," Chris said.

"We need Taro for this to work."

"I just want to know who I'm dealing with," Chris said. The two of them found an entrance to the subway and headed down. A homeless man sat on a pile of newspapers on the stairs, studying his blackened feet. "Is Taro the kind of guy that's going to explode and get in my face? Or is he going to let me walk all over him? Now I know."

"You don't know shit," Jessica said, "but I like the way you just said 'who I'm dealing with.' "

"Did I say that?"

The underground mall was a maze of businessmen in blue suits and loose ties, checking their watches, and groups of laughing young women in short skirts and sandals. Sandals and open-toed shoes everywhere. Chris had never stared at women's feet the way he did in Japan. They were so slender and delicate looking, the nails painted black or green or red. He couldn't take his eyes off them. It was turning into a fetish. He felt Jessica tugging on his arm.

"Are you listening to me?" Jessica said.

"What?"

"Stop staring. They're not *that* hot. I said, does this mean you're going to do it?"

"You mean, am I in?" Chris asked. "Am I on the team? Am I with the program? I don't know. What if I look at you the wrong way and get Taro all mad? He might bweak my widdle face."

Jessica smiled. "I wouldn't keep going out of my way to piss him off. Just because Taro didn't blow up at you today doesn't mean he won't tomorrow. I know he looks like a little geek, but this is a dangerous guy. He's been in prison, for Christ's sake."

"For stealing scooters."

"He's done more time than you have."

"You said he was a pussycat."

"I meant, for me. Maybe if you show him your tits, he'll like you, too."

"Might even like me better."

She stopped, gently pulling him around to face her. "What's it going to be?" she asked.

Around them, shopkeepers were using remote controls to ease down heavy metal doors. "Auld Lang Syne" was playing over the loudspeakers. It was eleven-forty. One of the subway employees shouted something, and there was a rush to the ticket machines.

"You're going to miss your train," Chris said.

"I'll take a cab."

"To Kobe?"

"Answer the question."

He grinned. "Which question was that?"

Jessica let go of his arm, shaking her head. "You're such a fuckup, Chris. You know that?"

"*I'm* the fuckup?"

"Acting like this is a movie. Like you're Bruce Willis, and you have to get all the good lines."

"I was thinking more John Cusack," he said, "and didn't you tell me once to come up with some good lines?" When Jessica turned away from him, putting her hands on her hips, he laughed. "I'm sorry, Jess, but I mean, really. We're going to have to have a sense of humor about this, or it's not going to work." When she still didn't look at him, he said: "I'm in, okay? Let's do this crazy thing."

He surprised himself, saying it. It was the night, he thought, the memory of the four girls at the bar, the seventy thousand stolen yen in his pocket. In the morning, he'd want to back out, but tonight he was invincible. Kidnapping? Extortion? Why not? Anyway, until they actually took the guy he could always tell Taro and Jessica *sayonara*.

Jessica still wasn't looking at him. Chris waited. As busy as the underground mall had been five minutes ago, it was nearly empty now. To the left of Chris and Jessica, the subway employees were shouting at the last few stragglers. Chris could hear the squealing of brakes as a train pulled up to the platform below. Jessica turned around slowly and looked over at him, her eyes thoughtful.

"Why?" she asked.

Chris said, "Why did I change my mind?"

Jessica nodded, coming toward him.

"You said it yourself," Chris said. "What's being good ever gotten me?"

"That was just a line I heard once on TV." She slipped her arms around his waist. "You've never been good a day in your life."

"Then there's no reason to start now."

"You're not going to give me a straight answer, are you?"

"Oh, I've got a straight answer for you." He pulled her closer. "Take me back to your place and I'll show it to you."

She smiled, the gleam back in her violet eyes, and Chris felt it again, the invincibility. What's more, he knew that he and Jessica were on the same page, and that whatever happened in the next few weeks, Taro Shimada was going to be the odd man out.

"Well," Jessica said, "if that's the only answer I'm going to get . . ."

Chris told Jessica to write the plan down so it would be easier to spot any flaws. Thursday after work, she took out a Kawanishi Report Pad ("The Path A Million Pens") and got started:

That night—Chris and Taro drive Taro's van to the Hotel Happy Casanova. (<u>Note:</u> The van should be painted a different color (easy), and we have to use one of Taro's stolen plates. They should try to get there before the place starts to fill up but AFTER it gets dark. 7:00? 7:30?

 <u>Clothes</u>

 Chris—suit, any color. Should look like a successful expatriate (kind of a stretch!) ★★★<u>Should let the goatee fill out to a beard</u>. ★★★

 Taro—nurse's uniform. (kinky date for Chris)

 Have to buy:

1. *uniform (what size??)*
2. *shoes (size???)*
3. *nurse hat*
4. *white stockings (thick)*
5. *gauze masks (2 or 3)*

Bags

Chris—briefcase (we have?). Inside: dark blue suit for Taro, video-tape*, red wig*, black ski mask*, black gloves*.

Taro—my green overnight bag. Inside: my black Donna Karan skirt and belt, low-cut blouse (which one?), leather bathing suit*, studded collar*, leather whip*, Walkman and MDs.

★ must buy.

Okay. Chris and Taro go into the hotel. Chris is the big important businessman, so he picks out the room. 3rd Floor if possible, pay for all night. Taro should be hanging on to Chris's arm, looking at him or at the floor. Don't look directly at the cameras. This goes for Chris, too—why take chances? Somebody will be watching 'cause Chris is a foreigner. ★★★IDEA★★★—Taro should act a little tipsy. Will help later. Once Chris has the key, the two of them should go up to the room and wait there. (Watch pornos and jerk off!)

I'll be at the club, doing my thing. I need to wear that long, black Moschino dress that I have—the really elegant one with the lace trim. Anybody watching will totally remember it. Zeniya and I will probably get to the hotel about 11:30, and we'll check into 301. (We always use 301.) Inside should take about ~~15~~ 10 minutes. Now, when he's done, Z always has to go to the bathroom, and he'll tell me to make us a couple of drinks from the minibar. (Those little airplane bottles. Johnnie Walker for him—straight, no ice. This guy is SO boring—every fucking time the same thing.) I'll make them, but

in HIS, he gets a couple of—what? (Chris's job—sleeping pills?)
He'll slug it down, and when I drink mine, I'll say it tastes funny.
He'll grunt or something and take a nap (he does this anyway—this
time he'll just sleep longer).

Now it's 12:00/12:30. Z is out. I go and unlock the door. Then,
I call Taro on the kei-tai, and he and Chris come over. ***Taro
should still be wearing the nurse getup, in case anybody's wandering
around outside.*** Once the two of them show up, all of us get to
work.

Taro—take off the uniform. Strip Z. Check to see if Z's suit will
fit. If it does, wear that. If it doesn't, put on Z's shirt and tie and the
dark blue suit from the overnight bag. (Zeniya always wears a dark
suit. If anybody's watching later from the surveillance cameras, they
won't be able to tell the difference. Cameras film in B&W). Get the
nurse's uniform on Zeniya.

Chris—take out the videotape and get started with the camera.
(Will be in the corner next to the TV.)

Me—put on S&M gear. (joy)

When we're all set up, I'll get in bed next to Z and pretend I'm
knocked out like he is. Chris films us. Need: close-ups of my face and
Z's and full shots of the two of us together. 2-3 minutes, max.

After the movie

Chris and Z have to leave first, dressed as Chris and Taro were before. (So—no changing necessary.) Now, here's where the tipsy part
from before comes in: Z, as the kinky nurse, is now SO "drunk" that
"she" "decides" to ride Chris piggyback right out the back door.
Chris takes "her" to the van and drives around the block. (Drive on
the LEFT!!! VERY IMPORTANT!!!)

Taro and I are still in the room. I put on the skirt and blouse and

put the dress on OVER it. We check the room and go downstairs.
I'm "drunk," too, and I ride Taro piggyback just like Z on Chris.
No, wait. That's a bad idea. Two couples doing the piggyback
thing . . . I'll just hang on to Taro's arm like I'm totally sloshed.
Taro—DON'T LOOK AT THE CAMERAS. We go out. As
soon as we're clear of the door and the camera, but still behind the
bushes, I pull the dress off over my head and put on the red wig.
(***Have to <u>practice</u> this, make it smooth.) Taro and I hit the side-
walk and hey! Who's that cool Japanese guy with Nicole Kidman!
We walk around the corner and Chris picks us up.

<u>Inside the van</u>

Taro—drive to Z's house (he knows the way, right?)—DON'T
SPEED.

Chris and Jessica—Tie up Z (rope?), put my earphones on him
(connect to Walkman, high volume, <u>bring MDs</u>: Robbie Williams?
Oasis?), put bag (we have?) over his head, and put him in the compartment under the bed. What else? Point is—he can't hear, he can't
see, he can't s—NEED SOME KIND OF GAG for mouth.

<u>At the house</u>

Z's house sits behind a wall and a wooden gate. No cameras. All
we do is drive by.

Chris—put on mask/gloves, jump out, and slip videotape inside
the mail slot on the gate. Get back in.

There is a convenience store a few streets down from the house
that's open all night and has a parking area. Taro pulls in and buys a
bento (?). He takes it back to the van to eat. (Everybody does this—
nobody will notice.) While he's eating, he calls Z's house on the kei-
tai. Z's wife answers. She's upstairs in bed, probably, 'cause it's 2 or 3
a.m. by now. Taro asks her in Japanese where her husband is. Of

course she doesn't know. Taro tells her to be very quiet, not to wake anyone up, then he tells her to hang up the phone and go downstairs. She's freaked out by now, so you know she's going to do it. Taro calls back after 10 seconds and asks if she's using the cordless phone (they've got one in the living room). She'll be so surprised by the question, she'll tell us right away whether she is or not. Next, Taro tells her to take the phone, don't hang up, and go outside and check the mail. She goes out there and finds the video. Taro tells her to go back inside, DON'T HANG UP, and put the video in the VCR. Be quiet. She does, and she sees her husband sleeping after a long night playing nurse and dominatrix. Taro says, what do you think? This is end of my new movie. Would you like to see the rest? (He's bluffing, but she doesn't know that, and it really doesn't matter anyway—I'll explain later.) She says, what do you want? Taro says, don't worry. We're not going to kill your husband. However, if you don't give us all the money in your husband's safe right this minute, we ARE going to take him and his foreign girlfriend down to Midosuji Boulevard and dump the two of them naked in front of . . . somewhere appropriate. Oh, and we'll be sure to call the news media beforehand. Oh, and copies of the video will be sent to all your husband's competitors.

Now, if she says "No, go ahead," I'll take a Seconal(?) right then and there and we'll go do just what Taro said we were going to do. But I am 99.9% sure she will say "Yes, I'll do it." Think of the humiliation for her husband (and herself) otherwise. Japanese people kill themselves over much less. Embarrassment is totally worse than death over here. "Saving face," etc. etc. Besides, they've got lots more money in the bank. She'll do it.

Potential Problem—she can't open the safe (doesn't know the com-

bination). Z TOLD ME BEFORE that it was her birthday, when he was drunk and being cute. If she says she can't open it, then A) she's lying or B) he lied to me. Either way, see "No, go ahead" above. ***IF WE DON'T GET THE MONEY RIGHT AWAY WE GIVE THE WHOLE THING UP. THERE IS NO PLAN B.***

<u>If she says "Yes, I'll do it."</u>

Taro tells her to take the tape out of the machine and put it in a garbage bag. Then he tells her to get the money. When she says she's ready, he tells her to go outside and put the bag in the shadows in front of the wall. She has to be quiet. If the neighbors wake up, then she'll be looking for her husband on the morning wide shows. Then he tells her to leave the front gate open, go inside, go to the bathroom, and lock the door. DON'T HANG UP! Now (this is still Taro talking), turn on the shower—I want to hear it. Good. Start telling me the story of your life.

She starts babbling and Taro drives up to the house. Chris gets out, gets the bag, and gets back in. Taro drives around the block while Chris and I check everything. (Mrs. Z is still on the phone.) If it's all kosher, I get back into the dominatrix outfit and Chris ties me up like Z. (Should I take a pill, or just fake it?) Back in front of the house now, Chris (mask and gloves on) throws me out (inside the gate, <u>small</u> bruises okay) and then throws Z out. Taro drives off, tells Mrs. Z thank you very much, count to ten before you hang up, then go check outside. Then he drives off!

<u>After it's all over</u>

Z and I "wake up." (He might be awake already.) I'm pissed. I want to call the police. They talk me out of it, 'cause they know the guy Mrs. Z talked to still has the original tape. It's over. Z has

learned to be more careful, and I've learned that Japan isn't as safe as
you read in Newsweek. I hang around at the club for another few
weeks, but I'm too shaky. I tell everybody I'm quitting and leave
Japan. AS A RICH WOMAN!!!!! OFF WITH TARO TO
PARADISE!!!!! THE END!!!!!!!

<u>Why it will work</u>

1. We are in charge the whole way. Mrs. Z has no time to think
about what she's doing or call the police.

2. Nobody, especially Z, gets a good look at Chris or Taro.

3. We don't have to bluff. Kidnappers always screw up when they
say they're going to kill the person they kidnapped. They don't want
to do that. That just makes everything worse. Our threat is totally
doable, and if we have to do it, so what? (Can you imagine the <u>pub-
licity</u> I'd get? Dumped naked on the street with a captain of industry? I'd have TV offers pouring in. If that happens, I promise to share
the wealth.)

4. There's no reason to suspect me, really. There are at least 4 other
girls who know about the safe and his stash, at least that I've found
out about; any one of them could have done it. In fact, those girls are
<u>better</u> suspects than me, because he's officially dumped them. He's still
stringing me along.

****

Biggest potential problem—police. I don't think they will get involved if Mrs. Z goes through with paying us, but Z might call them
anyway. A million dollars is a lot, even for this guy. If he calls the
cops, I'll be wetting my pants, but I think we'll still get away with it.
Why—A) The wife didn't see anything, B) Z and I don't remember
anything after we had drinks (and *remember*, I said mine tasted
funny), and C) The video cameras at the love hotel clearly show us

being "carried out" by two strange men—a bearded foreigner and a Japanese guy, both of them wearing sunglasses. After it's over the bearded guy won't exist—he'll just be Chris with his goatee, the Chris who doesn't have a gaijin card or a photo on file at Osaka City Hall—and as for the Japanese guy, who knows who that is? All Japanese look alike, especially when they've got their faces turned away from a camera stuck in the ceiling.

Jessica paused, nibbling on the end of her pen. What else? She had ten pages already. She looked at the clock and saw, Christ, it was almost five o'clock in the morning.

Fuck it.

On the bottom of the last page, she wrote:

Well? What do you think?

Taro didn't want to wear the nurse outfit.

It was Friday evening, about an hour before Jessica had to leave for the club. The three of them were sitting in her living room, reading, Jessica having gone down to the 7-Eleven and made copies of her "opus." Taro was on the floor, his head resting on a funky orange-and-gold pillow Jessica had picked up in Thailand. Jessica was sunk into a beanbag next to a large potted palm by the window. Chris was stretched out on the sofa, legs hanging over the side, smoking a joint and feeling comfortable. Chris liked Jessica's place. The night he ran into her at the bar, she had told him to come home with her, see how the other half lived. Kobe was a hike from America Mura, maybe an hour if you caught all the trains right, but it was different from Osaka all right: modern, shiny, cosmopolitan. The city was on a slope, running from Mount Rokko on the north to the Seto Inland Sea on the south. Jessica said Tokyo was the New York of Japan, Osaka was the Chicago, and Kobe was the San Francisco. Chris had been to San Francisco and thought this was a bit of a stretch, but Kobe was nice all the same.

Jessica's apartment was a few blocks from the south side of Sannomiya Station, on the top floor of a peach-colored building called the Sunny Hearts Mansion. It had auto-locks and cameras outside the front door and inside the elevators that you could check from your apartment, which Jessica said was still pretty unusual. Japan was a burglar's dream. Lax security, cheap locks . . . Jessica wasn't going to live like that. This building was new, built a few years after the earthquake. Chris said, what earthquake?

"You know," Jessica said, "the Great Hanshin Earthquake. Killed six thousand people? It was like the year before I came here."

Chris shrugged. Who kept track of natural disasters in Asia?

Jessica's apartment was a 2LDK, which meant there were two bedrooms and a bigger room with a sink and counter at one end that was a combination living/dining/kitchen. Since Jessica was on the top floor, she also had an extended balcony that was as big as one of the bedrooms. If you stood up on the rail in just the right place, you could see the wharf and the sea beyond it, so the realtors classified it as an "ocean view." Chris asked her the first night what the rent was, but she wouldn't tell him. She said: "A lot."

Chris believed her. The market down the street from her place sold watermelons for the equivalent of sixty dollars each.

Small watermelons. He couldn't imagine what an apartment with an ocean view would go for.

"Why he can't wear it?" Taro asked, jabbing his thumb toward Chris.

"Taro, honey—" Jessica said.

" 'Cause I'm not as sexy as you," Chris said.

"Chris, shut up." Jessica gave him a warning look. "Taro, Chris is too big to be the nurse. And he's a foreigner. Who's going to believe that? You walk in, nobody notices."

Taro said, "Nobody notice I wear the uniform anyway."

"Continuity, Taro," Jessica said. "That's a movie word. A nurse is going to walk *out* of the hotel, that means a nurse has to walk *in*."

Taro had his hands behind his head, staring at the ceiling. Thinking about it.

"Taro?"

"What is 'tipsy'?"

He was going to do it. Chris grinned and took a deep drag on the joint. He was starting to get a nice buzz going.

Jessica sat up on the beanbag. " 'Tipsy' is when you're just a little bit drunk." She put her thumb and forefinger close together. "Like, this much."

Taro scowled. "How I do that?"

"Just keep close to Chris, holding on to his arm—"

"Oooh," Chris said.

"Use your imagination," Jessica said, giving Chris a look. "Don't fall over or anything, just maybe trip on your feet a little. Laugh too much. Wrap your arms around him suddenly."

"Stop," Chris said, "you're making me all hot." He was trying to make smoke rings, but all he could manage were vaguely round puffs.

"Look," Jessica said, "we're talking two minutes here. When you get to the room, you can take it off."

"Oh, he's going to take it off," Chris said. He winked at Taro and was rewarded with a baleful stare, Taro about ready to take a swing at him. Chris giggled, then coughed up a cloud of smoke. He wondered why he was so intent on pushing Taro, wondered why he couldn't stop with the jokes. But every time he looked over at Jessica, there was Kathleen Turner from *Body Heat* again, or Annette Bening from *The Grifters*, and every time he looked over at Taro, there was . . . there was somebody. One of those wormy little guys that Bruce Lee beat up on before he had to face Yang Sze, somebody *tough*. The three of them were actors on a set, and pretty soon the director would shout "Cut!" and all of them would get up, stretch, and go out somewhere for a drink.

"If you're through being a wiseass," Jessica said, looking like she was pissed at him now, too, "do you have any problems with what's written down there?"

"You mean the master plan?" Chris said. He felt the giggles coming on again.

Jessica stared at him.

"Well," Chris said, grinning. "As a matter of fact . . ."

"What?"

Really pissed.

Chris sat up, feeling the blood rush to his head, and put what was left of the joint inside the can of Pocari Sweat he was using as an ashtray. He picked up his copy of the plan. "Okay, seriously," he said, shuffling pages. "Here. Page two. Why is it that he always gets 301?"

"What, at the love hotel?"

"Yeah. You say it right here: *We always use 301.*"

"The Japanese do something once, "Jessica said, "the next time they do it the same way. You should watch this guy dress. First the left sock, pull on it twice, then the right sock, pull on it twice—"

"No, no, no, no. I mean, why does he always *get* 301. Why isn't it occupied sometimes?"

Jessica thought about it. "He probably reserves it."

"You can do that?"

"He's rich," Taro said darkly. "Rich people can do anything."

"You said it, honey," Jessica cooed, and she stretched out and rubbed the top of his head with her bare foot. "After a few weeks, you, too. Chris, if we end up in another room, I'll just call on the cellular, the *kei-tai.*"

Something about it bothered Chris, but he couldn't figure out what. The dope was making it hard to concentrate. There was something else, too, something more important. He started shuffling pages again, thinking he should have been making notes.

What was it?

"Anything else?" Jessica asked.

There it was.

"The van," he said.

Taro started to sit up. "What do you mean?"

"We can't use the Astro." Chris tried to make his voice sound world-weary. "Frankly, I can't believe we didn't see this before."

Jessica looked up. "What are you talking about?"

"Think how easy it would be for somebody to trace that back to us. Say Z calls the police after I throw the two of you out the van. What's the first thing they're going to do after they talk with you?"

"Talk to neighbors," Taro said. He sounded bored, lying back down.

"Exactly," Chris said. "Ask if they saw anything suspicious. Then they're going to go to all the convenience stores and gas stations in the area and ask them the same thing. Then they're going to go to the love hotel. You think somebody's not going to notice a souped-up, Chevy Astro lowrider? It doesn't matter if you paint it a different color. When the cops don't find it, they're going to start checking the body shops. And," he said, pointing at Taro, "the police are going to ask themselves: 'Who do we have on file owning a customized van?' " He leaned back against the cushions, feeling clever.

"It doesn't matter," Jessica said.

"Really?" Chris leaned over the side of the couch, looking in his bag for another joint. "I hope you feel the same way about wearing stripes."

Ah, there was one, Jesus, big as a small banana. Now for the lighter. Wearing stripes. That was good. He had to remember that.

"It doesn't matter," Jessica said, getting up out of the beanbag, "because Taro's got that all figured out." She knelt down behind him and pushed him up, rubbing his shoulders. "Haven't you, babe?"

Taro said, "I think about that, first thing," giving Chris a look that said, *What a stupid asshole you are.* "Cops always want to make me guilty. I have to think better than them."

Taro Shimada, Chris thought. Master Criminal. Where was the fucking lighter? "Well?" he said impatiently.

Jessica couldn't wait. "Taro knows these other Filipinos in Wakayama. You know, on the Pacific? They've got a body shop."

"*Secret* body shop," Taro said.

"*Secret* body shop," Jessica said, winking at Chris. "They're part of this illegal setup that ships out old Japanese cars to the Philippines. Day before we're ready, Taro goes down there and gets the Astro painted. When we're done, he drives back. Nobody knows the difference. And," she said, jumping up, "it gets even better!"

While Jessica went to the bathroom, Taro told him about another scheme that the Iranians he worked with had thought up. The police, Taro said, would pick up Middle Eastern–looking guys on any pretext. Guy's riding a bicycle down the street? Stop him; maybe the bicycle's stolen. Maybe he's a terrorist. Bring him to the station, see what we can pin on him. And there wasn't anything the guy could do about it; it was perfectly legal. This was a big problem for the Iranians Taro knew because of all their warehouse jobs. They needed alibis for those times that the police wouldn't be able to question. One of the ideas they had, lots of them had relatives or friends working in Tokyo. Now, when you drove to Tokyo, the fastest way was to use to the expressways, and all of the expressways had tolls. The Iranians worked out a system where they could get toll receipts showing them on the road to or from Tokyo during any time in question. It was perfect. Even if the police took it a step further, and contacted the friends or relatives in Tokyo . . . well, you knew whose side they were on. Yes, Officer, he was with me the whole time. We ate *kabab koobideh* all weekend.

"Iranians," Taro said. "They're really smart."

Jessica was out of the bathroom. Chris said, "Why didn't you tell me all this?"

"I forgot. Taro and I had that part worked out before I even knew you were in Japan." She was looking at the unlit joint in Chris's hand. "Fuck, that's the size of a small banana. Let me see that."

"I can't find the lighter," Chris said, all of a sudden unsure of himself. He and Jessica were supposed to be the stars of this movie; Taro was the Actor in a Supporting Role. But there he was, lighting the joint for Jessica, the two of them grinning at each other, Taro putting the lighter in his pocket—he'd had it the whole time, the prick . . .

Chris felt his teeth clench.

He was feeling a little paranoid.

"Tell me this," he said, and he liked the sound of his voice: strong, in control. He started feeling better. "You really want 'sleeping pills'?"

"What?" Jessica had her eyes closed, the joint between her fingers.

Chris found the right page. "Here on page two. *I'll make them*—you're talking about the drinks in the love hotel—*but in HIS, he gets a couple of—what?* Then in parentheses, *Chris's job—sleeping pills?*"

"Yeah," Jessica said, eyes open now. "Sleeping pills, or something. Something to knock the guy out."

"You really think it's going to be that easy?"

"You're the local pharmacist." She took another drag on the massive joint. "This"—her voice strained—"this is fucking fantastic, by the way."

"Yes, well"—he took the joint from her—"getting 'something' isn't the problem. I'm talking about the whole idea. The pill-in-the-drink trick. The staple of every half-assed"—deep breath, holddddddd it, oh yeah—"made-for-TV mystery."

"You don't think it will work?" Getting defensive now.

"It might work." Chris put his arms up on the back of the sofa, feeling on top of things again. "All I'm saying is, on TV it looks easy. This is real life. We don't know what the drink will taste like after the pill's mixed in, how it'll work—we could kill the old fuck. Or, not do a thing to him. Most barbiturates, you fight against them, you can stay awake. They're not guaranteed to knock you out."

The three of them were quiet for a minute.

"Actually," Chris said, thinking out loud, "why are we making this so complicated anyway? Why don't we just break into the goddamn house?"

Jessica's head snapped up. "Are you insane?"

"I'm serious. We know the combination to the safe. You said the house doesn't have any security. Why do we have to go through this elaborate—"

"We *don't* know the combination to the safe," Jessica said. "Zeniya was drunk and being cute the night he told me. He might have made the whole thing up. And I never said the house doesn't have any security. I don't know that either. Even if it doesn't, there's no way I'm breaking into a house. That's way too risky."

"I'd call the pill thing pretty risky," Chris said.

Taro said, "Maybe we forget pills. We put, what can I say, gag in his mouth? So we don't care he's awake or not."

"A Ping-Pong ball or something," Chris said. "Put the nurse mask over his mouth." It wasn't a bad idea.

Taro's face fell. "If he wake up, maybe he start to kick or something."

"Stop," Jessica said. "Stop trying to think up new ideas. We don't have to be, like, original here. The pill thing is our best bet, and it *isn't* that risky. Look, this guy always has a drink after we do it, and he *always* takes a nap afterward. He's the fucking Habit-meister."

"Habit-meister," Chris said. The giggles were coming on again. "I like that."

"The purpose of the pill is to help him do what he does anyway. He's not going to fight it, and if you'd ever seen him drink, you'd know he's not going to taste *anything*."

"Say I grant you all that," Chris said. He giggled. "*Grant*. I *grant* you all that. Still, what do you give a—how old is this fart?"

"I don't know," Jessica said. "Sixty. Sixty-five."

"Say sixty-five. What do you give a sixty-five-year-old man to knock him out for a few hours? A sixty-five-year-old man with *alcohol* in his system?"

"You're going to have to figure it out," Jessica said.

"He could have a heart condition."

"The way he fucks, I doubt it. Look, if worse comes to worst, you're just going to have to experiment."

That confused him. "Experiment?"

Jessica smiled. "Yes, experiment. On yourself. Drink a couple of beers, then take something and see what happens."

"Dear God, madam"—Chris tried to affect an English accent—"you expect me to drug myself?"

"What's that in your hand? A lollipop?"

Chris looked at the massive joint resting between his fingers. "It's a banana," he said.

"All right." Jessica stood up and stretched. "I have to go. Taro, you're fine with what we've worked out?"

Taro shrugged. "Okay, Jessica."

"How about you, Mr. Anal?"

"Mr. Who?"

"You heard me. Any more objections?"

"I'm sure I'll think of something," Chris said. "But it can wait. Do you have a date in mind for the mission, Mrs. Phelps?"

Jessica looked at the calendar. "Today's what, the thirtieth? Z and I have a standing date on the second Friday of every month. That would be"—she flipped a page—"June fourteenth."

She looked back at Chris and Taro.

"Good for you?" she asked.

PART 2

8

Chris had the theme from *Mission: Impossible* running through his head all the way from the room to the van.

DUM dum, dum dum dum dum—

He had Zeniya cradled in his arms, the old man a transvestite's bad joke in the nurse outfit, white rubber-soled shoes bouncing up and down as Chris hurried to the elevator. Nobody in the hallway, that was good. He could just picture one of the cleaning women turning a corner, doing a double take at the foreigner with the nurse dead asleep in his arms. *My girlfriend, she's a little tired. Wink, wink.* Chris grinned, sweat starting to trickle down his face and into his beard. Christ, the old guy was heavy. He wasn't all that big, but he was *hard,* muscle everywhere. What did the piece of shit do all day, anyway? Chris didn't see him sitting behind a desk . . .

—da da DA, da da DA—

The elevator was a tight squeeze. Chris had to stand in the middle, holding Zeniya cattercornered, and nearly ran the old man's head into the side wall when he pushed the button for the lobby. The doors closed. Chris watched the overhead lights flash as the elevator went down, 3 . . . 2 . . . and—you have to be fucking *kidding* me—stopped at 2, doors sliding open, Christ, which button closed the doors, the wall connecting with Zeniya's head this time as Chris tried to get closer to the panel . . .

There was nobody waiting when the doors opened.

"Thank you, thank you, thank you," Chris said, looking up at the ceiling. "Thank you, *God*." Thinking whoever had pushed the button had taken the stairs, not wanting to chance a sudden encounter. Chris loved the Japanese. Timid, considerate . . . Still, he had to be careful. They were probably downstairs depositing their key right now, and after that, they'd have to find their car, so he needed to take it slow. Nice and easy. Nobody in a hurry here.

2 . . . 1 . . . L.

When the doors opened, Chris waited a few seconds, then angled Zeniya out, feetfirst. This was the tricky part. Using his right forearm, Chris bumped Zeniya's head up close to his own, trying to keep the old man out of camera range. Zeniya was making small wheezing sounds under the gauze mask. He smelled of garlic and whiskey. Their faces were close enough to rub noses, so that's what Chris did, rubbing Zeniya's nose and smiling at him, making it look as good as he could.

"Honey, you drank so *much*. Yes you *did*," Chris whispered, baby talk now, still smiling, trying to keep the heavy son of a bitch's head upright as he carried him to the exit. "Honestly, I couldn't tell if you were awake or asleep that second time. No, I *couldn't*. But look, here we are. We're going to stick the key in the slot here—watch your head, that's it—and push the door open . . ."

DA DUM! dum, dum dum dum—

Outside, the humidity hit Chris in the face, heat still rising from the pavement at one-thirty in the morning. His beard was starting to itch. Just get the old fuck in the back of the van, Chris thought, and he tried not to hurry as he made his way through the parking area. What happened to the couple on two? He kept his head down, looking at Zeniya's closed eyes, smiling like a lovesick asshole.

"Did it hurt when you got your head whacked in the elevator? I hope so, yes I do." He suddenly wondered if he should be talking so much, the man still not hooked up to the Walkman. Then thought: *Look* at him. The man was *out*. "Look, there's the van. License plate still covered up, that's good . . . Does Zenny-*san* want to take a widdle wide? Yes? Well, you're in luck, yes you are."

Once they were inside the dark carport, Chris propped Zeniya against the wall with his right hand while he fished the keys out of his pocket with his left. He heard the sound of an engine and froze, waiting. A white Corolla rolled past, a man and a woman sitting up front, then turned onto the street and was gone. Chris looked at Zeniya, the old man's head slumped to the side.

"You think they saw us?" Chris asked. "No, me neither." He

opened the rear door. With both hands, he lifted Zeniya inside and laid him down on the floor. His head hit the white carpet with a *thunk.*

"Oooh, twice now," Chris said. He climbed in, closed the door, and moved up to the driver's seat. He had driven the van a few times the week before, Taro wanting to make sure he didn't wreck it coming out of the parking lot. It wasn't all that bad, driving on the left, except for shifting gears. Chris put the key in the ignition and started the engine. Turned on the lights, started to edge forward, then heard the sound of a chain scraping against concrete and realized, Christ, he had forgotten to take the metal strip off the license plate. Leaving the engine running, he got out and pried the strip off. Got back in the van.

And sat there for a minute, heart thumping against his chest.

Had he forgotten anything else?

He didn't think so.

Pulling out of the lot, he turned right onto the street in front of the love hotel and drove slowly around the block. By the time he got back, Jessica and Taro were already walking along the sidewalk, Jessica pulling something out of her purse. . . .

Jessica was having a little trouble breathing.

She'd been okay until she walked outside. More than okay, really; everything had gone much smoother than she'd thought it would. She and Zeniya had had sex (Jessica bent over the vanity again, watching herself in the mirror), and later, while Zeniya was in the bathroom, her hand had been steady dropping the pills (Luminal, 100 mg) in his glass of Johnnie Walker.

She'd had just the right tone in her voice after sipping her drink ("This tastes funny."), and, as expected, he'd barely acknowledged her, swallowing the whiskey in one shot then falling back onto the bed. Five minutes later, he was snoring lightly. She'd snapped her fingers next to his ears, then taken him by the shoulders and shaken him. He'd hardly stirred.

It had been easy.

Easy getting Zeniya into the nurse getup, easy making the video, easy getting out of the black dress and into the red wig once she and Taro were clear of the cameras. Easy all the way until she saw the Astro turning onto the street and it hit her that there was a drugged old man in the back of that van. A drugged old man she was *abducting* . . .

Suddenly, her breath started coming in hitches, and she was trembling all over. The sidewalk started to curve up toward the sky. Taro had to grab her arm to keep her from falling.

"You feel sick?" he whispered.

Jessica didn't say anything right away. She dug in her purse for the black film case with the Luminal inside, and when she had the cap off she started shaking out pills.

"Hey," Taro said. "You're dropping those things all over."

She could feel the panic welling up from her stomach, forcing its way up her throat. The night before, she'd taken a knife and cut two of the green tablets into fourths, figuring if one would knock her out, then a quarter one would probably just steady her nerves. Christ, they were here somewhere. *There.* Jesus, all the way at the bottom. She dry-swallowed one of the jagged pieces and nearly gagged. Taro patted her on the back. He looked concerned.

"I'm all right," Jessica said. She had to say *something*.

"Sure?"

He was smiling, trying to reassure her. She wanted to hit him. What was wrong with him? Didn't he realize what they'd *done*? She felt her stomach do another slow loop, and she gritted her teeth.

The van pulled up next to the sidewalk, just past a streetlamp. Jessica put her hands on her knees and forced herself to take deep breaths—in, *out,* in, *out*—but it didn't help. She made the mistake of looking up when Taro opened the side door, and seeing Zeniya lying there, like some kind of grotesque doll, his head lolled to the side, his skin a sickly yellow in the ghostly light of the streetlamp.... She couldn't keep the panic back and threw up all over the sidewalk.

Taro could see that he had to take charge of the situation. The fuckup, Chris, was already starting to get out of the Astro. Opening his big mouth.

"Jesus, what the—"

Taro made a slashing motion across his throat. Chris got the message, retreating back into the darkness of the van. Taro quickly looked up and down the street. No one else was outside. A car went through a red light at the intersection to the north. Every window was dark among the scattered shops and sliverlike homes next to the Hotel Happy Casanova.

Jessica still had her hands on her knees, saliva dripping from the corners of her mouth. Her eyes were closed. Taro felt around the pockets of his slacks (Zeniya's slacks) and found the old man's handkerchief. He handed it to her, saying "Here," and when she took it, he put his hands on her shoulders. Gently. Trying to let her know he was there without crowding her. He wanted to say, *See? You see the kind of man I am? You think that stupid asshole sitting in the van right now could be so tender with you?* Tender. That was the word exactly. He was as tender as . . . he didn't know what. As Presley. Like that Elvis Presley song.

"Jessica," he said softly. "Jessica, we have to go now."

She looked up at him, eyes watery, handkerchief over her mouth. She nodded. Gently, no, *tenderly,* he guided her to the Astro, keeping one hand on her shoulder and putting the other one around her waist. She flinched once when she saw Zeniya on the floor again, but she didn't stop. That's it, Taro thought, keep going. He helped her step up into the van . . . and there was Chris, taking her hand and motioning for him to close the door and get up front. Get them the hell out there.

Fuck.

Chris decided he was going to have to get Jessica occupied, or she was going to curl up in a corner and go comatose on them. She still had the handkerchief Taro had given her pressed against her mouth, and her eyes were vacant, like she was in shock. Chris got some rope that they had stashed away in a box next to the bed, and pushed it into her free hand, closing her fingers around it. Then he snapped his fingers in front of her eyes. She blinked twice, finally looking over at him. He put a finger to his lips. Then he pointed to Zeniya's legs, gesturing for her to tie them up. It seemed to do the trick. She didn't acknowledge him, but she shuffled over and began wrapping the long rope around the old man's ankles.

Chris felt the van turn up an incline then begin to speed up, Taro already on the expressway. Working quickly, he took the nurse hat off Zeniya's head. He found the Walkman and, gently turning the old man from left to right, inserted the tiny earphones. Jessica had brought MDs, and Chris took a look at them, reading the titles in the intermittent light from the street: Robbie Williams, The Streets, Travis. Chris wondered if the old man was a fan of really cringe-worthy Britpop. Decided he didn't want to offend the old fart's sensibilities and found a radio station instead. Putting his head down next to Zeniya's, he fiddled with the volume until he thought it was right.

Next: head wrap. Expanding on the hospital theme, they had decided on Ace bandages rather than a bag to cover the top of Zeniya's head. That way, they could leave his nose and mouth free, and there was less chance of the earphones jiggling loose. Chris and Jessica had practiced on Taro, trying to figure out where to start. It was harder than it looked; if Taro moved his head enough, the bandages would start to loosen and eventually fall off. They added packing tape, and that seemed to do the trick. Taro nearly screamed when they pulled it off.

No pain, no gain, Chris thought. Wrapping the bandages around Zeniya's head, he found a raised lump that felt tender— a present from the side wall of the elevator in the love hotel. Pain *and* no gain, for this guy. With the bandages on, he looked like a trauma case in a war film. Dumb bastard. When he woke up and the bandages were pulled off, he would be a million dollars poorer. A million dollars plus *alpha*. Hey, you snooze, you lose. Literally.

Jessica was through with the legs and was working on Zeniya's hands, doing her best not to look back up at his face. Chris had to smile. She was feeling *sorry* for the guy?

"Hey," he said, crouching down next to her, keeping his voice low, "you gonna make it?" When she didn't answer, he added. "This guy fucked you over, you know that?"

"I'm not—" she whispered, then seemed to change her mind and shook her head. "Can we just put him in the bed?"

"Wait a sec."

Standing up in a crouch, Chris could see out the front windshield to the brightly lit expressway, sound walls curving up on both sides. Ahead, a truck's brake lights flashed as a group of bikers changed lanes. The bikers had purple hair, no helmets, dragon flags flapping behind them. A sign in English and Japanese slid by: SENRI NEW TOWN, 2 km.

Taro looked back. "Almost there," he said.

Taro drove the van past the house once, leaning over the steering wheel and looking for lights or people moving around outside. The second time around, he cut the lights and slowed to a crawl.

Chris was digging through his briefcase, looking for the ski mask. Jessica was crouched next to the side door, her fingers on the latch. She wanted this over with. Zeniya, lying inert on the floor next to her, was totally creeping her out; she hadn't been able to convince Chris to put him in the compartment inside

Taro's bed. (Chris: "The fucker's too heavy, and besides, we're practically there.") Once they passed the house and the gate, she found herself starting to hyperventilate again. It was about to happen. Why did everything seem so *loud*? The Astro's engine sounded like a Mack truck. Living in the city, she had forgotten how quiet it got in the suburbs; she was sure they were going to wake up the entire neighborhood.

Taro was looking back at Chris. "*Go*. What do you wait for?"

"Here it is. Christ." Chris pulled the ski mask over his face and nodded to Jessica. "Do it."

She opened the door, and he jumped out. He skidded a little on the gravel in front of the gate, and had to pinwheel his arms to keep from falling. Jessica held her breath. Pushing open the flap to the mail slot, Chris dropped the video inside, making a sound like a gunshot. From her vantage point inside the van, Jessica looked through the gate to the house.

One of the lights was on downstairs.

Jessica waved frantically for Chris to hurry up. When he climbed back in the van, she said to Taro, "Go!" and slammed the side door, no longer caring how loud it was. All she wanted to do was to get the hell out of there before whoever had turned on that light decided to take a peek outside. Taro accelerated and turned at the first signal, heading down the hill and out of the subdivision.

"Jesus, what was that all about?" Chris had the ski mask off and was leaning against the bed, breathing hard. Jessica kicked out at him, hitting his shin. "Ow!"

"Somebody turned a light on downstairs, you dickhead."

"How is that my fault?"

Jessica ignored him. "Taro, we can't wait. If she goes outside and finds the tape now, it fucks everything up."

Chris had his hands open. "Hey, excuse me?"

Taro said, "You want me call now?"

"Yeah, right now," Jessica said. "The scrambler gizmo's already hooked up. Here." While she was handing Taro the mobile, Chris grabbed her other arm and she flinched. *"What?"*

"I said, how is this my fault?"

"You were taking all fucking night!"

"I got out, I put the tape in, I came back. What's—"

"Before that. We were sitting in front of the house for, like, five minutes."

"Five *seconds.*"

"Shut up," Taro said. "It's ringing."

This was it. Jessica watched Chris lose the dumb wounded expression from his face and stare at the phone, all of them knowing that as soon as somebody picked up the phone on the other end, everything was going to be different.

The only question was how different.

"Moshi moshi," Taro said. *"Zeniya Mariko san desu ka? . . . Anata no goshujin sama, ima doko ni iruka shiteru?"*

Right from the script. *Hello? Is this Mariko Zeniya? Do you know where your husband is right now?* Next Taro would tell her to be quiet and go to the downstairs phone . . .

. . . but now he was pulling over to the side of the road, stopping suddenly and saying *"Moshi mos . . . dare desu ka?"* Now— what the *fuck*—taking off the voice scrambler . . . *"Moshi . . . Zeniya-san? . . . Zeniya Tamotsu-san? . . . Daijo kensetsu no shacho . . . Eh, chotto matte, Zeniya-san no jussho wa Senri Chuo, maruha—"*

Taro took the phone away from his ear and stared at it. Then he turned to the back and handed it to Jessica. She took it, open-mouthed.

Chris said, "What—"

Jessica put her hand over his mouth. She was trying to stay calm. "Taro, who was that on the phone just now?"

Taro seemed to think it over. "First," he said, "Mrs. Zeniya."

"Then who?"

"Her husband."

"Her *husband,*" Jessica said, "is on the floor next to your god-damn *bed!*"

"Maybe she get a new one," Taro said. "This one I talk to? He's pretty pissed I wake him up."

This was the conversation Taro had with the Zeniyas on the phone:

> WOMAN: HELLO?
>
> TARO: HELLO? IS THIS MARIKO ZENIYA?
>
> WOMAN: YES. WHO IS THIS?
>
> TARO: DO YOU KNOW WHERE YOUR HUSBAND IS RIGHT NOW?
>
> WOMAN: WAIT A MINUTE. I'LL GET HIM.

(This was when Taro pulled over to the side of the road and stopped.)

> MAN: HELLO?
>
> TARO: HEL—

MAN: WHO IS THIS?

TARO: WHO IS THIS?

MAN: WHAT? I CAN'T UNDERSTAND ANYTHING YOU'RE SAYING.
HELLO?

TARO: (TAKING OFF THE VOICE SCRAMBLER) HE—

MAN: IT'S TWO O'CLOCK IN THE MORNING.

TARO: IS THIS MR. ZENIYA?

MAN: WERE YOU JUST IN FRONT OF MY HOUSE?

TARO: TAMOTSU ZENIYA?

MAN: YES. WHO IS THIS?

TARO: THE PRESIDENT OF DAIJO CONSTRUCTION?

MAN: YES. NOW LOOK—

TARO: UH, JUST A MINUTE. YOUR ADDRESS IS SENRI CHUO,
MARUHA—

CLICK.

"Let's look at this logically," Chris said.

Taro had the Astro parked outside an all-night ramen shop, in the back near the kitchen. Even out here, inside the van with the windows rolled up and the air conditioner running, Chris could smell pig bones being boiled into soup. It was noxious, like the inside of a rotting barn. He tried to breathe with his mouth instead of his nose, but that took too much concentration and he gave up. It wasn't like he didn't have other things to worry about.

Chris was sitting on the bed. He had one eye on Jessica, slumped against the passenger door, her hand trembling as she smoked a crumpled cigarette. His other eye was on the old man on the floor. The old man was moaning softly. He was bleeding from a gash on his forehead. When Taro had started to drive away from the Zeniyas'—what else was he supposed to do?—Jessica had jumped up, screaming for him to go back, and tried to wrench the wheel from his hands. Before Chris could pull her off, the Astro skidded against a parked car, throwing them down. Chris had managed to twist away from the old man, but Jessica's heels had come down hard on his head, breaking the skin. Now there was a small pool of blood to his right that looked like an ink stain on the white carpet. He looked like he'd been shot.

"We should clean up that," Taro said. He had the captain's chair swiveled around and was leaning forward, gingerly feeling around the wound. "He's gonna need stitches."

"Stitches," Chris said. "He's not hurt that bad. All the blood, it looks worse than it really is."

"How do you know?"

"You can't see the bone, can you?"

Taro squinted in the dim light. "No."

"There you go. You can't see the bone, it's not serious."

Jessica's eyes were bloodshot, her voice exhausted. "What are we going to do?" she said.

"Let's wait on that," Chris said. "Let's see if we can figure out what happened first."

"He's Zeniya," Jessica said, pointing her cigarette at the prone body. "He has to be."

"He is or he isn't," Chris said. He was surprised at how steady his voice was. He wasn't tired. He wasn't even *scared*, and that made no sense at all. He should be scared. He should be practically out of his mind. There was an old man tied up and bleeding on the floor below him, for Christ's sake. All the police had to do was show up and open the door, and all of them would be sitting in jail for the rest of their lives. In a *Japanese* jail.

So how *did* he feel?

He felt *alive*.

"First things first," he said. "I really should have asked this before, but how do we know who this guy is?"

"Jesus, Chris." Jessica rubbed her eyes.

"How do you know? Who introduced you?"

"Fuck." She seemed to think about it. "It was the mama-*san* at the club."

"The hostess bar?"

"Yeah." Jessica exhaled. She put her cigarette out in the Coke can she was using as an ashtray. "Mama brought me to the table, said Zeniya was an old customer who hadn't been in for a year or two. Look, I'm not the only one who knows this guy. There are other hostesses, businessmen Zeniya sometimes came in with, his driver. The old fucker gives out business cards. I've got one. I showed it to you, remember?"

Chris thought of something. "You check his wallet?"

Taro was still wearing the old man's pants and jacket. He felt around the pockets and pulled out a thin, brown leather wallet. He riffled through it.

"Driver's license," Taro said, squinting again, "name of Zeniya. Address, okay. Picture, okay. Credit cards . . . all Zeniya."

"How much money?" Chris asked.

Taro fingered open the billfold. "Forty thousand. Not so much."

"He spent a hundred and fifty at the club," Jessica said. "At least. I saw him pull it out. Then ten or twenty at the love hotel. That's close to two hundred thousand right there."

"So he's not a bum," Chris said. "But I guess we already knew that. He's got money from somewhere, and he's got all the right ID."

"ID could be fake," Taro said.

Jessica kicked at the passenger door with her heels. "I was *inside* his goddamn house, Taro!"

"Hey, Jessica, relax, baby . . ."

"Fuck you, Taro! I will not fucking relax. I was inside the house. He showed me his fucking safe, and he knew the fucking combination. Who else could he fucking be?"

She was shivering all over. Chris figured she was about to bolt, so scared she wasn't thinking. She would open the door, and he wouldn't see her again until the police had rounded all of them up. He said, "Wait a minute. I've got an idea."

Taro and Jessica looked at him.

"Zeniya takes you out every second Friday, is that right?"

"Yeah," Jessica said warily.

"He's been doing this, what, six months now?"

"Five."

"Five." Chris rubbed his beard. "And you always go out on the same day, to the same place. You always leave at the same time the next morning. Zeniya's a creature of habit."

"So?"

"Well," he said, leaning back against the wall, "what's his wife do every second Friday night?"

He saw Jessica turning it over, the wild look in her eyes

starting to fade. "You think she's got something on the side, too?"

Taro looked dubious. "She's a housewife."

"Girls just wanna have fun," Chris said. "Let's say she's got a boyfriend. Tit for tat. Maybe a neighbor from down the street. Every second Friday he comes over, and they live it up. Now if somebody calls the house at, say, nine, and asks to speak to her husband, she can say that he's out. But if somebody calls at two in the morning . . . wouldn't it look funny?"

"No," Jessica said. "She'd still say he was out. This is Japan. Lots of men don't go home at night."

"Put yourself in her place. A strange man calls your house at two in the morning and asks you where your husband is. Are you just going to say you don't know?"

"She's not going to put somebody else on the line." Jessica's voice was getting higher. "She's going to be scared. She's just going to stand there."

"She don't hesitate at all," Taro added. "She say, 'Sure, wait a minute. I'll get him.' "

Chris thought it over. "Okay, you're right. It doesn't make sense to put the boyfriend on the phone."

" 'Okay, you're right'?" Jessica said. She was getting hysterical again. "That's it? That was your idea?"

Chris looked at her. "I'm trying to deal with the situation here." He was starting to get a little pissed off.

"Jesus, *fuck*!"

Jessica was sobbing now, her breath coming in hitches. She had her knees pulled up against her chest. Somehow it made him even more pissed. Like he was somehow responsible for all this. Like this wasn't all her idea to begin with.

"Well," he said. "I guess we'll just have to go with Plan B."

"There is no Plan B!"

"Hey, you know, that's right." He found the briefcase on the floor next to the bed and pulled out his copy of Jessica's original plan. "Now where does it say that?"

"Would you just shut up?"

"Here it is. Page eight. Quote, if we don't get the money right away we give the whole thing up. There is no Plan B, end quote." He held the paper in front of her. "Look, it's all in capital letters."

Taro grabbed the paper from him. The yellow knight coming to the rescue. "Hey, you leave her alone, huh?"

Chris held up his hands. "I just want to follow the plan." Opening his eyes wide now, laying it on thick. "*Jessica's* plan. Don't *you* want to follow Jessica's plan, Taro?"

"Look," Jessica said. Like she was getting back some control. "Things got fucked up, all right? I don't know how, but they did." Looking up at him now, wiping her eyes. "But you are not going to dump me off somewhere with him."

"But that's the plan."

"I *can't*. We don't know anything about him now! We don't know what he would do. What if he went to the police?"

"He's not going to go to the police."

"Why not?"

Chris pointed at the wallet in Taro's hands. "He's been *impersonating* this guy Zeniya. That can't be legal. He goes to the police and he's fucked."

Taro held up his finger like he'd just gotten an idea. "Maybe real Zeniya knows about it already."

"What?" Jessica said.

"Maybe real Zeniya knows this guy. Maybe they got some kinda business together."

Jessica threw up her hands. "Taro, that's fucking insane. There's a safe in this guy's house. Inside the safe is a million fucking dollars. And *this* guy," she said, pointing at the old man on the floor, "this guy knew the goddamn combination! Zeniya's going to tell his dumb-ass business partner something like that?"

Taro said, "Maybe he guess number."

Jesus Christ, Chris thought. "Maybe the aliens told him when they took him up in their shiny spaceship."

Jessica put her head in her hands. "I can't think right now," she said. "We have to, like, go somewhere and figure out what to do next."

"Where?" Taro asked.

Chris drummed his fingers on the edge of the bed. "We can't go to my place. It's only one room and there are six other people in the house. I think Jessica's place is out, too. She's supposed to have been kidnapped. Nobody should see her until this is all over." He looked at Taro. "What about you?"

"We could go my mother's house."

"Is your mother there?" Jessica asked.

Taro looked like he didn't understand the question. "She always there."

"Taro"—Chris was trying to be patient—"we've got an old man—we don't know who he is—tied up and bleeding in the back of your van. You want us to bring him to your mother's?"

Taro shrugged. "We keep him in my room. What's the problem?"

"*You* are. You're an idiot."

Taro started to stand up. "Hey, fuck you," he said.

"Fuck *you*."

"Stop!" Jessica said. She held up her hands. "Taro, I don't think your mom's is a very good idea." She threw a glance at Chris. "And I don't think we need to be getting counterproductive over here. Does anybody have any other ideas? Please?"

Nobody said anything for a few minutes. Chris looked out the back window at a concrete wall lined with garbage. Beyond the wall he could see neon signs over scattered rooftops. It gave him an idea. "What if we bring him to another love hotel?" he asked.

Jessica shook her head. "We'd have to get the guy in. Nobody cares when you check out at a love hotel, but they're always watching when you check in. How are we going to do that?"

"All right, we go to a motel. Taro checks in at the front desk—"

"There *are* no motels. Japan doesn't have them."

"You're kidding. Why not?"

"I don't know! They just don't!"

Taro had been looking down at the floor. Suddenly he jerked up his head. "Hey," he said. He pointed at Zeniya. "I got another idea."

This week, Masahiko Sato was driving a white Mercedes CL600.

He had an arrangement with XIV Osaka, a used-car dealership on Route 25 in Yao. XIV specialized in foreign luxury cars: Mercedes, BMW, Cadillac, Porsche. Sato knew the owner, Kenji Yamada. He and Yamada went way back; Sato had loaned him some money after Yamada got overextended in the late eighties, speculating on land. The arrangement was: Yamada let Sato borrow any car on the lot, or Sato beat the shit out of him.

The way Sato saw it, it was one of his more inspired ideas. There was none of the hassle that went with owning a car. He didn't have to register anything in his name, and if he got bored with the style or the color, all he had to do was drive to the lot and pick out something new. Sometimes he didn't even do that.

Just three weeks ago, all the way up in Shiga, he'd met an actress in a hotel bar and asked her if she wanted to take a ride in his new blue BMW convertible. She'd refused, claiming she only accepted rides from strangers with red cars; red drove her absolutely wild. Sato told her not to go anywhere. He called Yamada on his cellular, waking him up, and told him if there wasn't a red BMW convertible parked in front of the Shiga King Hotel in ninety minutes, then he would torch Yamada's house. Yamada made the seventy-kilometer drive with ten minutes to spare. Sato was impressed. So was the actress. She gave him a blow job as he drove over the Omi Big Bridge, the lights on the shore of Lake Biwa flickering in the darkness.

The reason he had the Mercedes now was the old man. When Tanaka told him that it was his turn to baby-sit, Sato traded in the BMW for the roomiest sedan that Yamada had on the lot. It was a matter of comfort. Little sports coupés were fine for zipping around town with actresses; shadowing the boss all day and night, you needed to be able to stretch your legs.

That was what Sato was doing now, quarter to six in the morning, stretching his legs and leaning back against the crushed-leather driver's seat, waiting with a moron named Fukumoto for the old man to check out of the Hotel Happy Casanova.

They had been sitting there for fifteen minutes, the car parked alongside the sidewalk a hundred meters from the hotel exit. The sun had been up for an hour, and even with the engine running and the air conditioner on, it was hot, sunlight streaming through the windows. Sato was wondering if he should change clothes. He was still dressed for business: purple suit, open-necked silk shirt, gold necklace, gold Rolex, gold rings, gold-rimmed sunglasses. He was going to be a puddle of sweat by noon, getting in and out of the car. And there was a polo shirt and slacks in the trunk . . .

But that would mean getting up, and he really didn't feel like it. Or making Fukumoto get up, which probably wasn't worth the trouble. The moron would be digging around back there for a half an hour. After tonight, Sato wasn't sure if the dumb shit could find his *chinchin* inside his pants.

Five-fifty. Sato lit a Mild Seven. Outside, the shadows were slowly receding, exposing the ravages of the night before. Looking out his window, he could see where someone had puked on the sidewalk. In the early morning sunlight, it looked like an orange puddle of curry.

"That's disgusting," Sato said, blowing out smoke. He hated looking at vomit. He hit Fukumoto on the arm. "Look at that."

Fukumoto had been dozing against the window, and when he looked up, his hair was plastered to the left side of his face. Sleepily, he said "What?"

"Somebody lost it over there."

Fukumoto raised his eyebrows. "Yeah," he said, seeing it. "Yeah, okay."

Yeah, okay. That was all Fukumoto ever said. He was nineteen, one of the new guys. Tanaka said he had been a member of a *bosozoku* gang in Neyagawa called the Bone Crushers.

"I heard they're the toughest in the suburbs," Tanaka said.

Sato had heard that, too. Extortion, kidnapping, drug running—the Bone Crushers were heavy-duty delinquents. Looking at Fukumoto, though, man, it was hard to believe it. He was tall but heavy, easily a hundred kilos without his leather boots and bomber jacket, with a round face and hair that went all over, like one of those teenage-idol singers. Sato said to him, the first time they met, "You fat piece of shit, don't you think you should cut your hair?" The kid said, yeah, okay, and stared at him, blank-faced, waiting for him to say something else. Not even realizing that he'd been insulted.

Sato had taken him out tonight to do some collections. Tanaka had ordered them to sit outside the love hotel all night, but Sato had nixed that idea. Nothing was going to happen to the old man while he was getting *laid*, come on. Besides, Sato had things to do. Maybe he could teach the kid a thing or two. So after watching the old man and his foreign whore make it safely to the entrance, Sato had given Fukumoto the keys to the Benz and asked if he was ready for a little fun. Yeah, okay, the moron said.

That had been Sato's first mistake, giving the moron the keys. The Bone Crushers rode motorcycles, mostly Suzuki 750s; Sato had assumed Fukumoto could also drive a car. After five minutes, the kid had knocked over two garbage cans, sideswiped a parked car, and run a red light. "You know that means stop," Sato told him, and the kid looked over with that blank expression of his and said, "What does?" After that, Sato drove.

Sato's second mistake was letting the kid do a collection himself. Sato loved collections; it was almost a religious experience. There was nothing like showing up at some poor slob's apartment in the middle of the night, dressed to the teeth, and watching the guy nearly have a heart attack when he opened the door to see who it was. It got even better if the slob didn't have the money he owed. Five hundred thousand yen or fifty thousand, Sato would shout at him, the guy bowing and groveling in his underwear, his wife and kids crying in the background. Then, just when he thought it was over, Sato would slip on a pair of brass knuckles and punch him the stomach, make him fall to his knees sucking wind. The guy would start blubbering then, saying *anything*, not making any sense at all, and Sato would crouch down and whisper something in his ear. "Next time," he would say, "I bring my knife." Then he would get up, maybe kick the guy once for good measure, and promise to come back next week. It was a terrific rush. Simple, too. Sato didn't see how Fukumoto could fuck it up.

The first place they went, the guy owed more than a million yen. Sato handled that one himself, the kid hanging back, watching. The second place was an apartment building full of college kids. Sato said, "There's an engineering student on the fifth floor, room 512, lost about eighty thousand betting on soccer. You think you can handle it?"

"Yeah, okay."

So Sato waited in the car, looking up at the apartment building. The doors to each apartment faced the street, and when Fukumoto got to the fifth floor, Sato saw him lumber down the open hallway, pause for a moment, looking confused, then stop in front of one of the heavy metal doors. He pounded on it, shouting, and when some kid opened the door—Sato couldn't believe it—Fukumoto threw him over the rail and held him there by his ankles. The kid started screaming, swaying upside down five floors over the street, and Sato saw doors opening one by one around the building, students poking their heads out to see what was going on. Fukumoto yelled, "You got it? You got it?" and the way the kid answered, screaming, "Got what? Got what?" made Sato get a pair of binoculars out of the glove compartment and take a closer look.

Fukumoto had the wrong kid.

When the moron came back to the car, he was smiling. He gave Sato an envelope. "Eighty thousand yen, just like you said. Who's next?"

It was all Sato could do to keep from bashing his stupid face in.

Five-fifty-seven. Sato tapped the clock on the dashboard with his fingernail, make sure it was still working. Another three minutes and they could get out of here. Then he remembered, fuck, the old man would want to drive the white bitch back to Kobe. That meant another two hours at least, more like three, fighting rush hour traffic both ways. Then back to headquarters. Sato saw how the rest of the day was going to be: sitting outside the old man's office on the black couch, reading old copies of *Friday* and the *Weekly Post* while Fukumoto, the moron, played video games on the *famicom*.

Sato drummed his fingers on the wheel. Like he didn't have anything better to do. It pissed him off, having to waste his whole day so the old man could play his games. And paired with a retard to boot.

When the old man hadn't come out of the hotel by six-ten, Sato started to wonder. The guy was punctual to a fault; Sato had heard he took a shit at the office every morning at ten-thirty; you could set your watch to it. When he hadn't come out by six-thirty, Sato got out of the car.

"Wait here," he said to Fukumoto. "I'm going to find out what's going on."

"Yeah, okay."

The first thing Sato did was look for the Nissan in the parking lot. It was still there. Nishida was asleep in the front seat, his cap pulled down over his eyes. Sato opened the door and honked the horn. Nishida jumped up, hitting his head on the roof.

"Fuck . . ."

Sato said, "How do you sleep out here, with the door unlocked? I could have stuck a gun in your mouth."

Nishida rubbed his eyes. "What time is it?"

"Six-thirty."

Nishida looked up. "Six-*thirty*?"

"Yeah."

Nishida told him the old man's room number. Sato went to the lobby and checked the board. Most of the pictures were black, the couples inside sleeping it off. His eyes scanned the slots until he came to 301.

The photo was lit up.

At the top of the board was a red button marked SERVICE. Sato pressed it, drumming his fingers against the display. Looking around, he saw the cameras suspended from the ceiling and motioned for whoever was watching to hurry up. He pressed the button again.

After about five minutes, a middle-aged mama-*san* with teased hair came out from a door next to the elevator. She was wearing a striped uniform that looked wrinkled, as if she'd been sleeping in it. She started to say something, sounding bitchy, eyes partly shut . . . eyes wide open then as she saw the sunglasses and the gold necklace and the purple suit.

"Oh," she said. "Are you here about Mr. Zeniya?"

It stopped him for a minute. Mr. Who? Then he rolled his eyes. "Where is he?"

The woman looked surprised that Sato didn't know. "He's been gone since about one-thirty. He forgot his tape."

"His what?"

The woman wagged a finger at him. "Wait here."

She disappeared behind the door she came in. Sato was confused. Why would the old man check out at one-thirty? Where did he go?

What tape?

After a minute, the woman reappeared, handing him a black Sony videotape. Seeing his expression, she said, "Of course I didn't watch any of it. I never do."

"Of course not."

Sato looked up at the cameras hanging from the ceiling, wondering if he should ask the next obvious question. When he looked back, the mama-*san* was smiling at him conspiratorially.

"You must be new. Don't worry about those. Those are just for show." She cackled. "They're not even real."

Then she tapped the top of the videotape and winked at him.

"This one, it's special."

"You have to be fucking kidding me."

That was the first thing Chris said, getting out of the van. Turning now to Jessica, jerking a thumb back at Taro and saying it again. "Is he kidding me?" The asshole. Taro had to keep telling himself not to take the crowbar he held in his hands and bash Chris's head in. Had to keep telling himself over and over.

Man, it was hard.

They were down by the wharf, where the Yasugi River emptied into Osaka Bay, in front of what had once been a small boathouse. It was all crumbling wood and sheet metal at the end of a narrow gravel road, sandwiched between the river and a new power plant with candy-striped smokestacks. The way Taro had heard it, the original owner had gone belly-up after the bubble and abandoned the place. For three years the local kids spray-painted slogans on the doors and threw rocks through the windows. "Then," Taro had told Chris and Jessica on the way over, "Khatani? He's the head of the Iranian gang I meet sometime? He find the place. He wanna use it to keep boxes and goods in while he's wait for customers. So he give this Japanese girl he know some money, she buy the lease. Really convenient. But now, hey, business is so good, they need a bigger place. So nobody use it."

Taro thought it was the perfect place to keep the old man while they tried to figure out who he was and what to do with him. It was old and a little run-down, but choosers can't be beggars, that was what his mom always said. But was that enough for Chris? No, he had to keep bitching about every little thing.

"It looks like it's about to fall in the water," he was saying now. "It's probably full of rats, and shit, and God knows what else." He put his nose in the air. "And what is that fucking smell?"

Taro looked at the luminous dial on his watch. It was almost five, which meant that the fishing boats were coming in. Taro had lived near here when he was a kid. His apartment had overlooked the big Osaka fish market, and when the men unloaded the barges in the morning, you couldn't smell anything else; it was like someone had dunked the city under the ocean and then put it out under the sun to dry. In the afternoons, the fish smell went away and you got a kind of industrial mélange: a little from the cement mixing plants, a little from the chemical factories, a little from the power stations. It wasn't all that bad. It was like anything else; you got used it.

Like most anything else, anyway. He was still trying to get

used to Chris. Taro was having a hard time reconciling his image of Jessica with the reality of Chris, knowing the two of them were friends and maybe more. Maybe more. That was the part that really killed him. It didn't make any sense. It was like ketchup and sushi. Maybe there was more to Chris than he knew. A good quality somewhere, something he hadn't picked up on. He had to assume there was, otherwise a girl like Jessica wouldn't have anything to do with him. Maybe you just had to get to know him.

Taro looked up. Chris had just noticed the crowbar. He looked incredulous. "You don't even have the *key*?"

Or maybe he was just a prick.

Chris heard Taro say something under his breath, probably a Japanese "fuck you," before going to work on the lock. The little guy was starting to get hostile. Still, he had his head down, his eyes on the job. It was a trick, keeping somebody cowed. Get on somebody's case too much, they were liable to take a swing at you. Don't get on their case enough, though, they would run right over you.

Chris saw it starting to happen, Taro starting to take over. Up until the phone call to the Zeniyas, Chris thought he and Jessica had things pretty much in hand. Taro was the guy handling the odds and ends. The problem was, now the whole plan was odds and ends. Let Taro dictate the action, they were going to be in trouble. The guy had been dropped on his head too many times when he was a kid. That idea about driving out to his mother's, and now *this* place . . .

The door squealed when Taro pried it open. Chris followed Jessica inside, stepping gingerly over the doorframe, wondering if he should start breathing through his mouth. But it wasn't as bad inside as he had expected. A little mildew. The briny smell from outside. It didn't look all that bad either. It was still pretty dark, sunlight just starting to creep in through the narrow windows below the roof, but there wasn't much to make out. It was all one big room, with a bare concrete floor that was mostly clean. Chris could see a stack of futons to the left, next to some boxes, and five straw mats spread out on the floor. There was a sink and kitchen counter stuck against the wall on the right-hand side. On the same side, in the corner, a shower nozzle was hanging down from the ceiling over a drain. The toilet, low and stretched long in the Japanese style, was right there, too. Everything was there, out in the open. Chris thought it didn't feel like a boathouse; it was more like one of those apartments that eccentric New Yorkers always had in the movies. Artists and lawyers who were trying to be hip.

Taro had his shoulders back, crowbar dangling from one hand, giving him a look. "Good place, huh?" Putting some attitude into it. "Like I said."

Chris didn't say anything right away. He looked over at Jessica, still standing in the doorway, biting her nails and staring off into space. Still trying to figure out how everything had gotten so fucked up. Not Kathleen Turner or Annette Bening anymore, not even close. The woman was going to be no help at all. He was going to have to do everything himself.

He looked up at the ceiling, putting his hands on his hips. "Place got any lights?" he asked Taro.

"No electric," Taro said.

"No electric." He walked over to the sink, turned on the tap. "Got water. Looks a little brown. We can use it for washing, but I don't want to drink it."

"So we gonna bring the old man in now?"

There, Chris thought. That was what he was waiting for, Taro asking him what to do. Acknowledging his leadership. The thing was not to agree with him right away. Let him know who was calling the shots. "Toilet work?" Chris asked.

When Taro walked over and pushed the lever, Chris knew he had him.

They spent the next few minutes taking an inventory of the place, trying to see what they could use and what they couldn't. There wasn't much. A half roll of toilet paper. A bottle of disinfectant next to the shower. A couple of chipped plates under the sink with rat droppings on top of them. Chris made a note to pick up some traps.

And food, now that he was on the subject. And water. Enough to last for what? A couple of days? He couldn't imagine it taking much longer than that to find out who the old man really was. Part of him was still hoping that Jessica was right somehow, that it really was Zeniya they had and not somebody else. That Taro had fucked up somehow or that there was a mix-up on the other end.

No matter what, though, they were probably screwed. Chris was having a hard time seeing anything good coming out of this. They'd already lost their chance to do something unexpected and original. What they had left was either a classic kidnapping or . . . what? Some kind of lost cause.

Put it that way, it wasn't an either/or situation after all. Classic kidnapping, lost cause—the two were one and the same. What he knew, he wasn't going to stick around if worse came to worst. Fuck Taro. Fuck Jessica, if it came to that. He wasn't going to stumble into doing something stupid, just to see this through.

Well, at least not something more stupid.

Taro had counted the futons. There were five, the same as the number of straw mats. Stained, but otherwise serviceable. Add sheets to the list. That left only the boxes. There were three of them, wrapped in packing tape. They were heavy; Chris tried to pick one of them up and nearly gave himself a hernia. He couldn't figure out what someone would take the trouble to wrap then leave behind. Even Jessica, wandering over, looked curious.

Taro pulled a slender butterfly knife out of his back pocket and flipped it open. Jessica flinched.

"Jesus, Taro," Chris said. "Think it's long enough?" Christ. He hadn't thought about knives.

Taro didn't say anything. He slid the blade down the middle of the top box and pulled it open.

"Hey," he said. "I remember this job."

It was like opening Ali Baba's treasure chest. Gold rings. Gold bracelets. Silver rings. Silver bracelets. A box full of them. And two more just like the first one.

"No good," Taro said. He picked up a silver bracelet and tossed it at Chris. "We go to this jewelry center in Kobe? Famous. Real expensive. Many alarm inside. We only have time to pick up three boxes of goods. After we come back, Khatani-*san* takes samples to this guy he know in Hommachi. Fake, this guy says. He says he don't give Khatani-*san* more than one hundred yen for anything. That was"—he counted on his fingers—"four, three months ago. Look at the bottom. Already be green."

Chris didn't like it. "So what if they aren't real? This guy's an honest thief? If the jewelers in Kobe can rip people off, why can't Khomeini?"

"Khatani," Taro said.

"Whatever. Guys sell this stuff on the street all the time." It was true. You couldn't walk out of a train station without seeing some foreigner behind a table lined with rings and bracelets.

"Those guys?" Taro made a face. "All of them Jews."

"Not all," Jessica said quietly, "but most of them. Israelis. They make a lot of money standing outside, maybe six or seven hundred thousand a month. They work here for a couple years, then go back to Israel and start up businesses."

"I still don't like it," Chris said. "There has to be some way for the Arabs to move this stuff. It *looks* real enough. Why leave it sitting here?" It made him think of something, and he gestured around the room. "Why leave any of this stuff here? The mats, the futons, the plates. What, did they go out and buy new stuff for the new place?"

"I think maybe they did. There is same thing over there," Taro said. "Just they forget about this. Nobody been here two months, at least."

How did *he* know? "You're sure about that?" Chris asked.

"Yeah." Taro nodded, not sounding sure at all. "Yeah, sure."

Chris wiped the sweat from his beard. He needed to shave; it was starting to itch. He had a picture in his mind of a gang of Iranians in mustaches and cheap white shirts bursting in and holding them all hostage, burning an American flag in their face. It was a stupid picture, but there it was.

Thought: Yeah, but where else are you going to go?

Maybe they wouldn't be bursting in today.

"Fuck," he said. "Let's get the old man and bring him in here."

All of them heard it going outside, a scraping sound coming from inside the Astro. Chris told Taro to open the door, quick, and Jessica saw both of them tense, waiting for something to happen. And—Jessica couldn't believe it—they looked like they were smiling. She heard the scraping sound again and she jumped. Her stomach turned over and she told herself she would not throw up, would not, would not, would not—

Then did, all over the front of the boathouse, when Taro pulled open the door and the old man fell out, his head raising a small cloud of dust when it hit the gravel.

After that she kept her eyes closed. She heard Chris say to Taro, wonderingly, "Bastard was trying to get out," and then she heard them set upon him, punching and kicking him until finally the only sounds she could hear were the two of them breathing and the soft lapping of the river against the flood walls. Grunting then, they carried him inside. As they did, something brushed against her back and her stomach heaved again, but there was nothing left inside but bile.

She didn't open her eyes until she was sure she was alone.

For a long time, she didn't move. She stood there, one hand resting against the boathouse, the building propping her up. It was getting lighter outside, the sun coming up behind her. She could hear the rumble of a train somewhere off in the distance, boats sounding their horns as they cruised down the canals, the city waking up. She struggled to hear those sounds. She wanted to hear them, the sounds of normal people doing normal things. But even as the sounds got louder, they seemed to grow farther away.

It was like her life saying good-bye.

After a while, she wasn't sure how long, she heard Chris and Taro step out of the boathouse, saw their shadows stretch out in front of her. Taro put his hand on her shoulder.

"Hey," he said. "You okay?"

She nodded, too exhausted to do anything else. From now on, what difference did it make if she was okay or not? She turned around, folding her arms across her chest. Squinting into the sun, she said, "What now?"

Chris shuffled his feet, putting his hands in his pockets. "Well, he's in there. We put him on one of the mats. Wrapped him up again tight, checked the ropes. He's not going anywhere."

"I take the van now," Taro said. "Go to the shop in Wakayama."

"Yeah," Chris said. "He's gotta get the blood cleaned out of there. Might as well get it painted again, get new plates, same as we talked about before. Somebody still could have seen the van. That might end up being important. Better safe than sorry."

"So what do we do?" she asked.

"Well," Chris said, "we're going to need food and water.

Some new batteries for the Walkman. Toilet paper. Maybe some fresh clothes. I'm going to go to my place, get some stuff, go to your place, get some stuff. I'm going to need your keys, your ATM card so I can get some cash."

"Leave me here, you mean," she said.

Chris and Taro looked at each other.

"Jessica," Taro said. "Baby—"

Chris put his hand up. "Jessica, you have to stay here. "

And went through the reasons. She'd been kidnapped, the kidnapping was on tape, odds were the police already knew about it. Nobody could see her now. She had to go in there, and they were going to have to lock her in. Jessica half listened to the rest, staring at the open doorway to the boathouse, the darkness inside like a hole that she was about to fall into. It mesmerized her. She didn't look away until Taro put something in her hand. It was the crowbar, the black iron already warm to the touch.

Taro was pointing at it, grinning. "Anything happen, you hit him with that."

"Yeah," Chris said. "Don't swing too hard."

No way Chris was getting in the Astro with Taro.

That was the last place he wanted to be, inside the van with all that blood on the carpet. No thank you, he told Taro. I'll walk.

Or jog, he thought, walking along the river's edge. No, run, *sprint*, that's what he wanted to do, sprint to the nearest train station. He could hear one somewhere ahead, near the rows of factories already belching white smoke, seven-thirty on a Saturday morning. It was funny, but he wasn't tired at all, antsy even, the adrenaline from last night still pumping. He felt he could run the hundred in world-record time, break the three-minute barrier for the mile . . . except he really didn't want to be sprinting in his suit; it was the only one he owned.

Then he remembered he had Jessica's ATM card in his back pocket. Shit, make her buy him a new suit.

After that, he started having fun, racing past the chemical vats and the grain elevators, not caring when he heard something rip. A couple of dockworkers in blue coveralls turned to stare at him when he passed by. He waved. He wondered what kind of image he made, a white bearded foreigner in a blue suit, running breathlessly through the industrial bowels of the city. It was a good opening—not for a movie, maybe a TV show. Get the audience wondering right away who he was and why he was running. Maybe what he was running *from*. Quick cut then to barking Dobermans gaining ground behind him, straining at their leashes, grim-faced men with leather gloves and automatics holding on, coming closer and closer . . .

Then all at once he thought he was going to have a heart attack and slowed down, wheezing. Fuck, he was out of shape. It was all that dope and beer, not enough exercise. He needed to stop for a minute, take a break.

He put his hands on the back of his head, breathing hard. He noticed—what the hell?—a rice field just to his left, deep in the shadows of an oil refinery. A farmer in a wide straw hat and yellow boots was bent over, fingering tiny buds sticking out of brackish-looking water. It made Chris wonder if Japan had zoning laws. He was always seeing things like this: refineries next to rice fields, factories next to ramshackle wooden farmhouses that had survived the American bombs sixty years ago.

Cicadas were buzzing all around him, several of them flopped on their backs next to his feet, trying to right themselves. It was already sweltering, the air hanging heavy in the sky, sweat running down his face and into his beard. All that running, trying to get away from the Dobermans. Chris took off his tie and wiped his face and neck with it. He was about to put it in his pocket, then changed his mind and threw it into the basket of a bicycle parked on the side of the road next to the rice field.

Stopped then and thought: *a bicycle.*

The farmer was facing away from Chris. He grabbed the handlebars, popped the kickstand, and started pedaling, rusted chain squealing, the farmer behind him splashing through the water now and shouting. Chris didn't turn around, just kept going, listening to the bicycle squeak and thinking that he was doing the old man a favor, taking the rusted piece of shit away from him.

This was better, pedaling along, the wind in his face fast enough to be almost cool. Then his eyes began to sting from the pollutants in the air, and he noticed the smell again, that fishy-incinerator smell. It never seemed to go away, that smell. Maybe that was what the cicadas fed on, what made them scream so loudly before falling dead on their backs.

He needed to get out of here.

Maybe go to Thailand or Nepal if things worked out with the old man. Fuck, if they didn't. Get out into the country. Stay in a guest house on a beach somewhere for fifty dollars a month, spend a couple of dollars a day for food, see how far he could stretch . . . how much? Before last night he'd had a nice, irregular number to work with: three hundred thirty-three thousand dollars and thirty-three and a third cents; his share of a million. Plus *alpha.* What was he looking at now? More? Less? Nothing?

He supposed it all depended on who the old man really was . . . and how clever the three of them could be.

The more Chris thought about it, the more he was sure they had the right guy. Jessica was right; there was no reason for anybody to be walking around pretending to be someone else. The whole idea was too implausible. Chris wouldn't have bought it in a movie, much less in real life. The old man had a driver's license in the name of Zeniya, credit cards, business cards, the key to the house they'd been to last night, and the combination to the safe inside. A safe with a million dollars in cash inside. What was that old expression, if it walked like a duck . . . ?

As for how clever the three of them could be, well, that was more of a problem. They'd done all right at the love hotel, spiriting the guy out of there, but they'd been able to map that one out, plan it down to the last detail. Now they were going without a plan, and Chris found himself curious as to whether they'd unravel. It was funny; it was like he was a part of this and he wasn't, able to look at the three of them like they were characters in a movie. Wondering what they were going to have to do next, trying to figure out where the plot was going.

Chris bicycled over a bridge, then past an air-conditioning factory. The place was busy even now, Saturday morning, men with close-cropped hair and gray company windbreakers and clipboards smoking outside, women walking together in packs of three in pink shirts and matching jackets, everybody with a SANYO patch on their front pockets. Like they were gas station attendants or part of a bowling team.

It made him nervous, looking at them, and he didn't know why.

Characters in a movie . . .

All at once his heart seemed very loud in his chest.

It struck him how little he really knew about what was going on, how much he had been relying on Taro and Jessica. Jessica knew Zeniya. Jessica had been to Zeniya's house. Jessica had seen the million. Taro had called the house last night. Taro had brought them to the boathouse. What had Chris done? What did he know firsthand?

Nothing.

If this were a movie . . .

It occurred to him, not for the first time but never so forcefully, that he had kidnapped a man completely on secondhand information. He hadn't done any preparation at all. He had taken everything on faith concerning the Zeniya deal. Without Jessica and Taro, in fact, there was no deal.

Carry that one step further.

What if the two of them were lying about it all?

The streets were narrowing now, everything getting more crowded, the concrete apartment blocks getting older and yellower. On balconies, housewives in Snoopy or Mickey Mouse T-shirts were hanging laundry on long plastic poles, or draping futons over the side and beating them with big spatulas. Chris was thinking back on everything that had happened so far, looking at it now in a different light. If he were *watching* this, if this were a movie and he was in the audience, he'd have doubted Jessica from the beginning . . . and wondered how the hero—himself—could have been so stupid. He had taken everything on faith, not doing any preparation on his own, believing that there was no reason for Jessica to lie about an old

Japanese man with a million dollars in a safe in his house. And hadn't she helped convince him by sleeping with him? What was that old line, a man's heart is through his stomach, but the way to his brain is through his dick? And now he was separated from both Jessica and Taro, no way of knowing what they were doing. If this were a movie, he thought, he'd be shaking his head by now, knowing that the poor sap on the bicycle was screwed.

He didn't feel very good.

He rode over a small canal with garbage floating on the surface, the effluvia hanging in the air. Ahead he saw a train pulling into a station, and he suddenly realized he had no idea where he was or how to get back. He had been riding more or less aimlessly, knowing that he couldn't go far in Osaka without hitting a train. He hadn't been looking for a specific train; he had been looking for any train. Going back, he had to find a set point, and he had no idea how he was going to do that.

In front of the train station was the obligatory *pachinko* parlor and convenience store. No English conversation school—that was a surprise. A row of shiny black taxis were parked on a side street, drivers slumped over behind the wheels, asleep. Two palm trees grew out of a tangled mass of weeds and crab grass, flanking a clock with a sign that read GIFT OF LION'S CULB. Chris dumped the bicycle next to the clock and walked up to the ticket booth inside the station. Trying to figure out how much it was going to cost to get to Sannomiya, he saw something out of the corner of his eye.

A bank . . .

* * *

Inside the bank, the ATMs were lined up against the wall next to one another. Chris stepped in front of one and it began to babble instructions at him in Japanese. He put Jessica's card in the slot and waited. At the machine next to his, a good-looking woman with streaks of brown in her hair kept sticking her card in, but the machine wouldn't accept it, telling her to try again.

He hadn't planned on getting any cash just yet, but he needed to think. If there was any possibility that Jessica and Taro were screwing him, then there was no way he was going back to the boathouse.

What were the possibilities?

What he was thinking now, maybe Jessica and Zeniya had planned something together, a kind of fake kidnapping. Get the money somehow from Zeniya's wife and then pin the crime on Chris. Maybe stick Taro, too; Chris didn't put it past her. He just didn't see how Jessica was going to do it. Of course, in the best movies, you couldn't figure out what was coming either, but he had never pegged Jessica as that smart.

He got thirty thousand out of the ATM and took a look at the receipt, wanting to see how much Jessica had in there. Had to look again when he saw the numbers—2,350,540—about ten times more than he had expected. Two million plus—sure, it was yen, but that was still more than twenty thousand dollars, sitting right there in a savings account. Just sitting there, not doing anything.

You could do a lot with twenty thousand dollars in Thailand.

Why not just go?

Really. Why not? Forget this whole disaster. This was heavy criminal stuff he was involved in here. Extortion, kidnapping—

Christ, kidnapping. He was a fool to even think about sticking around. Get out now while he still had time, while nobody could prove anything.

Chris stood there for a while, thinking about it. The good-looking woman at the machine next to his finally got her card accepted and clapped her hands together. Seeing Chris watching her, she blushed and looked away, but was glancing back before long, looking him over. Chris reciprocated, taking in everything from the silver chain with the name ROXY around her neck to her thin sandals. She had painted her toenails green. With sparkles. When he finally looked up, she waved at him, her hand close to her chest, not looking offended at all. "Bye," she said, and turned to go out, glancing back once over her shoulder. Jesus, he loved this country.

It helped him make his decision. He put Jessica's card back in the machine. He wondered how much you could take out of an ATM at any one time. For fun, he tried a million and almost fell on the floor when the machine began to whir. The tray opened and there it was, a million yen, almost eight thousand dollars, the wad of ten-thousand-yen bills so thick he felt like a gangster. It wouldn't fit in his wallet, so he stuffed the money down his pants. Was about to get out of there when he thought, what would happen if he tried it again? He punched in Jessica's code, entered a one followed by six zeros, and, how about that, got another a million yen. This *was* a wonderful country.

He decided that if he went back to the boathouse and felt funny about anything, anything at all, then he was taking off and getting on the first plane to Southeast Asia.

And if he was positive that everything was on the level?

Well, if Jessica got what she wanted out of this, was she really going to miss a few million yen?

It took him almost four hours to get to Sannomiya, mostly because he fell asleep and woke up out in the country, in Okayama, halfway to Hiroshima. When the conductor shook him awake, Chris was so disoriented he almost punched him. He was the only one left on the train.

When he made it back to Kobe it was nearly two o'clock. It was crowded, the streets jammed with shoppers. In the public squares, lined up at intervals from one another, young men with guitars warbled recent Japanese pop hits. Chris saw one guy slumped over, looking pooped, a Beatles poster plastered to the wall behind him. It was too hot to be singing in English.

As he turned onto Jessica's street, it occurred to him that Zeniya's driver had not seen the old man since before midnight last night. What was *he* thinking right now? Assuming he hadn't been to the police (a big assumption), Jessica's apartment was the logical place to come looking. Chris wondered if Zeniya was one of those rich guys who was always giving his help fits, sneaking off on them or doing something that wasn't on the itinerary. He pictured an elderly chauffeur with a hangdog expression shaking his head and saying to himself: *Here we go again.* Wandering all over town looking for the spoiled rich son of a bitch.

Chris walked past Jessica's building, glancing casually inside the lobby. No one was in there. No police hanging around outside. No Nissan Presidents parked along the curb either, though there was a sporty little Mazda in front of a cigarette stand and a white Mercedes sedan parked in front of what looked like a fire hydrant. Unlocked, too.

Not a hangdog in sight.

Face it, he thought, if the chauffeur had been by this way, it had been a long time ago. Chris was picturing it, punching in Jessica's security code and walking slowly to the elevator: the chauffeur, puzzled, walking inside the love hotel and finding his boss already checked out. Swinging by the office now, nobody there, starting to panic, feeling that knot in his stomach beginning to swell. Taking one last chance, stopping at the *gaijin* girlfriend's place, ringing the bell at least ten times. Finally swallowing his pride and calling the house, listening to the frantic wife scream something about a video over the car phone, stopping by the house, being invited inside, maybe his first time in there, taking off his shoes and hat, feeling a little tight around the collar, bowing repeatedly, watching the video now, sitting on his heels on the *tatami*, finally giving in to temptation and asking if it would be okay if he had a cigarette. Puffing on it, the wife looking anxiously at him. Finally saying that there wasn't much of a choice. It was time to call the police.

The scene was so vivid in Chris's mind that when he opened the door to Jessica's apartment, he felt as if he were at the Zeniyas'. Taking off his shoes and stepping into the hallway, he could *smell* the cigarette smoke. And damned if when the hallway opened up into the living room, damned if he couldn't *see* the black-suited chauffeur, hangdog expression and all, sitting down on the floor, mulling over what had happened.

Then the man on the floor stood up, and Chris saw that he

wasn't wearing black; it was a purple suit the man had on, with pinstripes. There was a gold medallion around his neck. And it wasn't a hangdog expression at all on his face—it was a smile. Chris took a step back, and bumped into something, another man, who grabbed his arms and held him there so he couldn't move.

The man with the purple suit said: *"Konnichiwa."*

Jessica dreamed she was taking a ride in the Astro with Chris and Taro. Taro was driving, and Chris was in the other front seat. The two of them were talking and laughing about something; Jessica wanted to know what, but she couldn't seem to lean forward far enough to hear. Every time she moved up, something would pull her back. For a long time she couldn't figure out what, then she noticed there was a handcuff attached to her left wrist. The person on the other end of the handcuffs was Zeniya. He was in the nurse outfit, bruised and bleeding from the gash on his forehead, moaning around the Ping-Pong ball stuck in his mouth. Hey, what is this? she asked. Taro and Chris didn't seem to hear. She screamed at them to take the handcuffs off, but they never once turned around to look at her. It was as if she wasn't there. She struggled to free herself but got nowhere.

Suddenly, the van stopped. Jessica looked out the window and saw that they were in the business district, across the street from Daijo Construction, Zeniya's company. It looked like it was lunchtime: salarymen and office ladies out carrying box lunches, sitting on benches, eating and talking. Taro and Chris put on black ski masks and got out of the van. Knowing what they were going to do, Jessica started to panic, jerking at her wrist to try to pull it free. The side door to the van flung open. Saying one, two, three, Chris grabbed the old man, Taro grabbed Jessica, and together the two of them threw her and the old man into the street. Then, laughing, they closed the door, got back in the van, and drove away.

For a few seconds, Jessica was too dazed to move. Her head was ringing. It was hot outside, the pavement burning her back. And there was this *smell,* like dead fish and urine. She gagged, clearing her head, and all at once she could see people starting to crowd around her and Zeniya, their faces blank, the women covering their mouths. Jessica noticed then that she was naked. She screamed, trying to get up, run, get out of there, but the old man was still stuck to her wrist. He wasn't moving. He didn't seem to be *breathing,* in fact, and now she heard police sirens getting closer and closer. Grabbing Zeniya by the neck, she tried to pull him to his feet, but it was so hot that he kept slipping through her fingers, layers of his skin coming off in her hands. At the same time, the crowd was moving in, its blank faces getting larger and larger, the police sirens becoming deafening. She screamed. Now the crowd was falling on her, burying her. She couldn't scream anymore, she couldn't breathe . . .

That was when she woke up, gasping, clutching her chest. For

an instant she had no idea where she was, completely disoriented, police sirens still pulsing in her head. Then she saw the
old man, bound and gagged, lying prone a few feet from her,
and she screamed. Realized she could still hear the police sirens
and screamed again, jumping up, her heart so far up her throat
that it seemed just behind her tongue. Stood there, frozen,
wide-eyed, until the sirens faded away and all that was left was
the buzzing from the power plant next door and her own
ragged breathing. When the panic broke, her knees gave way
and she fell to the floor, sobbing.

For the next several minutes she cried, feeling nothing, *thinking* nothing, her body shaking as the accumulated stress of the
past twenty-four hours tried to break free. Gradually, other sensations came back. The first thing she noticed was a dull pain
on the underside of her left wrist. Turning it over, she saw a
nasty-looking purple bruise. It confused her; she couldn't understand why it was there. Then she saw the crowbar lying on
the straw mat where she had she slept. She realized she must
have fallen asleep on top of it, her wrist trapped between it and
the rest of her body.

The second thing she noticed was that it was *hot,* sweat pouring down her face, her cute Donna Karan skirt and blouse sop-
ping wet and plastered against her body. It was hard to breathe,
it was so hot. She felt as if she were sitting in a sauna, her nasal
passages burning. She looked up to the windows lined up beneath the roof of the boathouse, and seeing them closed, she
forced herself to get up.

The windows were too high to open in the usual way, so
hanging down from each was a long metal chain. The chains

were rusted and filthy looking; Jessica didn't want to touch any of them. Making a face, she grabbed one and pulled down on it. When nothing happened, she pulled harder.

Tried to use two hands.

Felt the panic coming back then, pulling on the chain with all the force she could muster and getting nothing in return but grease and rust on her hands. She grabbed another chain, got nowhere with it, then another, gave it a vicious tug and fell to the floor as the chain broke and came flying back at her face.

"Fuck!" she screamed, no holding back the panic now, feeling it was two hundred degrees in the boathouse, sure that she was going to suffocate if she didn't find a way to get a window open. Saw the crowbar then and ran to it. Picked it up with both hands and ran to the wall, jumping up and swinging wildly. When one of the windows shattered, she covered her eyes. Shards of glass fell over her, sticking in her hair. She let the crowbar clatter to the floor and backed away, sucking in air, saying, "Jesus Christ, thank you God, thank you thank you thank you," over and over again until she felt her heart slow down to normal.

This was better. She turned back to the broken window and closed her eyes, feeling the sunlight on her face. She could hear the rumbling of trucks somewhere off in the distance, the low buzz of the power plant, louder now, even what sounded like voices, maybe from a boat out on the water or across the river.

Voices . . .

She wondered if someone had heard the window breaking.

She started biting her cuticles, tearing a jagged piece of skin off her thumb, thinking about it. There were people outside. On a boat? Across the river? Jessica tried to remember if there was a bridge nearby. Maybe a couple guys fishing. They see the window break, they call the police—

Christ, the police would come right in. They'd knock on the door, and when they didn't get a response, they'd knock the door down. Break the lock, see Zeniya bound and gagged on the floor, see her . . . she couldn't even get *out*. She was locked *in*.

"Christ, Christ, Christ!" she screamed. She ran to the door and wedged the crowbar between the front latch and the wall. A giant dead bolt. It would keep the police out for a little while . . . No, it wouldn't even do that; one of the cops would give another a boost so he could peek in through the windows and then she was going to be just as fucked as before.

She took a deep breath.

Then another.

Maybe nobody had heard anything.

The boathouse was next to a power plant; nobody hung around power plants. And the water on the other side, it was filthy. She wouldn't put her hand in it, much less try to catch fish. Nobody was out there. Everybody was at work, or asleep, or doing whatever normal people did on Saturday. Nobody had heard anything.

What if somebody had?

Even if somebody *had*, they weren't going to call the police. This was Japan, for God's sake; people minded their own business. You see a window break, it's not *your* window, you're not going to give it another thought. That's what you did in Japan: you kept your blinders on and you didn't pay any attention to things that didn't concern you. What was it she'd read? A hundred and thirty million people in a country the size of California, the amount of livable space about the size of Connecticut? You *had* to shut out the world; otherwise you'd go crazy.

She started to relax.

She was tired, that was the problem. She'd been up all night, things hadn't gone well—an understatement to redefine the term—and she was edgy. It was time to pull back. Get a little perspective on things.

Think about what she needed to do. Maybe that would help.

She checked her watch. It was almost noon. When had Chris said he was going to be back? She couldn't remember. Zeniya was going to be waking up again soon, if he wasn't awake already. God, she didn't want to deal with that. If he started moving around, she was going to freak. But she had to keep an eye on him somehow . . .

Jessica forced herself to turn her head and look at him.

Zeniya was still lying on his side, curled up, his body a vague, limp form in the shadows. He wasn't moving. Actually, as she looked at him more carefully, it struck her that he hadn't changed positions at all. He hadn't moved since . . . when? Since at least the time Chris and Taro had left. It was, ha ha, almost like he was dead.

Ha ha.

Rushing over to him, Jessica pulled him onto his back. She could see the sweat running around the caked blood on his forehead and down the sides of his face. Dead men didn't sweat. That was right, wasn't it? Christ, she wasn't sure. Maybe they did; maybe the water in there had to run out or something.

How would she know? She wasn't a doctor. She bent over his nose, listening. Couldn't hear anything at first except the morning show on FM 85.1 coming from the earphones under the towel around Zeniya's head, the chirpy DJ mixing in English expressions like "Get down to the funky music" and "We are so happy!" with a steady stream of Japanese patter. A huge wave of panic broke over her. Then there they were, the old man's quick intakes of breath, coming into focus. Shaking, she stood up.

"Oh God," she said, and the scratchy, hoarse sound of her voice, that brought another jolt to her heart.

She started to wonder if she was going to make it.

Opening up her overnight bag, she found a half-empty bottle of mineral water and drank it, letting the last few drops run down her chin and onto her neck. It felt good, the cool water against her skin. She looked over at the nozzle on the wall and thought a shower would be nice, maybe just what she needed. Now was the time to take one, too; without Chris or Taro around, she had a little privacy. And she had the Moschino dress she could change into.

One thing she wasn't going to do was walk barefoot on the floor of the boathouse, which meant the heels were staying on. Reaching around her back, she unzipped her skirt. She nearly tripped stepping out of it, the wet fabric clinging to her body. Her blouse and bra were even worse. Finally, pushing down her panties, she hesitated, self-conscious, looking back at Zeniya on the floor, her hands automatically moving to cover herself.

The man had Ace bandages and tape over his eyes.

And besides, it wasn't like he had never seen her naked.

The water from the nozzle was cold and brown and smelled

of brine, but it felt good all the same. Jessica thought she was going to fall, standing in her heels, so she squatted down next to the floor and let the water run over her. She closed her eyes, brushing back her hair. She didn't want to move, didn't want to think. She wanted to stay right there, under the spray, until she was washed away.

Then she started wondering if Zeniya was dead again.

She kept her eyes closed, feeling the water rushing over her back. Why would Zeniya be dead? She had just checked him five minutes ago. He was fine. She was just being paranoid.

She was *not* going to go over there and check on him.

She opened her eyes, squinting over at the old man through the spray. He was exactly as she had left him, lying on his back. She tried to see if his chest was moving up and down and couldn't tell.

He wasn't breathing.

"Yes, he is," she said. She closed her eyes again. This was ridiculous. She told herself she absolutely, positively was not going to give in to the compulsion to check him again.

She opened her eyes, looked over there again.

"Fuck," she said, and stood up and turned off the water. Irritated with herself, she wobbled over on her wet heels to where Zeniya was lying down. Kneeling on the mat next to him, she bent over and put her ear next to his face. Water from her wet hair dropped onto his forehead and he moaned. Jessica jumped up, startled, and her left heel broke, causing her to fall on her ass on the dirty concrete floor.

"Shit!" she shouted, more scared than hurt. She rubbed her ass and her hand came away black. She thrust it at him. "I just took a shower, you asshole," she said. Her feet and the back of her legs were black now, too. She kicked away her other heel. A lot of good it was going to do her now. She stood up.

"Fucking piece of *shit!*" she shouted, looking down at Zeniya. "I'm dirty again, I'm all worked up—" She stopped, rolling her eyes. "Christ, and now I'm talking to you."

It felt good, though, listening to somebody talk. Even if that somebody was her. She thrust a finger at Zeniya.

"You're not going to die on me, you got that? You got a little cut"—she put her thumb and forefinger about an inch apart—"about *this* big, from my heels. My heels that cost fifty thousand yen in Tokyo that you made me break. You're not going to die, nobody ever died from a cut like that. You know it, I know it, so stop making me all fucking crazy."

Okay, that didn't sound so good. In fact, it sounded pretty bad, like she was losing control or something.

"Let's talk about something else," she said. "What do you say?"

Zeniya didn't say anything, just lay there like a lump.

"No objections?" she asked. "Good. I'm going to rinse off again and put some clothes on."

This was better, keeping her sense of humor about the whole thing. She washed the dirt off her backside and hands, then dried herself off with a handkerchief from her purse. Looking over at Zeniya, she said, "I want to know what happened last night. You listening? I mean, what the fuck was that? Did Taro screw up somehow?" She held up a hand as she reached in her overnight bag for her dress. "Don't get me wrong, he's a cute guy, but he doesn't have it all together. Did he call the wrong number? Did he hear your wife wrong on the phone?" She slipped into the dress, pulling the straps up over her shoulders. "I couldn't understand what he was saying; it was all in Japanese. Yeah, I know, seven years in Japan, I ought to know the language better, but I don't. I have to assume that what he told Chris and me was right."

But it wasn't. That was the obvious explanation. And now she was stuck in this filthy, hot boathouse while Zeniya's wife was probably being interviewed by the police. The police were probably looking at the videotape right now, winding it and rewinding it, making sketches of the blonde in there in the dominatrix outfit. Or scanning the tape into a computer and printing out pictures; they could do that now, couldn't they? They were going to find out who she was, where she lived. She was never going to get out of this.

"You know what the problem is?" she said. "It's that asshole, Chris." Chris, the one who had forced Taro to drive away from Zeniya's house. Chris, who thought that Zeniya wasn't even Zeniya.

Jessica nibbled on another cuticle, staring off into space. She felt a pang of fear worm its way down to her bowels, giving her cramps. She had to face it. She should never have brought Chris into this. It had seemed so right, like fate, meeting him again after all that time, but he had been a problem since the beginning. Not taking things seriously, generally being a fuckup. And Jesus, she suddenly thought, she had given him her ATM card and the key to her apartment. What if he cleaned her out? There wasn't anything stopping him; it made sense, in fact. Clean her out and keep on going, leave her stuck here with Taro when everything came crashing down.

And, shit, what if Taro didn't come back?

"No," she said, "I am not going to think about that."

But the thought was there now and it stuck, growing like a tumor until she couldn't think of anything else. Go over what happened last night again. When had everything gotten fucked up? After the phone call to Zeniya's. Who had made the phone call? Taro had.

Now look at it in another way.

What if Taro wasn't so dumb after all?

He knew she and Chris didn't speak Japanese. He could have said anything about the phone call and she would have believed him. He had been pretty convincing, but that didn't mean he hadn't made it all up.

Taro wouldn't do that.

Why not?

He was a *criminal*, for God's sake.

He was. She could dress it up any way she wanted, but the fact remained: this man was a criminal. He was a thief and a drug dealer and he had been to prison. What did she know about what a guy like that would do?

"Yeah," she said, looking at Zeniya, "but he's crazy about me."

She imagined Zeniya awake, keeping up his end of the conversation. *Really?* he was saying now. *Just like you are about him? Just like you are about me?*

The cramps were coming on strong now and she ran for the toilet, lifting up her dress. Squatted just as the diarrhea exploded out of her. Didn't move again for several minutes, her eyes closed. It all made sense, what Taro had probably done. He had called the Zeniyas and there hadn't been any mistake. Left

Zeniya's wife with a quick message: There's a package for you outside; take a look. Call the police and bad things will happen. Then he had hung up and concocted a story for her and Chris.

Then—it was perfect—drove them out to a place that neither she nor Chris knew anything about. Pretended to let Chris take charge, and then agreed to take the Astro to Wakayama and give it a makeover. But before doing so, he'd headed right back to Senri to call Zeniya's wife and give her the original scenario: put the money in a plastic bag and put it outside with the garbage or your husband's on the front page of every tabloid and weekly magazine in the country. She did, of course, and now Taro had it.

And without two people to split it with.

It was so perfect, Jessica started to cry. Cleaning herself up, she walked over to Zeniya and lay down next to him. She cried until she was worn out and only the dry heaves were left. Then, exhausted again, she fell asleep.

The big guy behind him took Chris's wallet out of his back pocket then gave him a hard shove, sending him flying. Chris managed to keep himself from falling down, then edged back toward the couch, hands in front of him, trying to put some space between him and whoever the hell these two guys were in Jessica's apartment.

They were here about the old man, that much he was sure of. And, Christ, they looked like mobsters—*yakuza*—the one in the purple suit wearing at least a pound of gold on his fingers and around his neck, the other one—the one who had shoved him—maybe two hundred and fifty pounds in his black boots and leather jacket, a big fucker. Purple Suit was older—in his late thirties?—and looked like he was the boss, hands behind his back, barking a question now at the other guy but keeping his eyes on Chris. Big Fucker—he looked like a high school kid on steroids—had Chris's driver's license out and was trying to read the name.

"Chulee . . . Chuleesutopuher," he said, trying to sound out the letters, "Chuleesutopuher Lion." Then, almost as an afterthought, "—*san*."

Chris couldn't decide what to do first, his head darting back and forth. Were these guys actually *yakuza*? What in the fuck did the *yakuza* have to do with Zeniya?

No, he didn't have time to think about that now. He had to take the initiative somehow, try to put some doubt in their minds. And make sure they didn't find the two million yen stuffed in his pants. Unless he could convince them right now that he had nothing do with what had happened to Zeniya, he was screwed.

"Hey!" he shouted. He stood up straight, spreading his arms wide. Being the indignant American, waving his arms around, stepping forward now and getting in Purple Suit's face. "What the fuck are you doing in here? Who the fuck—"

Wanted to finish with "—are you guys?" but before he could get it out, Purple Suit pulled a steel baton from behind his back and slammed it into Chris's right knee.

It was like a bomb going off inside his leg. He screamed and fell back on the couch, grabbing for his knee. Touched the spot where the baton had hit and nearly passed out, black clouds blowing in from the corners of his eyes. Purple Suit was yelling at him, the man's saliva hitting Chris in the face. He smelled of perspiration. Chris couldn't have formed a coherent answer even if he had wanted to; instead he cried "I don't speak Japanese! I don't speak Japanese!" until the other man finally backed away, scowling. Then he threw the baton to Big Fucker and said something, motioning with his head.

Big Fucker walked over to Jessica's TV stand and pulled it away from the wall, so it was facing Chris. Then Purple Suit got a videotape out of his bag and fed it into the VCR. Chris rocked back and forth on the couch, groaning and asking who they were and what they wanted, trying to sound as butt-fuck scared as possible. It wasn't hard. His knee felt like a train had run over it. It was already puffing up, the pain settling into a pulsing throb.

Purple Suit put a finger to his lips. He pointed the remote control at the TV and the set came on. Chris heard the tape inside the VCR start to turn.

For several seconds the screen was blank. Chris fought to keep an innocent look on his face; he suddenly had a premonition of what he was going to see. It was the tape he had put in Zeniya's mailbox.

He was wrong.

The picture was in black-and-white, and very clear, like something from a high-definition surveillance camera. It was of Zeniya's room at the love hotel. The big double bed was in the center of the frame, just below eye level, which put the camera behind the mirror on the dresser. You couldn't see much else of the room: the door to the shower on the right and nothing at all to the left.

Chris had the presence of mind to say that he didn't understand and where was Jessica, and Jesus, right on cue, there she was walking into the picture in front of Zeniya. Opening her mouth now, saying something, no sound coming out of the TV. Chris almost said "Thank God" aloud; it came out as a whimper when he stopped himself. Purple Suit was looking at him closely. Chris was sure that the guy could see right through him, that the shock was all over his face, and that he was dead.

Zeniya was sitting on the bed now, Jessica helping him take off his clothes. He had his eyes closed, a serene expression on his face. When Jessica reached around his back to take off his shirt, he snuck his left hand up under her dress. She bent her head back, jaw going slack as he stroked her. Chris started to squirm on the couch, getting an idea.

Purple Suit pointed the remote at the screen. "Romano," he said very slowly. He pointed the remote to the floor, gesturing with it, then back to the screen, tapping Jessica's image. "Romano."

Jessica Romano. Porn star. She had her dress off now and was letting Zeniya take off her panties. Chris said, "You bastards!" and made a move like he was going to get up, the white knight defending his maiden's honor. Before he was even close to his feet, Big Fucker had come around behind him, putting the steel baton over Chris's head and pinning him to the couch by the neck. Christ, this was working too well. He couldn't breathe. "You fucks, where is she?" he managed to get out, but that was it. He thought he was going to pass out. Purple Suit put a finger to his lips again. Now he was pointing to Zeniya with the remote and saying "Ozawa."

Who? Chris struggled against the baton. He wasn't acting anymore. "I can't breathe!" he said, starting to panic.

"Ozawa," Purple Suit said, showing teeth this time. He got in

Chris's face again, shouting, while Ozawa, or whoever he was, started giving it to Jessica from behind, her face up close to the camera. "OZAWA!" Purple Suit screamed again.

Big Fucker let up slightly on the baton. Chris gasped for air, choking. Purple Suit was still screaming "Ozawa" over and over. Chris didn't even want to acknowledge that he understood "Ozawa" was a name. He started moaning "Where's Jessica? Where's Jessica?" and hoped he sounded at least as clueless as he had obviously been his whole life until now.

Sato was thinking that he really should have applied himself more when he was a student. Six years of English—at least five classes a week through junior and senior high—and he couldn't understand a thing the bearded foreigner was saying. Granted, he'd skipped a lot of schooldays, but you'd think he'd have retained *something*. Come on, think . . .

Sato ran his fingers through his hair in frustration. He gestured with his palm, and Fukumoto slid the baton away from the foreigner's neck. He fell back against the couch, choking. Sato was starting to think the guy didn't know anything at all. Maybe he was just one of the Romano whore's boyfriends. Comes over on Saturday morning, all dressed up, the two of them have plans . . . instead finds out about the woman's secret life.

Not so secret anymore. There she was on the TV, still getting plugged by a sixty-five-year-old geezer. Impatient, Sato pressed the search button on the remote control, watched the two of them speed it up. Still doing it, still doing it, there—the old man finished at last, saying something to the Romano woman, walking into the bathroom. Now the Romano woman turning over a couple of glasses, opening up the minibar, getting two of those little airplane bottles of booze: Scotch for him, some kind of cocktail for her. Sato couldn't get over the woman's tits bouncing up and down. And those nipples, they had to be two or three centimeters long. Poke somebody's eye out, they weren't careful.

There. Sato took his finger off the search button; normal time now. Watched the bearded foreigner on the couch watching Romano, the woman turning her head furtively toward the bathroom, turning around now—look at that ass!—and digging through her purse on the end table next to the bed. Shaking something into her hand, walking quickly back to the dresser, now dropping whatever it was into Ozawa's drink. Sato paused it there, Romano's hand coming up. Ran it back, made the foreigner watch it again.

"You see that?" he shouted. The bearded foreigner flinched. Sato shook the remote control at him. "We know what your little tramp of a girlfriend did! Where is she? Where did you take him?" Watched as the idiot kept shaking his head and saying something over and over, his eyes wide. Sato looked over the foreigner's shoulder at Fukumoto, who was starting to knock things onto the floor with the baton. Sato said, "Do you have any idea what he's talking about?"

"Who?" Fukumoto said.

The moron. "Him!" Sato said, pointing at the foreigner. "Him! Who else do you see in here? Do you understand what he's saying?"

Fukumoto seemed to consider it, cocking his head. Then he said "No," and went back to knocking things on the floor.

Sato was starting to lose his temper. This had been a shitty day so far, and it stood to get shittier if he didn't find Ozawa fast. He checked his watch. Almost four. That made it six hours since he'd called headquarters and told Tanaka that the old man had developed a sense of spontaneity and was taking the Romano woman shopping. Had been sitting in this whore's nest ever since, climbing the walls while Fukumoto sniffed the woman's underwear and broke things.

And now what was he supposed to do? Finding nothing substantial missing from the woman's apartment—she'd even left her passport—Sato had assumed she'd be back, or that she would send someone back. Was the bearded guy that someone? Everything would be a lot easier if he could just figure out how the bearded foreigner fit into the big picture. A little interrogation, that usually did the trick, but this dumb fuck didn't understand any Japanese at all. Didn't seem to at least. That was the real problem: Who could tell what the guy knew and what he didn't? Foreigners were so inscrutable. Whenever you thought you knew what they were thinking, that's when they surprised you. Japanese could be the same way, of course, but Sato wouldn't have bothered trying to figure one of them out; he'd have just beat the shit out of him and found out whether the guy knew anything useful. Why not? What was the guy gonna do? Foreigners, though, especially Americans like this one, they went to the police, they went to their embassy, it got in the papers . . . beating up foreigners was more trouble than it was worth. You had to kill them.

And that was even more of a hassle.

Fukumoto was working on the walls now, taking out hunks of plaster. Somebody was going to call the police eventually. Sato let the foreigner see the rest of the tape on fast-forward, watched his eyes jerk when the Japanese-looking guy in his underwear came in and put the outfit on the old man. Who was that? Another good question. Irritating, too; the guy never looked directly at the camera. What was more irritating: Sato was sure there was another person in the room as well, someone off to the left and out of camera range entirely. The Romano woman kept looking over there and saying things, even when the guy in his underwear was on the other side.

Watching her talk to the invisible man gave Sato an idea.

He told Fukumoto to throw him the baton. The moron gave it up reluctantly. Sato told him to stand behind the foreigner and hold him down. Fukumoto bent down and put him in a headlock. The foreigner started to shout. Sato gripped the baton by the rubber handle and held it in front of him, where the foreigner could see it. Then he raised it over his head and swung it down toward the foreigner's swollen knee, enjoying the look of panic on his face as he struggled to break loose from Fukumoto's grip. At the last minute, he changed direction and smashed the baton into the TV screen.

The picture tube blew with a satisfying *whomp!*, licks of white flame shooting out from the inside. Sato watched it crackle and burn, then calmly bent over and popped the cassette from the VCR. He heard Fukumoto giggling behind him, saying "Hey, yeah," and the sound of the foreigner's shoes beating against the floor. Turning around, Sato held the videotape in front of the foreigner's ridiculously long nose and tried to dredge up all the English he could remember.

"*Say Romano,*" Sato said. "*Ozawa give me. This night. Police no.*" Gave the videotape to Fukumoto and reached in his inside suit pocket for a business card with his cell-phone number on it. Dropped it in the foreigner's lap. "*I name Sato,*" he said. "*Call telephone. Until this night.*" Then he put his mouth next to the man's ear. "Yakuza," he whispered. Then he whispered it again.

Sato stood up. The foreigner was looking at him, scared, like a trapped animal. Sato said to Fukumoto, "Let's go," and pointed to the videotape. "Don't forget that."

He wasn't going to waste any more time here. The bearded foreigner might not have anything to do with this, but Sato was betting he knew someone that did. These *gaijin,* they all knew one another. Let this guy do the work. Maybe have Fukumoto follow him, see who he talked to. Somebody would get the message to Romano, Sato was sure of it. And when she found out what she was mixed up in, she would fall all over herself to cooperate. If she called tonight, Sato decided he wouldn't hurt her before he killed her.

After all, anyone could make a mistake.

The big problem now was how to keep everything secret for a few more hours. He was going to have to call headquarters again. Talk to Tanaka and hang up before there were any questions. Sato was so busy thinking about what he had to do next that he didn't notice Fukumoto staring at the videotape, still giggling. Was way too late to stop him then when the moron took the cassette and slammed it into the bearded foreigner's face.

Sato heard the plastic casing splinter first, then the foreigner's garbled scream, blood from his nose spurting up and over the sides of the cassette. When Fukumoto took it away, it was dripping, blood falling on the floor in little *plops!* The foreigner had his hands to his face, crying, looking like he was trying to keep his nose from falling off. It seemed to be hanging down as if from a hinge, yellow pieces of cartilage poking out of the nostrils.

Fukumoto was looking at Sato, grinning, like a dog waiting for a treat. It was all Sato could do not to pull the Tec-9 out of his black bag and shoot him. "You *idiot*," he said. He pointed at the tape. "Look at that. It's useless now. That was our *evidence*."

He continued berating him, shoving him out the door, Fukumoto protesting that they'd already seen the tape and why did they need it anymore. The *moron*. Sato gave up. He couldn't decide which was worse, Fukumoto's idiocy or Ozawa's lack of common sense. Between the two of them, it was enough to make a guy want to give up the life, go out and be an accountant.

Jessica woke up to the sound of rustling, like that of a giant rat crawling across the floor. She jumped up in panic, not knowing where she was.

Realized it and said, "Oh."

Then, "Fuck."

Inside the boathouse, the shadows on the walls had changed directions; it was getting darker. Zeniya, the giant rat, was rolling back and forth on the straw mat, groaning beneath his gauze mask. Now what? Jessica knelt down to check the cut on his forehead, but it had already scabbed over. Then she noticed that the old man was no longer sweating, despite the heat, and when she put the back of her hand on his cheek, it felt clammy.

"Great," she said, sighing.

She got up, frowning. Stretched. God, her whole body felt

disgusting. It was as if she had taken a bath in a tub full of lukewarm sweat; her pores were oozing perspiration. She needed to get out of here. Digging through her bag, she found her watch; it was almost five in the afternoon. Jesus, five already. Where the fuck was Chris? And just like that, the fear was there again, pushing needles into her bowels, making her run for the toilet. Squatting, eyes closed, she thought: This paranoia has to stop. Right now. She was not going to think about Chris and Taro not coming back. They *were* coming back, and that was *final*.

Getting up, her legs felt weak and rubbery. Across the room, Zeniya was still doubled over and groaning.

"What is your *problem*?" she asked.

She wished she had a book. A magazine, maybe. Anything. Restless, she started rummaging though the boxes of jewelry next to the futons, trying on rings and bracelets. Some of the stuff was pretty nice; she couldn't tell the difference between it and the real thing. She held a necklace out in front of her, watching it sparkle in the lingering sunlight.

"Didn't you buy me something like this?" she asked Zeniya. "Had little gold hearts on it?"

He moaned again, louder this time. Seeing him down there, all tied up and helpless, like a sick joke in the nurse outfit, Jessica started feeling sorry for him again. He wasn't a bad guy really. He was interesting to talk to. He'd bought her a lot of nice things. Even at the end, showing her all that money . . . maybe he hadn't been trying to scam her. Maybe he would have bought her the apartment. Maybe he would have spent the million dollars on her.

Just not in the way she wanted.

So who was the bad guy here?

Jessica nibbled at a thumbnail, thinking about it. Suddenly wondered if maybe Zeniya was thirsty. Realized, Jesus, nobody had given him any food or water for—she checked her watch again—fifteen hours.

Inside her bag she still had half a bottle of Evian. Looking at it made her thirsty herself, and she had no way of knowing when Chris or Taro were coming back.

If they were coming back.

No, stop that. Rewind that sentence. She did *not* think that.

No way of knowing *when* they were coming back. It could be a while. If she gave the Evian to Zeniya, she was going to have to drink the brown stuff from the tap.

Who was the bad guy here?

She didn't feel *that* sorry for him.

Opening the cabinet under the sink, she found a rice bowl with what looked like an oil stain on the underside. Inside were two dead flies. She shook them out on the floor, making a face.

"This place is a hole," she said.

Rinsing out the bowl, she filled it with water and, holding it with both hands, brought it across the room. Siting down Indian-style next to Zeniya, she gently picked up his head and laid it on her lap. His head jerked at her touch. She put her fingertips on the edge of the gauze mask, then pulled them away, frowning.

"I don't want to hear any screaming, okay?" she said. "If you scream and scare the shit out of me, I'm going to drop you on your head and I'm not going to give you anything. I've been scared enough today, and I'm tired of it. Are we clear?" She paused. "I'm going to take your silence as a yes."

She lowered the mask, said "This is going to really hurt," and pulled the packing tape from Zeniya's mouth. The old man gasped, and the Ping-Pong ball popped out of his mouth and onto the floor. Jessica made a face, thinking about picking it up. Decided to leave it there. Cradling Zeniya in her arms, she tilted the bowl to his mouth. As soon as the water touched his cracked lips, he sucked at it greedily, choking once ("That has to taste terrible," she said), then drinking the rest of it down.

"What a maternal scene this is," Jessica said. "You never have a camcorder when you need one."

Water was running down the corners of Zeniya's mouth and onto the straw mat. Jessica automatically reached for something to wipe it up with, then thought: What, and make a clean spot? Then Zeniya coughed violently and she lost her grip on the bowl, which rolled onto the floor.

"Shit," she said.

She bent over him, trying to reach it. It was right there at her fingertips. If she just stretched a little more . . .

"I must use toilet," Zeniya said.

Jessica froze. Had that just been her imagination, or had—

"Toilet, please," Zeniya said. He coughed again into her chest.

She sat up, looking down at him. Jesus Christ, he *had.* And in *English,* why had he used *English,* why would he assume that—

"Toire e itte mo ii desu ka? Onaka ga itai kara."

She lifted his head from her lap and put it back on the mat. Stood up, thinking. Okay, he wasn't sure. He'd used English *and* Japanese. He'd used English *first;* she wasn't sure how she felt about that. Did that mean he assumed she was involved? Started replaying the events of the night before in her mind, putting herself in his shoes. Decided, yeah, obviously he was going to assume she was involved. She hadn't given him any reason to think otherwise. If the original plan had gone according to plan, she'd have already talked to him, put the seeds of doubt in his mind, maybe even have talked to the police . . .

She kept forgetting how far they were from the parameters of the original plan.

Take this situation, for example. None of them had talked about this. How was she supposed to take Zeniya to the toilet? First she was going to have to untie his legs; it wasn't like she could pick him up and carry him over there. But what if he started running all over the room? Or kicked her? Or . . . *something*. Even if he didn't do *anything*, she was going to have to lead him over there, lift up his skirt, pull his stockings down, and whip it out . . . Christ, she was going to have to *hold* it there, just like that IRA guy had to do to Forest Whitaker in . . . What was that movie? The one where the guy's girlfriend turned out to be a man?

Zeniya was moaning, louder now with the Ping-Pong ball out of his mouth, alternating pleas to go to the toilet in English and in Japanese. Shit, did she have any alternative? What was she going to do, let him piss all over the floor? That would be a fine addition to the boathouse's collection of smells. Worse, what if he had to—

Her eyes widened. She had just made the connection: the moaning, the way the old man was doubled over. How was she going to help him do *that*? He was going to have to hold on to her . . . she was going to have to wipe his fucking *ass*, no way, the hell with that, she was waiting until Chris and Taro came back . . .

It was worse than she had imagined.

Jessica was standing in front of Zeniya, straddling the porcelain toilet bowl, the old man's white skirt draped over her head. She was trying not think about what she had just done, one hand hugging his naked, yellow-stained waist, the other struggling to pull up his white stockings. They were bunched up around his knees, stuck there. She gave the right one a jerk, swearing at it, hearing it rip as it slid up, *finally,* now for the left . . .

That was when Zeniya kneed her in the stomach.

Jessica felt the air rush out of her body, her lungs collapsing in on themselves. Her hand came up to her chest and she started falling to one side, Zeniya trying to shake her off. Then he lost his balance, slipping on the rim of the toilet, and came down on the handle. Jessica, half on top of him, heard him grunt as his head hit the water pipe. Shouting now in Japanese, he moved his body violently and sent her tumbling off him and onto the concrete floor.

Jessica's mouth was open, but nothing was coming in or out. She couldn't move. She remembered being with her mother at the supermarket when she was ten and falling off the front of the shopping cart and onto her back. She tried to say, *Mommy, I can't breathe,* but she couldn't get the words out. It was like she was inside a bubble. Her mother was hovering over her, shaking her frantically, trying to help but only making the bubble tighten around her, pushing it down into her throat and *oh Mommy please stop, please STOP—*

Jessica coughed once, twice, and the bubble popped, the air rushing back into her lungs, her mouth making whooping sounds as she drew in her breath. She rolled onto her side, holding her stomach, choking as she tried to bring in air. She had to get up. She had to move her head. Where was Zeniya? She had to get up and stop him, or she was dead.

Zeniya was standing up against a wall, moving his upper body up and down. He was trying to loosen the ropes. Jessica staggered to her feet, tripping once, one hand still holding on to her stomach. Saw Zeniya pull his left hand free and ran for the door, grabbing the crowbar and pulling it out, thinking *No, not the mask, don't let him get to the mask.* Turned then and saw him ripping the packing tape from around his head. She screamed, charging at him. His head jerked up, the Ace bandages falling to the floor. He blinked once, pupils dilating, looking straight at her, and that was when she swung, catching him just over the ear with the pointed tip of the crowbar. His head snapped to the right and she swung again, grazing his scalp as he fell to the floor. She raised the crowbar over her head and brought it down, aiming for the top of his skull. But now she was too close to the wall, and the pointed tip skidded against wood, making the crowbar fly out of her hands and clatter to the floor. Jessica brought her hands to her mouth, stifling a scream. Christ, this was it. She was dead.

Looked down and saw that Zeniya wasn't moving, blood oozing from his head onto the floor. She took a step back, then another, then ran for the sink and stood there, heaving, until she no longer had the strength to stand.

Chris was thinking that it had been ten years since he had graduated from high school.

Ten years. This month. In fact, maybe even today. When had he graduated? June something. June 15? June 14? That sounded right: June 14. What day was it today? Jesus, it might be *exactly* ten years.

It was a strange thing to be thinking about, lying on the white sofa in Jessica's apartment, blood oozing down the sides of his face. Not that he was *always* thinking about it. He wasn't always conscious, for one thing. Every once in a while he would drift away, and when he came back he would think *Where was I?* and have to find his train of thought again. For another thing, even when he was awake and fully alert, it was kind of hard to concentrate.

His nose felt shattered. Chris didn't think that was possible—noses *broke,* they didn't shatter—but it felt that way all the same. Blood was still bubbling up from inside, and it seemed like there were hard pieces of bone or cartilage floating in there. Sometimes one of the hard pieces, a big one, would get stuck in one of his nostrils. The first time it happened, he instinctively tried to sniff it back; the stabbing pain that resulted made him pass out. Now when it happened, he let the piece stay there, float back eventually on its own. He was breathing through his mouth anyway.

Ten years. Man, it didn't feel like that long. Chris remembered being a kid and thinking *one* year was an eternity; ten had been almost inconceivable. Now ten years had gone by and what? He'd blinked and missed them. What had he done with himself all that time?

Start at the beginning: June 14, graduated from high school. Had spent the summer . . . Wow, he couldn't remember most of that summer. Going out mostly. Drinking too much with Doug and Sean and the other guys from the football team. Spending time with Cindy. There was somebody he hadn't thought of in a long time. He wondered what she was doing now. She had looked a lot like Jessica: same big eyes, pouty lips. What had happened to her? He had a vague recollection of driving down a narrow country road at midnight, turning off his headlights to show her how well he could see in the dark. Flipping the car in a ditch and putting Cindy in the hospital with a concussion. He hadn't seen too much of her after that.

Let's see. Next: five years at Jefferson College. No, five and a half—he'd had to make up those two credits and hadn't graduated until December. College hadn't been what he had expected. He had gone to school thinking he would have to buckle down and discipline himself. Found out if you showed up for classes and turned in papers on time you got B's. Not that it was so easy; there were so many distractions: girls, parties, late-night bull sessions. Drugs, naturally. Was than when he had started selling? He hadn't planned on it; it just happened somehow. Jefferson was a funny place. Drugs were everywhere, just like in high school, but no one seemed to know what they were taking. It was a Midwestern kind of thing. Chris remembered sitting in one of the TV rooms, watching a rerun of *Sanford and Son* and listening to a couple of freshmen behind him complaining about how tired they were. As a joke, he turned around and asked them if they wanted some speed, keep them up all night. They looked at each other, looked back at him, and said, "How much?" He took some of his roommate's caffeine pills, popped them out of their packaging, and said: "Ten bucks." To his amazement, they bought them. What's more, by the end of the week he had people lining up outside his door.

It stopped him, thinking about it. Tell the story that way, it was like he had been a *dealer*. That wasn't right. He was more like . . . a con artist. Like Paul Newman and Robert Redford in *The Sting*. He wasn't doing anything all that bad. He was just taking advantage of other people's stupidity. That wasn't being a *drug dealer*. Sure, he had also had connections that gave him good stuff for his own personal use and to sell to friends, but that wasn't the same thing. He shouldn't even use the word *connections*—those guys were just friends, too. Friends helping friends. What were friends for?

Moving on.

Graduated from college with a degree in Mass Communication. Went to Europe for two months—London, Paris, Nice, Switzerland, Prague ... Prague, that had been a blast, the slacker capital of Eastern Europe. Everybody wearing grunge even though it was out of fashion; it was too much trouble to change clothes. He remembered trying heroin there for the first time because everybody else was doing it. Couldn't get into using a needle and never did it again.

Was he still in Prague when Dad called him about starting the fly-fishing company? His father had moved to Wyoming while Chris was away. He remembered thinking Dad had gone off his rocker, listening to him talk about *A River Runs Through It* and how the two of them were going to tap into the coming fly-fishing boom. Turned out he had rented a factory down in Mexico with twenty-five middle-aged señoras ready to work for sixty cents an hour. Could Chris come back and help oversee the production? Be vice-president?

The fly-fishing business had taken up, shit, the next four years. Chris tried to think what he had actually done during that time. There wasn't much to the business. His father did all the sales work, lining up companies and writing contracts; he had a number of other projects going at the same time, so he was out a lot. Chris did the accounting and went down to Mexico every couple of months to see how things were going and bring back random cases for quality control. It wasn't very demanding. Thinking about it now, Chris guessed he had only spent two or three days a week actually working. The rest of the time, he ... played pool? Went mountain biking. There were a couple of girls he saw every now and then. It was *Wyoming;* it wasn't like there was a lot to do. That was it.

No, that wasn't exactly true. There was the one other little thing. A couple of guys he played pool with asked him once how the weed was down in Mexico, and was it as good as everyone said. Without even thinking about it, he'd said yes, even though he'd never had Mexican marijuana before in his life. Just like that, he had orders from practically everybody he knew. When he came back from the next trip, he was five thousand dollars richer.

Actually, that had ended up taking a lot of his time, getting weed for everybody. He'd had to do all that work on the car, making smuggling compartments. Then there were the trips themselves; he was eventually spending twice as much time in Mexico as he needed to for his dad's company. And how many hours had he sat down in the basement, taking off buds and weighing bundles and rolling joints for people who were too lazy to do it themselves?

Spending all that time in the basement, that's what had gotten him in trouble eventually, his father coming down there when he wasn't supposed to be home and finding about ten pounds of Tijuana Gold drying out in the storeroom. Chris remembered him burning it out in the backyard (and weren't there a lot of people poking their noses outside *that* afternoon), telling Chris to get out, that if he saw him again he would call the police. Chris figured he was just mad. Who had he spent the night with? Andrea? Chris couldn't remember. But he remembered showing up at the house the next day and watching his father dial 911, his father saying that he had a drug dealer for a son. Could they send a squad car over right now?

And that was about it. He'd left town fast, trying to avoid the twenty-seven people who had given him money for dope that was now part of the atmosphere. Spent a month in Colorado with Jacqueline, from college, before she threw him out. Then two months in California, living off his savings, eating in coffee shops and running out without paying the bill. Finally here, Japan, flying over free with a buddy who worked for United Airlines. Working in the bar, selling some pills and a few joints now and then to bring in extra cash. There it was, ten years.

Oh yeah, and kidnapping some kind of *yakuza* goon, don't forget that.

That made ten years.

And getting his nose and right knee smashed into pulp.

That brought him right up-to-date.

Ten years. It still didn't feel like that long. How would a historian sum it up? Chris tried to separate himself from it, look at it objectively.

What did he see?

Not much that was productive. Certainly slacker-ish. A lot of shady characters for friends. Too many drugs; wow, he had sold a lot of drugs. Now this catastrophe. Kidnapping, he still couldn't believe he had done that. How had that happened? Mixed up somehow with the *yakuza* . . . Hell, the only reason he wasn't *dead* now was blind luck: being off camera while Jessica and Taro did their thing at the love hotel. If Taro hadn't carried the old man over to him, if Chris had gone to get him himself, the *yakuza* would know he was in on it.

In on it . . .

Christ, he was a *criminal*.

"Jesus Christ," he said aloud.

It shocked him, thinking it. He told himself to step back, look over everything again. Was he overstating things, being a little melodramatic?

Lay there thinking.

Decided *criminal* pretty much hit the nail on the head.

How else could you describe it? Crime was the only common thread in the past ten years of his life. He had spent the majority of his time engaged in criminal acts or criminal behavior. That he had never seen it as such didn't change the fact; there it was.

What was interesting to him now was why he had never seen it.

Drug dealing, that was easy. He had never thought of himself as a dealer because he was just getting drugs for friends. Or friends of friends. It wasn't like he was standing on a corner. And he had never thought of drugs as criminal because, well, everyone did them.

No, everyone *he knew* did drugs. That was different.

Had his perspective changed?

What was it he had said to Jessica, looking over the love hotel? "We're not criminals. We don't think like criminals." If that were true, why had he even been listening to her? She was talking about kidnapping and extortion. Wouldn't a normal person have walked away?

Take it a step further: When everything had gone wrong, wouldn't a normal person have given up?

A step further: What would a normal person do now?

Would a normal person even have to ask?

He lay there a while, considering it.

Imagined Lee Marvin from *Point Blank* was sitting on Jessica's sofa, looking down at him on the floor.

Lee Marvin said, *Zeniya's real name is Ozawa.*

Right, Chris said.

And the men who beat you up were yakuza.

Yeah.

They want Ozawa back.

Right.

Lee lit a cigarette and blew out a puff of smoke.

Said, *So how much is he worth to them?*

It was a good question.

It was very dark in the boathouse.

Not pitch-black; everybody said pitch-black; pitch-black meant no light at all. There was a little bit of light coming in the dingy windows from the river on one side, and from the power plant on the other. It was enough to see the windows. Also the crack beneath the door. Nothing else though. Not a single, solitary, goddamn thing.

Jessica was sitting on the straw mat next to Zeniya. After she'd gotten herself under enough control to deal with things again, she'd dragged him back there and retied him. Then gotten the crowbar and crouched over him, waiting for him to move. He hadn't. Now it was ten o'clock, and as far as she could tell, he still hadn't. She wasn't worried that he was dead anymore, though. She was too tired for that. Also too hungry; she hadn't eaten for twenty-four hours and during that time she had thrown up repeatedly. And anyway, she could hear him. There was nothing like near-total darkness to give your ears a workout. She couldn't see, but she could hear everything: Zeniya's breathing, water lapping against the underside of the boathouse, something scurrying across the floor.

Someone walking down the gravel road to the boathouse.

Her heartbeat, she could hear that, too. The sounds of her body tensing. The steps got closer. They didn't have to mean anything. Somebody out for a walk. Only there wasn't anywhere to walk *to*—it was a dead end. Which left Chris or Taro . . . God, she hoped so. Or maybe it was a homeless guy looking for a place to sleep. That would be all right. But what if it was a policeman? Shit, or one of Taro's Iranians? Great, there was something she needed to be thinking about. That was the other thing about darkness; it gave your imagination a workout, too.

Not that she needed one at this point in her life.

The crowbar was somewhere on the floor next to her. She felt around until she found it. Picked it up by the wrong end and made a face—it was still sticky with Zeniya's blood. She turned it over and gripped it with both hands. Then stood up slowly, hearing her knees pop.

The footsteps had stopped. Whoever was out there was right in front of the door, his feet—Jessica was sure it was a he— blocking the faint light coming in through the crack below. She was too scared to move. She held the crowbar like a club, her eyes as wide open as they had ever been, straining to see something, *anything*.

When the person outside jiggled the padlock on the door, the noise loud and immediate, she almost wet her pants.

It was Taro's lock. He'd replaced the Iranian one before he and Chris had left. Taro had one key, Chris the other. If the person outside was Taro or Chris, why didn't he just unlock it?

The jiggling stopped. She heard the sound of a zipper being pulled. A rustling, like a bag being opened and looked through. Then a *click*. There were suddenly pinpricks of yellow everywhere, light coming in through cracks and holes that she hadn't noticed before in the door and the wall around it. A flashlight. The feet at the door took a step back, then two, and the field of yellow pinpricks expanded. It was like looking at stars in the night sky. Then the footsteps crunched over glass, and the stars disappeared. After a beat: the light at the window she had broken hours earlier.

It was one of the Iranians. She was sure of it. He had stolen something, that's why he had a bag and a flashlight, and he was looking to stash it. But he'd seen the new lock on the door, the window broken from the inside, and now he knew something was wrong.

She could not let him in. If he tried, she was going to have to stop him. Whatever it took. Swing the crowbar as hard as she could right at his skull. She tiptoed forward, knowing she was trembling, the sweat coming off her hands making the crowbar wet and slippery.

The stars came back. So did the feet at the door. Jessica stopped. She was close enough.

Come on . . .

She heard Taro say, "Jessica?"

She screamed, dropping the crowbar on her foot.

★   ★   ★

Taro had half expected police. Or an empty boathouse. It had taken him too long to get back, and while he trusted Jessica, Chris was another story. A real snake in the class, as his mom liked to say. With Jessica tired and scared, who knew what she might believe?

What he hadn't expected: Jessica alone with the old man in the dark, wide-eyed, twitching like a wild animal caught in a trap. She'd pounded on the door hysterically until he got it open, then almost knocked him over, throwing her arms around him.

"It's been *hours*!" She was almost sobbing. "What happened? Where have you been? I was all alone and he tried to escape!"

"Took time," he said. "Get Astro painted, drive back."

"You couldn't call?"

"Denchi ga nakunatta," he said. His cell phone had gone dead, and he hadn't been able to charge it. "Sorry."

She would not let go. He forced her to get back inside and closed the door. Wow, it was dark. He swept the room with the flashlight. Shower, toilet, boxes, futons, Zeniya. Or whoever he was. "Where's Chris?" Taro said.

"I don't know."

It was after ten o'clock. "He don't come back?"

"No." She took a step back, wiping at her eyes. "He didn't call either."

"He should be here, long time ago."

"Yeah, Taro, I know." Jessica getting an edge in her voice. "You were supposed to be back a long time ago, too. I've been locked in here for like sixteen fucking hours."

"I told you," he said. "Have to drive to Wakayama. Everybody's busy, then I have to drive back. It took time." It was true. There had been a line of stolen Mercedes at the body shop, the guys down there getting them ready to be shipped out the next day. Plates from Tokyo, Osaka, Kobe, Nagoya, even as far as Ishikawa. He'd been lucky to get in at all. He said, "I did everything, it's as fast as possible."

"You still could have called me from a pay phone or something. He tried to attack me!"

She sat down on one of the futons and started crying, telling him the story. Taro listened, patting her on the back. She'd had a rough day all right. What he didn't like: it was possible Zeniya had seen her. All the way back to Osaka, Taro had been trying to think of a way to get Jessica out of this, but if the guy had seen her, that really limited their options.

When she was finished, Jessica wiped her eyes again, then looked at her hands in the beam from Taro's flashlight. "God, I'm filthy," she said. "And tired. And *hungry*. Did you bring any food?"

He had some dried squid in the bottom of his bag. She took it from him and tore open the packaging. "I'll even eat this," she said.

While she chewed, he gave her his flashlight and got out another one. Then he walked over to Zeniya and looked at him carefully. There was blood on the bandages on the right side of his head, but not too much. Taro listened. Still breathing.

Taro crouched over him, thinking again about what they could do.

When he walked back, Jessica was riffling through his bag, dried squid sticking out of her mouth like a cigarette. "Anything to drink?" she said.

He sat down next to her. "Calpis, *kamo shiranai.*"

She found it. "Liquid yogurt and squid. I'd throw up, but there isn't enough in my stomach yet."

"Jessica—"

"You know what foreigners call this?" She held up the plastic bottle. " 'Cow Piss.' You know, cows, milk . . ." She took a drink. "Jesus, that's awful."

"Jessica," Taro said. "Listen me."

Taro wanted to leave. Put Zeniya in the Astro—now an anonymous white, it was parked three blocks away—and get out of there. Drop him off somewhere in the suburbs, then drive back to Wakayama. Taro had friends who could put them on the boat with the stolen cars headed for the Philippines. People were smuggled *into* Japan all the time; it wouldn't be that hard to smuggle two people *out*.

Jessica said, "I can't go to the Philippines. I don't have my passport, I don't have any money—"

"Nobody check passport," Taro said. "Just go."

"Go to the Philippines without money or a passport."

"Sure. I have money, a little. Go out into a jungle somewhere, find some group, ask them, they want to make some money."

She was having trouble following the conversation. "What are you talking about? What kind of group in the jungle?"

"You know, rebels. Terrorists."

"Terrorists."

"Sure. There are lots of different kinds. We pick one."

"What for?"

"So they kidnap you."

This was the kind of conversation that was only possible in a dark, run-down boathouse after the worst day of your life. Maybe not even then. Jessica wondered if something was being lost in translation, Taro trying to go from Japanese to English in his head too quickly. She said, "I'm supposed to *ask* some terrorists to *kidnap* me?"

"Sure," Taro said. "All the time people do it. Make a video, send to U.S.A. embassy, ask for two, three million dollar. Say you were kidnapped in Japan, with this guy Zeniya. Then you become—how to say?—innocent."

"How am I supposed to explain me hitting him? And who's supposed to pay the two million dollars?"

Taro shrugged, saying, "Your parents." Like he was apologizing.

"My parents don't have two million dollars. They wouldn't spend it on me if they did."

"*Ask* for two million," Taro said. "Get one hundred thousand, two hundred thousand, like that. Then give half to terrorists."

Was he serious? He was, look at him. Jessica closed her eyes and pinched the bridge of her nose. This was ridiculous. "Taro," she said, "I'm not going to the Philippines. Give myself over to a group of terrorists, you have to be kidding."

Taro said, gesturing at Zeniya, "You wanna stay here? With him?"

"No, I don't want to stay with him!" Starting to lose it again, voice rising. She forced herself to take a deep breath. "Listen, another fake kidnapping is not the way to go. It's not going to solve anything. Anyway, we can't just leave Chris."

Taro gave her a look. "You think he's coming back?"

She didn't know what to say to that. Yes. No. Maybe. She had absolutely no idea. After a pause, she said, "Chris wouldn't just leave."

"Yeah? You give him your bank card, right? Tell him your secret number?"

Yeah . . .

"How much you got in there?" Taro said.

He was staring at her, his face hard. She didn't want to tell him. He'd laugh if she did. Two and a half million, or something like that. Didn't want to tell him either that she'd already thought of this possibility. Even with the new restrictions on withdrawals, Chris would be able to take her for everything she had by eight A.M. tomorrow morning. It wasn't three hundred–plus thousand dollars, but it was enough for him to get out of the country and disappear for a while, that was for sure.

Leave her and Taro to face the mess the three of them had gotten into.

God, would he do that?

Was he already doing it?

Jesus, the fucking Philippines . . .

Jessica held up her hands. Enough. "Look," she said, "maybe something happened to him. He got into an accident, he got lost—"

"Went to Kansai airport, maybe there right now."

"Taro! Stop. Let's just wait a little bit longer."

But Taro kept pressing, saying "Now is best, *to omou*. Nighttime, nobody outside—"

"Stop!" Jessica stood up and walked away, wringing her

hands. Goddammit, she didn't want to have to deal with this. Chris was coming back. He *was*. She opened the door and took a peek outside. Didn't see him, but that didn't mean anything. "A few more hours," she said, as much to herself as to Taro. "He will come back."

Chris finally found the narrow gravel road in front of the power plant at one-thirty in the morning. His knee was killing him. He did a quick glance around and didn't see the Astro anywhere. Which would have been a good thing—Taro smart enough to put it somewhere else—but Chris couldn't see any lights through the boathouse windows. Taro had flashlights in the Astro—why wouldn't he have brought them? Why wouldn't he and Jessica be *using* them? Were they sitting there in the dark?

Unless they weren't there at all.

He had forgotten about that, the possibility of Taro and Jessica screwing him. Paranoia was hard to maintain when you were getting the shit kicked out of you by *yakuza*. But it was back now. He took a flashlight out of the backpack he'd found at Jessica's apartment and turned it on, shining it against the front of the boathouse.

One of the windows was broken. From the inside; there were shards of glass all over the gravel road. Had Jessica gotten out? He took a closer look. It wasn't a clean break; jagged remains pointed out from the frame like spikes. Ow. The hole was big enough for a person to get through, but Jessica was in pain if she had.

He brought the beam down to eye level. Saw it right away—the padlock was off the door. Son of a bitch. She *was* gone. Taro, too, had to be; he had the only other key. He'd come back and they'd left. Chris slammed a fist against the door and said, "Mother*fucker!*"

Heard Jessica say, "Chris?"

He jumped, startled, and felt it all the way through his injured knee. "Jessica," he said. "Jesus Christ, you scared the hell out of me."

Now he heard Taro's voice: "Where you go?" Taro trying to be gruff.

"Open the goddamn door," Chris said. He tugged at the knob, banging the door against the frame. "It's been a bad fuck-ing day."

They had padlocked it from the inside. Chris heard metal clacking against metal, then the door opened. It was Jessica he saw first, her face pinched and angry, then shocked as she got a good look at him. "What happened?" she said.

"It's my new look," he said. His nose was in an aluminum splint. There was a bandage under his left eye, where a piece of plastic from the videotape had cut the skin. He had shaved. Changed clothes, too, put on a T-shirt and shorts, trying to make the brace on his knee as comfortable as pos-sible. He said, "You like it? The doctor said the kneecap was broken. A horizontal fracture; he'd never seen one before." It was going to have to be wired together. The doctor had wanted to put him in the hospital immediately. "Hurts like you wouldn't believe."

"No, I believe it," Jessica said. She helped him inside, Taro watching with a more skeptical expression. The little fucker. Jessica said, "What, did you fall on something?"

"Yeah," Chris said, "a steel baton. Why is it so dark in here?" His was the only flashlight that was on.

"Taro thought it was safer that way."

"Keep away police," Taro said. "They come by, see lights in here, maybe they think strange."

Chris said, "If I bang my knee into something cause it's so frigging dark, the whole neighborhood's going to come by— that's how loud I'm going to scream. Turn on some flashlights."

They did, pointing them at the floor. Chris followed the beams to one of the futons, where he carefully sat down. Jesus, that was a relief. He exhaled and said, "How's our guy?"

"He's alive," Jessica said. Giving Taro a look. "What do you mean, 'a steel baton'?"

"I mean a steel baton," Chris said. "About a foot long and this wide." He made a circle with his thumb and forefinger and showed it to them. "Swung right into my kneecap by a guy in a purple suit and gold chains, while a big teenage fucker held me down on your sofa."

Jessica looked alarmed. "Somebody attacked you in my apartment?"

"Listen," he said, and proceeded to tell them the whole story. Everything, from the moment he'd left the boathouse. Well, except for stealing all of Jessica's money. He was holding that one in reserve. He told them instead that he'd taken out a couple hundred thousand yen and had it stuffed it in his pockets when the *yakuza* attacked him. They'd taken his wallet—along with Jessica's bank card—and missed the cash. It sounded believable.

Mixed in with the rest of the story, it didn't even stand out. When he was finished, he said, "I'm sorry it took me so long to get back, but I had to find a clinic that was open on Saturday, then pick up some things that I thought we'd need. It's all in the backpack: clothes, water, some food. Other stuff. Then I got lost trying to find this damn place again. I've been walking outside for hours."

"Wait a minute," Jessica said. "Can we back up? These guys in my apartment, you said they were *yakuza?*"

"Right."

"How do you know?"

"Come on," Chris said. "Purple suit, gold chains . . ." Wincing, he wiped at his nose; it was dripping again. "Plus they told me. Hell, Purple Suit gave me a business card."

"Show me," Taro said.

Chris took the card out of his pocket and handed it to him. "I can't believe even the mob carries business cards over here. The guy said his name was Sato."

Taro held it under his flashlight. "It's real," he said.

Jessica said, "You've seen one before?"

Taro nodded. "Yano Corporation. It's mean Ono-*gumi*." Taro explained that because of laws passed ten years ago, *yakuza* could no longer officially call themselves *yakuza*. They had to hide behind dummy corporations. But everybody knew what was what. "Card says assistant manager," Taro said. "So Sato is maybe *wakagashira*."

"Which means what?"

"Like little boss," Taro said.

"A crew chief."

Jessica slumped down next to Chris and buried her face in her hands. "Oh God," she said, "and they've got a video of me tying Zeniya up and taking him out of the love hotel."

"Ozawa," Chris said. "They *had* a video." He pointed to his nose. "What's left of it is on the floor in your apartment. On the way out, this Sato guy was yelling at the one who broke it against my face—I'll bet it was their only copy. The original, straight from the hotel."

"But they know who I *am*," Jessica said. "They know what I *did*. What if this Zeniya/Ozawa is working with them somehow? They'll *kill* me."

"I think he *is* working with them," Chris said. "In fact, I think he's *yakuza,* too. Think about it. The muscles, the car, all the scars on his body—I'll bet those were tattoos that he got removed."

"What for?"

"I don't know, maybe it's a con. Maybe he and the real Zeniya are mixed up in something together. That's not the point. What I'm trying to say is, the *yakuza* want this guy back."

"*That's* the point?" Almost yelling at him.

"No," Chris said. "The point is, how badly do they want him back."

She looked at him like she didn't understand what he meant. Then, realizing it, she looked at him like he was out of his mind. She said, "You can't possibly want to try and blackmail the *yakuza*."

"Why not?" Chris said. "Tell me what other choice we have. You think if we give him back and say we're sorry, they're going to let it go? Besides, I've got an idea."

"You are insane," Jessica said. "Taro, tell him he doesn't know what he's talking about and is going to get the three of us killed."

Taro was still looking at the business card. "You told me"—glancing at Chris now—"Zeniya's name Ozawa?"

"Yeah. Sato kept shouting it. Finally said, 'Ozawa give me.' Really fucking pissed about it, too."

Taro said, "Ozawa Shinji?"

"What does *shinji* mean?"

"It's a name," Jessica said. "A first name. Taro, who's Shinji Ozawa?"

"I didn't hear a Shinji," Chris said.

Taro pointed at the business card. "This *meishi* for Ono-*gumi*. Yamaguchi-*gumi*, they are the most big. Ono-*gumi* is like *yonbanme*."

"What are you talking about?" Chris said.

"Rankings," Jessica said. She had gotten very quiet. "Taro said this Ono gang's the fourth largest in Japan."

"*Oyabun* of Ono-*gumi* is Ozawa Shinji," Taro said.

"*Oyabun*," Jessica said.

"Big boss. Top."

Nobody said anything for a minute.

"Taro"—Jessica cleared her throat—"are you trying to say that Zeniya—Ozawa—*this* Ozawa"—she pointed at him on the floor—"is the head of the fourth-biggest *yakuza* gang in Japan?"

Taro seemed to think about it. *"So,"* he said. *"To omou."*

They looked at one another. Finally, Chris started to laugh. It hurt, but he did it anyway.

"This isn't funny," Jessica said.

But it was. Actually, it was better than funny. It was perfect. Somewhere, Lee Marvin was proud.

Somehow, completely by accident, they'd kidnapped the Godfather.

This was the conversation the three of them had on the floor in the boathouse, Sunday, two o'clock in the morning:

JESSICA: NO. ABSOLUTELY NOT. NO WAY.

TARO: I AGREE JESSICA'S OPINION.

CHRIS: OKAY, FINE, BUT WHAT ARE YOU GOING TO DO?

JESSICA: GET OUT RIGHT NOW. LEAVE THE COUNTRY.

TARO: THERE IS BOAT TOMORROW. GO TO PHILIPPINES.

JESSICA: TARO, I AM NOT GOING TO THE GODDAMN PHILIPPINES!

CHRIS: SO WHERE ARE YOU GOING TO GO? YOU THINK THERE'S ANYWHERE IN THE WORLD THAT SOMEBODY CAN'T FIND YOU? EVEN IF THERE WAS, WHAT ARE YOU GOING TO DO THERE? WHAT ARE YOU GOING TO LIVE ON?

JESSICA: IF WE STAY HERE, THEY WILL KILL US!

CHRIS: WHAT'S THIS *US*? THEY'LL KILL *YOU*. KILL TARO, TOO, IF THEY FIGURE OUT WHO HE IS. YOU TWO WERE IN THE VIDEO AT THE LOVE HOTEL, NOT ME. THEY BEAT ME UP, SURE, BUT THEY DON'T KNOW I'M INVOLVED. I COULD WALK OUT OF HERE RIGHT NOW.

JESSICA: SO WHY DON'T YOU! GET OUT!

TARO: HE DON'T WANNA DO THAT.

CHRIS: TARO'S RIGHT, I DON'T. FOR ONE THING, IF THEY CATCH YOU, YOU MIGHT TELL THEM.

TARO: TELL THEM EVERYTHING.

CHRIS: YEAH, LOVE AND KISSES TO YOU, TOO, BABE. FOR ANOTHER THING, THIS IS TOO GOOD AN OPPORTUNITY TO PASS UP.

JESSICA: AN *OPPORTUNITY*? WHAT, TO GET YOURSELF BUTCHERED? CHRIS, THIS IS THE FUCKING *YAKUZA*!

CHRIS: EXACTLY. LISTEN, YOU WERE WILLING TO RISK SPENDING TWENTY-TO-LIFE BEHIND BARS FOR A THIRD OF A MILLION DOLLARS. THIS WAS WHEN YOU THOUGHT OZAWA WAS ZENIYA. I KNOW YOU HAD YOUR PLAN AND YOU THOUGHT IT WAS FOOLPROOF, BUT IT WAS STILL KIDNAPPING AND EXTORTION. DEEP DOWN, YOU KNEW IT WAS POSSIBLE FOR THINGS TO GO WRONG, AND YOU WERE WILLING TO DO IT ANYWAY.

JESSICA: WHAT DOES THIS HAVE TO DO WITH ANYTHING?

CHRIS: JUST THIS: YOU WERE WILLING TO RISK YOUR FREEDOM FOR ABOUT THREE HUNDRED AND FIFTY THOUSAND DOLLARS. SO MAKE IT AN EVEN MILLION. MAKE IT TWO. NOT SPLIT THREE WAYS, I MEAN TWO MILLION, ALL FOR YOU. *SIX* MILLION, SPLIT THREE WAYS. WHAT ARE YOU WILLING TO RISK FOR THAT?

TARO: YOU CAN'T KIDNAP *YAKUZA*.

CHRIS: BUT WE *HAVE*. IT'S A DONE DEAL. WE DIDN'T MEAN TO, BUT WE HAVE. AND ANYWAY, WHY NOT? IN SOME WAYS, IT'S BETTER

THAN KIDNAPPING SOMEBODY NORMAL. SOMEBODY NORMAL, THEIR FAMILY GOES TO THE POLICE. THESE GUYS ARE CRIMINALS; THEY'RE NOT GOING TO GO TO THE COPS.

TARO: *HAI,* BUT EVEN YOU GET MONEY NOW, LATER THEY KILL YOU.

CHRIS: WITH TWO MILLION DOLLARS APIECE, IT'S GOING TO BE A LOT EASIER TO HIDE. BUT THE WAY I'M THINKING NOW, WE MIGHT NOT EVEN HAVE TO.

JESSICA: WHAT DO YOU MEAN?

CHRIS: WHAT IF OZAWA AND HIS TOP BRASS THINK SOMEBODY ELSE IS RESPONSIBLE FOR THIS?

JESSICA: LIKE WHO?

CHRIS: LISTEN . . .

They made a ransom tape the next day.

Jessica still couldn't believe she was doing this. Every instinct told her to run, get out of there, and not look back. But Chris was right; the *yakuza* would find her. And if she left now, she'd have nothing. Not even—she was pretty sure—the twenty or so thousand dollars in her bank account. That was gone. She couldn't prove it, not yet, but she was willing to bet Chris had it.

He'd given Taro two hundred thousand yen to buy the video camera, tapes, and other odds and ends that morning. When Taro was gone, she'd said, "I thought you said you'd only taken two hundred thousand out of my account. Did you just give Taro all our money?"

"I think I said a couple hundred thousand," Chris said.

Checking on Ozawa, not looking at her. "Meaning two, three, four."

"Three or four is a few, not a couple."

"Okay, a few hundred thousand, Jesus."

"I'd like to know how much. In an actual number this time."

He looked at her now. "What do you think, I ripped you off?"

"I just want to know how much you took. Since my card and the receipt conveniently disappeared along with your wallet."

"Then I could say anything and you'd have to believe me, wouldn't you?"

She kept her eyes steady. Her voice, too. "How much?"

He shook his head and turned back to Ozawa. "Four hundred and fifty, Christ. I spent twenty getting over here the other night and gave the two hundred to Taro. The rest is in the back-pack. Go and check if you want."

She did. Found two hundred thirty thousand and change in an envelope beneath some clothes. Which seemed to back up his story, but why four-fifty? What was the point of the fifty? When you were withdrawing a lot of money, you kept things even. Plus, the envelope the money was in was one of hers: cream-colored with little squiggly lines down the side—she kept them in her desk drawer. Every ATM in Japan had envelopes in a slot next to it for people making large withdrawals. If Chris hadn't wanted one then, why had he gone looking for one in her apart-ment? *After* getting his nose and knee smashed in.

Answer: He needed another one.

And wait a minute—how had he paid for the clinic?

The money was gone.

What else was he not telling her?

Shit.

The problem was, there wasn't anything she could do about it. She couldn't trust him, but she had to trust him, at least until this was over. It was frustrating. And scary. It had always irritated her watching movies where you knew, you *knew*, that one character was going to stab the other in the back. Somebody told a lie, that was how it started, and as soon as Jessica heard it, she wanted to say to the idiot on the screen: *Get out! Leave!* But they never did.

Something she had realized over the past twenty-four hours: leaving was harder than it looked.

She didn't say anything else about the money. If there wasn't much she could do, she could at least not give away what she was thinking. Maybe then if Chris was trying to screw her, he'd make a mistake. And it was possible that she was just being paranoid. She doubted it, but it was possible.

It had been that kind of weekend.

Taro came back from Den Den town with a passport-size Sony and they got to work, Chris arguing about camera angles like he was Steven Spielberg. Actually saying things like "Take One" and "Take Two." They finished at two. Taro left with the digital cassette to get it dubbed over to videotape (Chris: "Don't take it to Fotomart." Taro: "What?"), and she went over what she was going to have to say. The plan was to talk to Ozawa tonight; the longer they waited, the greater the risk of something happening: Taro's van getting stolen, the police or the Iranians dropping by, Ozawa dying. He didn't look or sound good at all, and if he died everything would fall apart.

Of course, everything would fall apart if he didn't believe her story either. At least believe most of it. Jessica thought Chris's plan had a chance to work, but this part was the weak link. Looking up from the notes he'd prepared for her, she said, "Chris, we need to do something about this."

He was lying on a futon with his eyes closed, his T-shirt stained with sweat. They'd managed to open two of the windows, but it was still nauseatingly hot. He said, "Do something about what?"

"This plan. What I'm supposed to say." She held up the notepad. "I just don't understand why he'd believe it."

Chris sat up, holding on to his knee. He rubbed his face. "Yeah, I know. I've been thinking about that, too."

"I mean, I hit him," Jessica said. "With a crowbar."

"It needs something, doesn't it?" Chris said. "A little extra *oomph*. Something to really convince him."

"It can't be something I would just say."

"No, you're going to have to do something."

It stopped her. "I'm not sleeping with him again."

Chris smiled. "No, I've got a better idea."

He motioned for her to come over and sit down next to him, to his right. There was a plate on the floor with an apple core on it, and he dragged it over. Threw the core away in the bag they were using for trash and handed her a tissue. "Can you wipe off the plate? I want to get something."

"What for?"

"Can you just wipe it off?"

So while he dug through the backpack, she wiped off the plate, thinking he was going have get it through his head that she wasn't anybody's maid. "There," she said. Put the plate back on the floor. "Are you happy?"

He picked it up and balanced it on his right thigh. "Put your hand on it."

"The plate?"

"Right in the middle."

"Why?"

"This will help your story, I promise."

Giving him a look, she put her hand on the plate. What had he taken out of the backpack? She didn't see anything. Now he was grabbing her wrist with his right hand, pressing her hand against the plate, something coming up in his left . . .

She said, "What are you doing?"

That was when he brought down the knife and cut off her little finger.

It was weird doing it. Like cutting a wet twig. There was a tiny *snap* when the knife passed through bone, then a quick spray of blood. As soon as he was all the way through, Chris dropped the knife and wrapped his arms around Jessica, clamping a hand over her mouth to keep her from screaming. She screamed anyway, getting his palm all wet, holding her hand up in front of her face while blood ran down her arm and onto the floor. Her eyes bugged out like a chick in a horror movie. She tried to twist away from him then, kicking out with her legs, but he held her fast. Managed to get the Ace bandages out of his pocket without letting her break free and slowly wrapped them around her hand, whispering that she was all right, she was going to be fine, telling her this was the only way and why someday she would thank him. After all, it was only a finger. She wouldn't even miss it. He pointed out that she still had nine left.

When he thought she had calmed down, he loosened his grip, thinking to give her some space. Before he could react, she slammed her fist onto his injured knee. He howled, clutching it, as Jessica scrambled away and picked up what was left of her little finger on the floor. Then she ran for the door. Was almost outside before he caught up to her, grabbing her hair and yanking her back in. Turning her around, he slapped her, twice, knocking her to the floor. Twisting her wrist, he forced her to drop the finger. Then he took it and threw it out a window, hearing the faint *plop* as it fell in the water.

He didn't want her to get any ideas, so he took the crowbar and the knife and sat in front of the door, blocking it. Jessica was on her knees on the floor, crying, clutching her hand. Finally she leaned forward and screamed at him, loud enough for everyone in Osaka to hear her, calling him a motherfucker and a piece of shit and every other obscenity she knew. He held up the crowbar and said if she didn't stop screaming, he'd knock out a few teeth as well. How would she like that? It took her a few minutes to wind down, but she finally shut up. Crawled over to one of the futons and curled up on top of it, sobbing.

She cried for a half hour. Then she was quiet. He tried to engage her, get her to talk about it ("Jessica? Nobody will notice really. Anyway, with two million dollars, you can get a prosthesis."), but she was unresponsive. She wouldn't even look at him. After several attempts fell flat, he limped over there and patted her on the shoulder. She jerked away and said, "Would you just shut up and leave me alone?" Not screaming anymore, though—more resigned, like she was coming to terms with it.

It seemed like progress.

Taro came back at five with steel cuffs for Ozawa and a VHS copy of the ransom tape. Did a double take seeing the blood on the floor and asked what happened. Chris couldn't believe it when Jessica ran to the little Filipino fucker and threw herself in his arms, showing him her bandaged hand and crying about how Chris had cut off her finger. Not bothering to tell Taro *why,* not giving him *any* of the extenuating circumstances. Making it sound like Chris was some kind of violent psycho. It was irritating. Chris thought he and Jessica had come to an understanding.

Taro threw the first punch. After that things got ugly. They didn't get any better until Chris grabbed the crowbar—Ozawa's dried blood still all over it—and crushed it onto Taro's left forearm. Chris heard the snap and knew the fight was over. Both of them ended up going to the same clinic Chris had been to on Saturday, Taro for the arm, Chris to have the doctor look at his nose again. ("Another bike accident. Can you believe it?") They left Jessica with Ozawa, Chris making sure to lock her inside. On the way to the clinic, Taro told Chris that he was a "cocksocker." Chris told him the word was "cock*sucker,*" and that if he was going to insult someone, he ought to at least get it right.

Taro didn't say anything else to him for the rest of the day.

None of them was in any shape to deal with the Ozawa situation anytime soon, so they decided to put off setting things in motion until Tuesday night. Well, Chris decided; Jessica and Taro sat sullenly in a corner, ignoring him. Which convinced him that he was right. Forty-eight hours, that's what they needed, a chance for everybody to catch their breath and calm down.

But it wasn't as easy as he thought. That night, especially. Chris pulled one of the futons in front of the door and slept there, one hand on the crowbar, the knife buried under clothes beneath Jessica's backpack *slash* pillow. Not that he really slept. Jessica and Taro were on the other side of the boathouse, and who knew what they were plotting? He wanted to keep an eye on them, but he couldn't. In his haste to secure the crowbar and the knife, he'd forgotten to get a flashlight; now they had them all. Once it got dark, they disappeared from view, the boathouse about as bright as the inside of a tomb. He could hear them whispering. It bothered him, wondering what they were talking about. Once he called out, "Jess? Taro? We're going to deal with this situation like professionals, right?"

It was quiet for a few seconds, then the whispering started again.

Finally, Chris couldn't stand it. As quietly as he could, he inched off the futon and onto the floor, then over to another corner of the boathouse. With any luck, they'd think he was still in front of the door. If they tried anything, he'd know about it. He stared into the darkness as hard as he could, body primed, waiting. Around midnight, the whispering stopped. Soon after that, he heard Taro snoring. Which was the oldest trick in the book; Chris wasn't going to fall for that one. He waited, but nothing happened.

At two, he dozed off. Woke up fifteen minutes later, panicked. Dozed off again at half-past three. When he woke up this time it was after five, light starting to stream in through the boathouse windows, and he was so startled that he jerked the crowbar into the wall behind him. Jessica—he could see her now, across the room—raised her head sleepily and said, "Do you mind?"

"Sorry," he said.

But he was encouraged. Even a complaint at this point was a good sign.

That day he stepped around them carefully. Things seemed to get better. On one level at least—Ozawa—Jessica and Taro had to deal with him. It was hard work, kidnapping. It was like having a baby in the house; you had to keep on top of everything. They had to help Ozawa go to the toilet, help him eat, help him drink. There were all kinds of other things, too. Checking the Walkman to make sure the batteries were all right, checking the towel to make sure it was still wrapped tightly around his head, checking the cuffs, keeping an eye on the old guy's head wounds—it never stopped. Not only that, the mental pressure was growing. Chris found himself constantly keeping an ear open for sirens; the slightest sound out of the ordinary made his heart jump right out of his chest. It was affecting Jessica and Taro, too. A few times Jessica came over to talk to him, nervous about this or that. It was another good sign, Jessica seeming to realize that they were all in this together and had to let bygones be bygones. Taro wasn't as forgiving—he still hadn't said a word to him since Sunday afternoon—but Chris wasn't too worried. If Jessica could get over having her finger cut off, so could Taro.

That night after dinner (ramen from 7-Eleven, again), Chris was exhausted. He was asleep before it got dark. He dreamed that he was one of the cooks at a ramen shop, in charge of making the pig-bone soup. It was disgusting, standing over the pot with a ladle and stirring the awful stuff while the smell rushed up to his face. Every so often he'd try to take a break, but a half-dozen *yakuza* were watching him, scowling, their hands on their hips. All of them looked like Taro. They were stripped to the waist, and when Chris turned away from the soup he could see the tattoos spread across their chests.

Ozawa was there, too. He was wearing the nurse uniform and sunglasses and grinning from ear to ear like a madman. The handcuffs were dangling from his right wrist, the ankle cuffs lying open on the floor. Ozawa never seemed to move, but somehow every time Chris turned around, the old man was a step closer. Chris wanted to get out of there, make a run for it, but couldn't figure out how. Jessica was no help. She was standing in the entrance to the restaurant, wearing a pink camisole and spiked heels, pretending to be a waitress. Occasionally she would come in, tell him the orders. She'd stare at all of the *yakuza,* then give Chris a look, challenging him with her eyes to do something. He'd look back as if to say, *Do what?* and she would shake her head and walk out. Like he was being a pussy. All the while, Ozawa kept getting closer and closer, and when Chris felt the old man's hot breath on the back of his neck, he gripped the ladle with both hands, ready to turn around and smash it right in the fucker's face. But before he could move, the other *yakuza* had surrounded him, knives glinting in their hands. One of them made a move, and Chris couldn't hold on to the ladle; it slipped through his fingers and into the boiling soup. Now the *yakuza* had his hands, spreading them open—

Chris woke up and saw Taro above him. Taro had one foot on Chris's right hand; he had Chris's left hand spread open on the floor in front of a flashlight. Chris tried to shake him off, shouting that he was a motherfucker, but couldn't move; Taro had all the leverage. Somewhere in the darkness, Jessica was crying, telling Taro to stop. The next thing Chris knew, he felt a searing pain running up from his left hand to his shoulder and he nearly bit off his tongue, clenching his teeth. Then Taro was looking at him, grinning, showing him part of a finger, *Chris's* finger, letting it drip blood all over his face.

"Cock*sucker,*" Taro said.

Chris felt he should have seen it coming.

His first reaction was to get up and fight. He didn't. For lots of reasons. One, his hand hurt like a son of a bitch. Two, Taro stepped on his knee getting up; that hurt almost more than the finger. Fighting with both injuries was out of the question. Three, Taro had taken the crowbar. Four, he had the backpack with the knife in it, too.

But none of those reasons was very important. What *was* important: He needed Taro for the plan with Ozawa to work. If Taro was satisfied, having got his revenge, that was fine with Chris.

It was only a finger.

There would be time to settle things later.

"*That was Evening Daughters with their million-selling smash, 'GO! GO! Best Love!,' falling to number eight this week on the countdown. Keiko-chan, you met lead singer Takako just a few days ago, didn't you?*"

"*I sure did!*"

"*What kind of person is she?*"

"*So cute! Cute fashion, cute personality—of course that cute face. Cute, cute, cute!*"

Shinji Ozawa lay in the darkness, listening to the Osaka Hot 100.

It was the third time they had played the countdown this week. Coming up at number seven, he knew, was Mr. Hip Hop Drive's new hit: "Machine Gun." After that, Keiko-*chan* had an interview with the girl from Okinawa, Ami, about life with her new baby. Then Ami's new song, "Wonderful Life," that was number six. Ozawa couldn't remember number five or number four. He was waiting for number three: "Lucky Seven," by PAP (People Artist Power). He liked that one.

He was learning a lot of new songs.

It was funny; he couldn't remember the last time he had listened to the radio. It just never occurred to him to turn it on. He supposed he was out of touch. What made it funnier was that the Organization had a controlling interest in four or five Kansai radio stations, including (he thought) this one. He should have been tuning in every once in a while just to monitor the investment.

Now, of course, he was tuned in twenty-four hours a day. He couldn't believe the number of times they would play certain songs: twice, sometimes three times an hour. They even had a special word for it, *heavy rotation,* which Ozawa was sure was an American expression. He wasn't sure why they bothered, since most of the songs sounded the same. A producer who came in for an interview said he wrote all the songs for his singers using a computer. He had a program that would take a basic melody and put it in different arrangements; all he had to do was sit back and wait until he heard something he liked. Ozawa thought: And kids liked this? But the producer had seven different groups with songs in the Osaka Hot 100.

Every morning at seven and eleven, then at six in the evening and at midnight, there would be a fifteen-minute newsbreak. It was nice; he could keep track of things. The Hanshin Tigers were winning; that was a pleasant surprise. The stock market was still down. There had been nothing about him, which he thought was interesting, but then the station did seem geared toward kids and teenagers. Maybe on another station. Somebody had to have reported something.

It had been four days now.

The last thing he remembered clearly was sitting naked on the bed in the love hotel, drinking a Scotch. Hearing Jessica say, "This tastes funny," but not paying much attention to her, swallowing his drink and putting it on the end table next to the bed before lying down and going to sleep. After that he wasn't sure of much. He didn't remember waking up. Instead, it was as if over a period of time he gradually became aware that certain sensations he was feeling were real. There was the blare of the radio, of course, the headphones stuck deep in his ears. His forehead throbbed and felt as if it had been cut. Some kind of ball was stuck in his mouth and resting on top of his tongue; he could taste the plastic. A thick tape was keeping the ball in place, and there was something over the tape as well, like a doctor's mask. Something else (more tape, he was sure, and possibly a thin towel) was wrapped around his head and over his eyes. His hands and legs were bound with rope. He was wearing clothes, but they weren't his clothes; it felt like long underwear, but that couldn't be right. Whatever it was, it was hot and uncomfortable, and the next thing he noticed was that he was drenched in sweat.

He hadn't panicked. He remembered feeling very calm, thinking, *Well, it looks like I've been kidnapped.* Like it was the most natural thing in the world. Had he been drugged? Looking back on it now, four days later, he thought that he must have been. That was why Jessica had said, "This tastes funny"; she had been drugged as well.

But if she had been drugged, then who . . .

No, take things in order.

His current theory was that he had first been put in a van or a truck. He remembered lying on what felt like deep-pile carpeting, which at the time made him think he was in an office. Or—this made more sense—that he was still in the love hotel. But then, struggling to sit up, he backed into what felt like metal, like aluminum. There wasn't anything made of aluminum in the love hotel. He was trying to figure it out when whatever it was gave way and he fell backward, head leading the way, hitting the ground hard, rocks scraping against his face, breathing in gravel dust. Realizing that he was outside but no chance to think about it, not then, something like a boot striking his side, his stomach, something else hitting his head when he blacked out.

When he woke up the second time, he was somewhere else—the place he was in now. He remembered the DJ on the radio saying it was three in the afternoon; he had been out for close to twelve hours. He was inside, lying on a thin *tatami* mat. The ropes binding him were tighter than before, digging into his wrists and ankles. It was brutally hot, like the inside of a sauna, and when he breathed he smelled dead fish and diesel oil. Where was he? Somewhere near the water. He didn't feel well. He ached all over from the beating the night before. There was something sticky running down his right cheek that he was sure was blood; his head felt like it had been squeezed in a vise. Inside his mouth, the plastic ball felt glued to his tongue and the back of his throat; he couldn't swallow, couldn't get any moisture circulating. Worst of all, his lower body was cramping, sending shooting pains through his bowels. He lost some of his control then, he knew. How long had he lain there, moaning and rolling from side to side? He wasn't sure. That period was blank. The only thing he remembered now was coming out of it when the woman put his head on her lap.

Ozawa was sure it was a woman. He could smell her, his head right there next to her sex. He did not remember thinking it was Jessica. He was not considering Jessica as one of his captors, not then. He only knew that it was a woman, a slender woman, a young woman. Her legs were hot and wet with perspiration. He felt her take his mask off and pause, like she was considering whether or not to keep going. Then she pulled off the tape. It was like she was pulling off his lips, but he didn't care, happier than he could have imagined to feel the plastic ball popping from his mouth and rolling down the side of his face. He was rasping, drawing in air, breathing in at the same time she poured brackish water down his throat, making him choke.

The water was terrible, but it was cool and wet and he drank it all. He wanted more, but he asked to go to the toilet then, his bowels ready to explode. He asked in English first, not thinking clearly, and felt the woman pause, leaning over him. Caught himself and asked again in Japanese, more urgently this time, the woman moving away from him suddenly and making his head fall to the floor. He saw stars in the blackness. He asked again. Could she understand what he was saying? He couldn't tell. He couldn't hear himself speak, the radio so loud in his ears, and he felt himself losing control again, thrashing about on the floor as much as it was possible to thrash with your hands and feet bound with heavy rope. Then, all at once, his feet were free.

Had someone untied them, or had they come loose on their own? He couldn't concentrate, his bowels screaming. He felt two hands slip under his armpits and then he was being pulled to his feet . . .

Afterward, when he could think again, Ozawa realized that there was only one person helping him. It was the woman. She was trying to hold him steady, one arm around his waist, the other wiping his ass. It surprised him. Why wasn't anyone helping her? He was not that tall, he knew, but he was solid; he could feel the woman shaking with the effort to keep him balanced. Was she alone? He decided she must be. He could feel her shift around to his front, trying to pull up what he now guessed were thin nylon stockings and not long underwear.

Ozawa did not hesitate. Once his right leg was free, he brought it up hard into what he hoped was the woman's stomach. He felt her fall forward, slumping against him, and realized, shit, he had lost his leverage. She was dragging him down. He tried to shake her off but it was too late; his foot slipped on the wet rim of the toilet and he fell, knocking his head on what? A pipe, something hard, the towel or the blanket around his head cushioning the blow but not enough. He shouted curses to keep himself from blacking out. The woman was still on top of him. Putting everything he had into it, he lurched to the left and felt the woman slide off.

He had to get the ropes off. He managed to get to his feet and stumbled forward, keeping his head back and out of harm's way, trying to find a corner, something angled. Ran into what felt like a rough wooden wall and turned himself around, working his way to the left. Something sharp dug into his side, pierc-

ing the skin, and he gasped in pain. It felt like a hook. Quickly
Ozawa brought up his hands and began moving them up and
down and from side to side, cutting his skin but sensing the
ropes starting to fray, feeling them loosening enough then that
he could pull his hands free. He remembered thinking *Hurry up,
old man,* grabbing at the towel around his head, ripping the tape
away, feeling the headphones fall out of his ears and onto the
floor. He heard the sound of metal scraping against metal, the
woman close. Then the tape was away from his eyes and he was
blinking furiously, the sudden light painful, trying to focus, and
then there she was in front of him, the woman, shit, swinging
something at him—

When he woke up the third time it was Sunday.

Now, two days later, things had settled into a kind of routine.
In the mornings, around seven, two men—Ozawa was sure they
were men—would take him to the toilet to do his business. They
would take him again sometime in the afternoon and again
around nine P.M. Ozawa suspected they were the same men each
time, but he couldn't be sure. They did not clean him as the
woman had; instead, they sprayed him with water, so that now his
ass was constantly damp and raw. They did not bathe him or
brush his teeth. They had yet to change his clothes. The ropes
around his hands and feet had been replaced with steel cuffs.

Breakfast was at nine and dinner at five. There was no lunch.
Someone would prop him up against a wall in a sitting position
and feed him with a plastic spoon. Convenience-store food
mostly, he was sure: stale rice and limp fried chicken, fried noodles, rubbery *sushi.* Always the briny water to wash everything
down.

The rest of the day he had to himself.

He spent most of his time thinking, trying to blot out the constant noise from the radio. Where was he? That was one good question to think about. Ozawa was certain that he was near the water. Probably still in Osaka. The taste of the water was one indication; the odors in the air were another. He would lie on his back taking deep breaths, trying to figure out what he was smelling; the odors were not always the same. In the mornings, the smell of fish was strong, but by midafternoon it would fade and be replaced by something more industrial. Diesel oil— he had caught that right from the start—tar, rubber . . .

It smelled like the wharf.

Which was nice to know, but the wharf was pretty fucking big.

Who had him? That was another question. He had no idea who the two men were, or if there were more than two men. But the woman who had hit him, she was white, a foreigner. Maybe. He had had less than a second to look, and the light had been so bright in his eyes; he couldn't be sure. Assuming she *was* a foreigner, what did that tell him? Was it Jessica? That made sense, but Ozawa knew a lot of white women who were equally good candidates and some who were better. It was sort of fun, thinking about all of them, trying to guess which one had the nerve to go through with something like this.

Which led to the last question: What did his captors want? If one of them was Jessica, he knew what she wanted: the million-plus that "Zeniya" had in his safe. Jessica. He hoped it was her. The woman was so obvious, the best of all of them so far. Ozawa wondered what she had done when she found out things weren't quite as she had expected. He wished he could have seen her face.

Then again, maybe she still didn't know. Maybe that was why things were taking so long, the woman not smart enough to figure it out.

Then again, maybe she was tied up in the room with him, scared out of her wits.

It was possible.

But he doubted it.

On the radio the countdown was over. It was ten o'clock, time for the weather report. Ozawa was thinking about trying to sleep when he felt someone beside him. It surprised him. It couldn't be for a meal or the toilet; he had already done both. He felt himself being pulled up to a sitting position. Two hands, one smell—the woman. Ozawa waited. Then felt her hands on his face and was surprised again when the tape over his mouth came off and the bandages started to fall from around his head . . .

22

Jessica didn't think she was going to be able to cry on cue. But then when she pulled the last of the tape away and saw Zeniya's—*Ozawa's*—face in the yellow beam of the flashlight—the drool stuck to his gray stubble, the bewildered eyes, the ugly scars on his forehead and next to his left ear—her hand went to her mouth and there were the tears, welling up over her eyelids and falling freely down her cheeks. She threw her arms around his neck.

"I'm sorry," she sobbed, whispering it. "I'm so sorry. I never meant for any of this to happen this way." She kissed the side of his face, tears still coming, not faking it. Truly regretting everything that had happened. She held him until the feeling passed. Then noticed how bad he smelled and backed away, wiping her eyes.

Ozawa looked disoriented. He wasn't saying anything, his head moving all around, eyes blinking rapidly. Jessica put the flashlight down on the straw mat, pointing the beam at the wall. In the shadows, Ozawa looked gaunt and old, like a homeless man. She took his chin and turned his head to face her, watching his eyes come into focus.

"Listen," she said. "We don't have much time." Saw him drifting away and said, "Ozawa-*san*?" Saw him come back and stare at her between blinks. "Listen," she said, "they're going to be back soon."

"Who?" he rasped.

Jessica took a deep breath. "Sato," she said. "And the others."

She had his attention now. The blinking was slowing down, his black eyes trained on her. This was the hard part. The old man was cuffed around both his wrists and ankles—and Chris and Taro were right outside—but she was still scared out of her mind. She felt her stomach flip and she turned her head as if she had heard something so that she wouldn't have to look at him for a second. When she turned back, her hands were trembling. She showed one of them to Ozawa. "Look at me," she said. "My hands are trembling."

Ozawa didn't say anything.

If she was going to do it, she had to do it now, before she completely lost her nerve. Jessica said, "Look," and then she told him, blurting it out, everything that Chris had told her to say. She said, "I know who you are. You're Shinji Ozawa, and you're like one of the top guys in the Ono-*gumi*. I don't know why you said you were Zeniya, and I don't know what you really wanted with me, but about a month ago I came back to my apartment and there were these three guys in there." She was giving it to Ozawa fast, too nervous to slow down. "Two of them were really big and they had bleached hair. Brown, you know. *Chapatsu.* The other one was wearing this purple suit. He grabbed me and threw me down on the floor. I didn't know who they were. I thought they were burglars. I thought they were going to rape me. I was screaming and crying. Then the one who threw me down said his name was Sato and that he was *yakuza.* Then he told me about you, that you weren't Zeniya, you were some kind of *yakuza,* too. I didn't understand everything he said, his English wasn't very good. He kept slapping me, calling me names, saying I was a foreign whore who should have never come to Japan. I was crying. I didn't know what to do, I was never so scared in my life."

Jessica paused, breath hitching. Ozawa was still staring at her. She looked away, lowering her voice and saying, "He had pictures of us. Videos, you know, of us having sex. I guess there was a camera somewhere in the room at the love hotel. He said he was going to make pornos out of them, send them to my parents in America. He had my address book. He said he was going to cut my face if I didn't help him.

"He"—and now she looked down, thinking *Look at the floor, look at the floor*—"he also said that if I did help him he would give me twenty percent of the money he was going to get for you. Twenty percent of the ransom."

She hadn't wanted to say that, but Chris told her she had to. He said she had to tell Ozawa things that would make her look bad so that it would seem like she was telling the truth. She said, "I didn't want to go along with his plan, and I was scared to death, but . . . I wanted the money, too. I thought about trying to run but I wanted the money."

Jessica took another deep breath, looking at Ozawa now. She said, "Sato's trying to get six hundred million yen for you. I don't know who he's talked to or how he's going to get the money. He made a video of you a couple days ago, just you lying on the mat over here. I don't know if he sent it to somebody or not. I don't know very much, but he's really confident. He thinks he can win no matter what happens. If your people pay, he gets six hundred million yen and everybody will think you're weak or something. If your guys don't pay, he can kill you. I think that's what he wants actually, I really do. Kill you, I mean. I don't know why, but he's really angry at you. Maybe it's about you being Zeniya or something about me—he's always calling me 'foreign whore,' 'foreign bitch.' He doesn't like foreigners." She stopped. Gave him what she hoped was a bitter smile. "You probably want to know why I'm telling you all this."

Until now she had kept her bandaged left hand hidden; now she showed it to him, watched his eyes focus on it. The tears came back then, real tears, and her voice cracked as she said, "I don't think Sato's going to give me anything. I told you he's always calling me names, putting me down. The day after he did it, the day after he took you, he went out with his guys and left me here with you." Crying harder now, thinking of Chris. "The son of a bitch. I was so scared and you looked sick, like you were going to die. I tried to give you some water, but then you wanted to use the bathroom and—you know the rest. I'm sorry I hit you, but I didn't know what else to do. When Sato came back he was drunk. He saw you on the floor and there was so much blood. He went crazy. He started slapping me around. He—he pulled out a knife—" And she had to stop for a minute, breath hitching again. "He pulled out a knife and told the others to hold me down on the floor. I thought he was going to cut my face like he said before and I was screaming. One of the others put his hand over my mouth and I was screaming into his hand. Sato kicked me and told me to shut up. Then he said, 'Stupid. You know what happens to stupid *yakuza*?' "

There was more, but Jessica couldn't get it out. Shaking, tears flowing, she unwrapped the bandage around her hand and showed Ozawa the stump where her little finger had been. She held it out in front of him and cried, closing her eyes.

She cried for a long time.

When she finally looked at him again, Ozawa was leaning forward. "More close," he said. Confused, she wiped at her tears and put her hand closer to his face.

Pursing his lips, Ozawa kissed the stump.

"*Sugoi*," he murmured.

"What?" she asked.

Ozawa didn't answer. He looked at her and said: "Where are we?"

Just like that. Not sounding mad or anything. He tilted his head up toward the windows, rain beating against the glass. Said it again: "Where are we?"

For a minute she couldn't think of anything to say. The kiss, the "*sugoi*," the question—they had caught her off guard. She said, "What?" just to give her some more time to think.

"Where are we?" Ozawa asked again.

Jessica shook her head, having trouble getting the words out. "I don't know," she finally managed to say. "Kobe, I think. I've been locked in since we got here."

"You come here," he said. "What did you see?"

"When I came here?" she asked. Her mind was blank. Come on, get on track, get on— "I don't—I was sitting on the floor next to you in a van. You were drugged," she said, suddenly remembering what Chris had said about the video. Shit, she was making a mess of this. "I put something in your drink at the love hotel. I don't know what it was, Sato gave it to me. It was green. Then I helped his men tie you up and get you out of there. But they didn't tell me where we were going." She paused. "I think we're in Kobe because it took a while to get here. Also I heard someone say Port Island, I think. I can smell the ocean, but I don't know where we . . . I don't know."

This was awful. She had to stop him from asking any more questions. He was going to trip her up eventually (trip her up *worse*); she couldn't think straight. She had to get back to the script. What else did she have to tell him? Ozawa opened his mouth to say something, but Jessica put her hand over it.

"I don't know anything. We've been here for four days. They brought me some clothes," she said, gesturing at the jeans and T-shirt she was wearing, "but I don't know how long they're planning to keep you here. Or me. I'm locked in here, too. I can't get us out, and I don't have the key to your cuffs. There might be something in this place that could get you out of them, but if somebody's watching outside they might see the flashlight moving around." She moved in closer to him then, whispering, "Look, I'm really scared. I don't believe anything that Sato says anymore. He might kill us both no matter what happens. I've been waiting for a chance to do something to help us, and now I've got an idea."

Her black Prada handbag was lying on the floor, just out of sight. She pulled it over by the strap and popped the snap. Then she took out a cell phone and showed it to Ozawa.

"One of them forgot this when they left a little while ago," Jessica said. "Not Sato, I don't know his name. I almost called the police, but I didn't know what I could say. I don't even know where we are; I mean I think we're on Port Island, but I'm not sure. Anyway, the police can't protect me from Sato." She lowered her eyes. "Or from you, if you make it out of here alive. I know that." She looked at him again. "My idea is, give me a number to call, somebody you trust. I'll hold the phone up to your ear so you can talk. Tell them about Sato, about what's going on. Maybe one of your guys can do something, I don't know. Just tell them to be careful or Sato will find out."

"And you?" Ozawa asked softly.

"What about me?"

"What do you want? For helping?"

Jessica shook her head.

"I don't want anything," she said. "I just want out. I want out alive. I hope that someday you'll be able to forgive me."

She pressed a button, and the LED on the cell phone came alive, glowing brightly in the darkness.

"Well?" she asked.

Chris and Taro were huddled outside in the rain in front of the boathouse, waiting for Jessica to come out.

The way Chris figured, Ozawa didn't have many options. The man was a criminal; he wasn't going to call the police. He wasn't going to call his family either; this didn't have anything to do with them. No, Ozawa was *yakuza;* he was going to call one of his lieutenants.

Chris had been reading up on the *yakuza.* There were a lot of books out there; they were an interesting bunch. Chris thought they were a lot like the Mafia. Each organization, or *kumi,* was highly insular and rigidly structured. On the bottom were the *chimpira,* the "little pricks," who weren't yet full-time members and who did all the shit jobs. Next up were the rank and file, then the crew chiefs like Sato. After that were the *kumi-cho,* the heads of the smaller gangs within the big gang, then the real big guys: the subbosses, the counselors, the advisers, and finally the boss himself. The *oyabun*. The Godfather. The Big Kahuna. That was Shinji Ozawa. Taro was right; according to all that Chris had been able to find out, Ozawa was a big-time gangster asshole.

Ozawa would call his *saiko komon*, his senior adviser; there wasn't any other real choice. Once he did, what was he going to say? Again, Chris thought the options were limited. Assuming Ozawa bought Jessica's story, he seemed likely to do one of two things: tell the gang to go after Sato or tell them to pay up. Either way, Chris thought he came out ahead. If Ozawa told the gang to go after Sato, then Sato and all of the guys who worked with him were going down. Chris wouldn't be able to complain about that. He liked imagining it, picturing the motherfuckers being tortured before they died, especially Sato and the other guy, Big Fucker; it was the least the bastards deserved. Chris's nose still hurt like hell; it was all yellow and purple beneath the aluminum splint and kept leaking some kind of rust-colored fluid. When he talked, he sounded like Elmer Fudd.

Yeah, Ozawa telling the gang to go after Sato, that would be perfectly acceptable. Sato and Big Fucker would end up dead, and Chris would still have the old man. But Chris was betting it wouldn't happen that way. Ozawa was smart; he wasn't top dog for nothing. Why risk having Sato killed before he was in the clear himself? If Chris were in Ozawa's shoes, he would tell his *saiko komon* to pay up—at least *pretend* to pay up—and go after Sato later. It was safer that way. More dramatic, too. Chris imagined the whole thing all over, Ozawa safe and sound, Ozawa calling a meeting of all his top guys. Chris pictured a circular table, gangsters in gold-rimmed sunglasses seated around it, Ozawa walking behind them with a baseball bat—like Robert De Niro in *The Untouchables*—telling them that he knew who was responsible for his kidnapping. Then taking the bat and bashing Sato's head in. Asking, deadpan, if anybody had any questions.

Sato getting the blame—and the three of them getting the money—would be a decent-enough ending, however it happened. But to get this movie Oscar-worthy, Chris thought something was going to have to be done about Jessica. It was possible Ozawa would forgive her, due to all her "help" getting him free of Sato, but Chris didn't want to bet his future on it. If the guy was like Vito Corleone, sure, but what if he was like Michael? They couldn't take that chance. She was going to have to disappear before Ozawa was turned loose, and even then she was going to have to disappear in a way that would convince Ozawa that she could not be found. Otherwise, he was going to send his guys out to track her down, and when they did, she would tell them everything. About the plan. About Taro.

About *him*.

Chris hadn't figured out how to do it yet, but he was working on it. Maybe pull a *Sting,* make Ozawa and the rest of the *yakuza* think she was dead. It was an idea.

Anyway, they would cross that bridge when they came to it. First order of business: getting Ozawa to believe Sato was behind everything. Second order of business: getting the *yakuza* to pay up.

With money, everything would seem easier.

*　*　*

Chris was starting to wonder what was taking so long, Jessica having been in there for something close to an hour. Then he checked his watch and realized, wow, it had only been twenty minutes. It *felt* like an hour, waiting out here in the rain, nothing to do, watching Taro play with his finger. *Chris's* finger—Taro had tied a string around it and kept twirling it around. Like that was supposed to be intimidating, the little prick thinking he was in charge. Chris let him think so. If everything worked out with Ozawa, who cared what Taro thought?

At last, ten-thirty, Jessica stepped out of the boathouse, the door creaking as it swung closed. She had her hands in her pockets, walking over. Taro moved the umbrella to cover her, leaving Chris to get wet.

"Well?" Chris asked.

Jessica shrugged. "He called somebody."

"Know who?"

"No," she said, shaking her head. "I think it was a man. Other than that . . . they talked for about six or seven minutes."

"What did he tell you?"

"Not to worry. That everything was taken care of."

"Let's hear it."

Jessica reached behind her and pulled a slender digital recorder out of her back pocket. It was a Sharp, silver, about the size of a candy bar. It had cost another twenty-five thousand of Jessica's yen. Chris looked at it as insurance. Along with having her finger cut off, the best way for Jessica to earn Ozawa's trust was to give him the phone. He'd be convinced she was on the level; what self-respecting kidnapper would allow the kidnappee the chance to make an unmediated phone call? Which made it a risk, too—Ozawa could call *anybody,* say *anything*—but it was a risk Chris was willing to take. Who could he realistically call? What could he tell them? He didn't *know* anything. So as long as Chris had a way of listening in . . .

Jessica held the recorder up to Taro's ear and pressed a button.

Chris heard Ozawa's rasping voice say *"Moshi moshi,"* the Japanese way of saying hello on the telephone. After that he was lost.

Taro stood there, head cocked, his eyes closed.

Seven minutes later opened his eyes. He looked at Chris.

"You were right," Taro said.

"About what?"

"He tell them to pay."

Seven-thirty in the morning, rush hour, Sato was on the Loop Line platform at Osaka Station, dressed like a salaryman. Blue polyester suit, cheap tie with silver tie clip, battered loafers, briefcase. He even had his hair in the traditional "seven-three" style: seven-tenths to the right, three-tenths to the left.

He felt like an idiot.

Guys dressed just like him shuffled past, faces pinched, not smiling, inching their way through the crowd. Sato knew all about their day just by looking at them. Cigarettes and coffee for breakfast. An hour standing in the train from the suburbs. Time for work now, twelve hours of staring at the OLs in the company skirts and wondering when the next wave of restructuring was going to hit.

Zombies with homemade box lunches and penny-ante contracts in their leather briefcases.

Sato had six hundred million yen in his.

Yesterday, Tanaka *kumi-cho* had called him into his office. Kawaguchi *saiko komon* was there, too. The *oyabun's* right-hand man. It was the first time Sato had ever met him. He didn't say anything, just stared at him, and Sato thought, Shit, here it comes. But all that happened, Tanaka said, "I got a phone call this morning," and pressed a button on the tape recorder that was hooked up to his phone. Sato heard Tanaka saying *"Moshi moshi,"* then heard the guy on the other end ask to speak to Ozawa *oyabun*. Sato didn't recognize the guy's voice. He heard Tanaka say that the *oyabun* was busy this morning. The guy said, "You're right. He *is* busy. He's all tied up, in fact. Wouldn't you agree?" Tanaka said, "I'm not sure what you mean." The guy on the other end said, "Take another look at the video you got yesterday. Refresh your memory. I'll call back." Then there was a *click* as the guy hung up.

Sato asked Tanaka, "What video?" Tanaka looking strangely at him from behind his desk. Tanaka nodded at the TV and video deck in the corner. "See for yourself," he said.

Sato did, picking up the remote and pressing play. The TV screen flickered and came to life, showing a man propped up against a dingy wooden wall. It was Ozawa. He was wearing the nurse uniform that Sato had seen before, in the video from the love hotel. The old man looked like shit. His head was filthy, and there was an ugly wound the size of a five-hundred-yen coin on his forehead. His eyes and mouth were taped shut. Dried spittle clung to the beginnings of a beard. Black wires were hanging from his ears; Sato couldn't figure out what they were for, until suddenly it came to him: headphones.

Tanaka asked, "Is that how he looked when you saw him?"

Sato nodded, still watching. "It's the same outfit. He looked a lot better. The beard, you know. He didn't have the head wound." On the screen, Ozawa seemed to moan, slumping to one side. Sato asked, "Is this all there is?"

"No, they show him in a couple more poses."

Three poses, in fact. The next was a close-up of Ozawa being fed from a Styrofoam bowl by a black leather glove, what looked like curry dribbling from his chin. The one after that was another close-up, the old man lapping water from a bowl with his tongue. The final segment started as a close-up, Ozawa's head wrapped in a towel, a gauze mask over his mouth. Then the camera pulled back, showing Ozawa taking a shit. He was naked, straddling the toilet while two men completely covered in black—ski masks, sunglasses, ponchos, gloves, boots—held his arms. When he was finished, one of the men left the screen, then came back with a hose running water. He stood behind Ozawa and sprayed his ass, drops of water flying up and hitting the lens of the video camera. The image tilted and the screen went black.

"Romano," Sato said. "The whore. The men in black, they were with her at the love hotel. I'm sure of it. I only saw one of them, but I know there were two."

Tanaka nodded, lighting a cigarette. Kawaguchi said nothing. He was making Sato nervous. Tanaka pressed the button on his tape recorder again. "I got this call ten minutes ago."

What Sato heard:

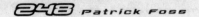

TANAKA: HELLO?

MAN: WELL?

TANAKA: YES, MY MEMORY IS CLEARER.

MAN: GOOD. I HAVE A BUSINESS PROPOSITION FOR YOU.

TANAKA: I'M LISTENING.

MAN: YOU CAN HAVE OUR COPIES OF THE VIDEOTAPE AND YOUR *OYABUN* BACK FOR SIX HUNDRED MILLION YEN.

TANAKA: SIX HUNDRED MILLION.

MAN: THAT'S RIGHT. WE WERE GOING TO ASK FOR TEN, BUT— YOU'VE SEEN THE VIDEO. HE'S SO PITIFUL. WE DON'T THINK HE'S WORTH ANY MORE THAN SIX.

TANAKA: IF WE REFUSE?

MAN: THEN YOU CAN HAVE HIM BACK FOR FREE. BUT THE TAPE GOES OUT TO EVERY NEWS ORGANIZATION IN THE COUNTRY. NOT TO MENTION EVERY . . . ORGANIZATION. I THINK THEY'LL RECOG- NIZE HIM FROM THE PICTURES, DON'T YOU?

Sato said, "They want to humiliate us."

"Yes."

TANAKA: WHAT WOULD YOU LIKE US TO DO?

MAN: TOMORROW, HAVE SOMEBODY ON THE LOOP LINE PLAT- FORM AT OSAKA STATION AT SEVEN-THIRTY.

TANAKA: IN THE MORNING OR THE EVENING?

MAN: WHAT?

TANAKA: SEVEN-THIRTY IN THE MORNING? SEVEN-THIRTY IN THE EVENING?

MAN: OH. IN THE MORNING.

TANAKA: THEN?

MAN: TELL HIM TO DRESS LIKE A SALARYMAN. NO PUNCH PERMS
OR JEWELRY. NO *YAKUZA* SHIT. COUNT HIS FINGERS—MAKE SURE
HE'S GOT TEN. DO YOU HAVE A CELL PHONE?

TANAKA: YES.

MAN: WHAT'S THE NUMBER?

TANAKA: YOU WANT THE NUMBER TO MY CELLULAR PHONE?

MAN: YES, ASSHOLE. WHAT IS IT?

TANAKA: 090-8790-95XX.

MAN: GIVE THE PHONE TO THE GUY WHO COMES TO OSAKA STA-
TION. TELL HIM TO BRING THE MONEY IN A BRIEFCASE. AT SEVEN-
THIRTY, I'LL CALL AND TELL HIM WHAT TO DO . . . YOU GOT ALL THAT?

TANAKA: YES.

MAN: ANYTHING NOT CLEAR?

TANAKA: NO.

MAN: GOOD.

CLICK.

"Well?" Tanaka said, pressing the rewind button. "What do
you think we should do?"

"What do I think?" Sato said. He was surprised. Tanaka had
never asked for his opinion before. A *kumi-cho* never asked for
anything; he ordered. Now here Tanaka was, asking Sato
whether or not the gang should pay six hundred million yen to
have the *oyabun* set free. Not that Sato was complaining; it was
about time he was given a little more responsibility. But why
now, especially when he was the one who had lost the old man
in the first place? And what the fuck was Kawaguchi doing
here, sitting in a corner and staring at him? Glancing over there,
Sato said, "I think we should pay."

"Naturally." Tanaka took a long drag from the cigarette in his hand. Now he was staring at Sato intently, too. "Then what?"

This was too strange. "Then we go after them," Sato said, wondering what was going on. "We know who they are. It's that foreign bitch and her friends. They won't be that hard to track down. We pay, let them think they're getting away with it. Then, when it's over, we bring down the hammer."

Tanaka seemed to consider it. "Any ideas on how we can do that?"

"They'll be easy to find, *kumi-cho*. If you like, I'll take care of it personally."

Tanaka nodded. "Then take care of it."

Sato backed out of the room, bowing. The whole time, Kawaguchi had not said one word.

Sato wondered if somehow he was being set up.

He had a team of six at Osaka Station.

Uemura and Sunabe were at the other end of the platform, milling around and keeping their eyes open. Kato was at the kiosk in the middle sipping at a canned coffee. Wakebe was just a few meters away, smoking a cigarette and trying to keep the toupee covering his punch perm from falling off. Two more, Okuda and Yamamoto, were watching the main entrance on the off chance that the Romano woman would show up.

Sato was sure the exchange would take place somewhere else. Another *yakuza* might walk right up to him and stick a gun in his face, but the Romano woman was an amateur. She'd have her Japanese boyfriend call and make Sato jump on and off trains for the next hour. Make sure he wasn't being "tailed," or whatever it was they said in the movies. Sato wondered if somebody was watching him right now. Well, they might pick out one or two of his team, but not all six. And Sato had another ace in the hole besides . . .

His cell phone rang. He looked around carefully before picking it up.

"Yeah?" he said, eyes still moving.

"Who is this?" It was the Japanese man from the audiotape in Tanaka's office.

"Sato." He put his other hand up to his ear as the train on the outer loop rumbled into the station.

There was a pause on the other end. Sato pictured the guy cupping the phone, mouthing the name to the bearded foreigner, the color draining from the white fucker's face. He heard the man say, "You got what we want?"

"Yeah," Sato said. "How's your friend's knee?"

Another pause. "There's a train coming into the station now."

"How about his nose?"

"Get in the third car. Don't use your phone."

The guy hung up. Now he had something new to think about. The little prick, taking orders from foreign whores and pimps. Sato decided that when he caught him he would save him for last, make things as painful as possible. Cut the guy's balls off or something.

The outer loop train slowed to a stop. Sato got in line at the door to the third car. Putting his head down, he spoke into the microphone attached to the underside of his lapel. "Everybody on the train. Watch for me."

After all the exiting passengers were clear, the line began to move forward. The station employees in their white gloves were on both sides of the door, ready to push the last few stragglers inside. Sato caught a whiff of Chanel No. 5, then felt someone pinch his ass. He didn't turn around. He heard his girlfriend Misato murmur, "You bastard, do you know how much I hate riding the train?"

"Shut up," he said. "Keep your eyes open."

The departure bell sounded, and Sato felt himself being swept into the train. He almost lost the briefcase, a couple of high school kids with duffel bags shoving past him. When the doors closed, he found himself stuck in the middle of the car, crushed inside a pack of zombies. He couldn't move, his arms pinned to his sides. He felt like he was breathing perspiration. He'd forgotten how bad the trains could be.

Craning his head to the left, he caught a glimpse of Misato sandwiched between a couple of high school girls. She looked pissed, arms wrapped around the black Issey Miyake one-piece he'd picked up for her last week. Well, he'd told her to wear something casual. She didn't look like she was paying attention either, which was the other thing he'd told her. Ozawa's kidnappers might spot another *yakuza,* but they wouldn't be looking for a woman. Come on, he thought. Look around. This might be it right here.

Sato hadn't expected the guy on the phone to tell him to board a specific car. It made him wonder if the exchange was going to happen sooner than he expected. The train comes to a stop, everybody starts to shove their way out, somebody grabs the briefcase . . . Sato stood up on tiptoe, looking down the length of the car. He saw a foreigner sitting down, arms folded over a green backpack. It wasn't the bearded guy. A friend maybe? As the train slowed, pulling into Fukushima Station, Sato saw the foreigner stand up and start pushing his way forward. Sato tensed, his eyes narrowing, thinking to himself, Okay, get ready . . .

The foreigner brushed against him and kept going, out the door with the rest of the wave.

Shit.

Nothing happened at Noda or Nishikujo Stations either. At Bentencho, a mass of passengers got out and he managed to get a seat. Misato was still standing, her eyes smoldering. Sato ignored her. He put the briefcase in his lap and drummed his fingers on the top of it. He looked at his watch. It was a quarter to eight.

At five after, just before Tennoji Station, his cell phone rang.

"You are a little fucker," Sato said. He felt the businessman sitting next to him flinch.

"Get out at Tennoji," the voice on the other end said. "You've got five minutes to get on a subway train headed for Senri-Chuo. If you're not on your way by eight-ten, your boss loses a finger."

Then, shit, before Sato could say anything, the little prick hung up.

The train was already inside Tennoji Station, slowing down, about to stop. Sato stood up, bending his head down to whisper instructions into the lapel mike. As the doors slid open, he grabbed Misato's arm.

"You're going to have to run," he said.

"Are you kidding?" she asked. "In these?"

He looked down. She was wearing black pumps with spiked heels.

"Fuck," he said. "Get on the subway to Senri-Chuo as fast as you can."

Pushing his way through the crowd, he heard her shout: "Now I have to ride the *subway*?"

Running down the stairs to the subway platform, he heard the conductor's whistle. Thrusting the briefcase in front of him, he stopped the train doors from closing and wedged himself into the crowded car. He was breathing hard, rivulets of sweat running down the sides of his face and his back. He wondered if this was the right train. He caught a glimpse of the platform clock as the train pulled away: eight-twelve. Eight-twelve, fuck, that had to be wrong. He'd made it.

He thought he'd made it.

Sato was getting pissed. This was bullshit. He was riding back to where he started, the kidnappers sending him around in circles. That he'd expected it didn't make it any less annoying. The fucking Romano woman, thinking she knew what she was doing . . .

The train lurched around a bend. The crowded mass of passengers fell to the side, pressing Sato's face against the glass of the sliding doors. When he managed to right himself, he felt something flapping against his chest. He put his hand inside his shirt and found the end of the body wire pulled loose from the transmitter. Son of a *bitch*. He wondered how long it had been out. Had the others gotten his last message? He tried to plug the jack back in but didn't have enough mobility and couldn't find the socket.

How had the body wire come out in the first place? Everyone crushing against him . . . that was the logical explanation, but Sato couldn't help thinking back to the foreigner brushing past him at Fukushima Station, wondering if the *gaijin* had deliberately knocked it loose. Then thought: But how could he have known about it?

He needed to call back to headquarters, let them know what was going on. Working his hand up to his inside jacket pocket, he pulled out the cell phone and turned it on. Saw the flashing message on the screen and realized, damn, he was in the subway. The phone wouldn't work.

This was turning out to be another in a long string of bad days.

At eight-fifty, the train surfaced at Shin-Osaka. It was elevated from here to Senri-Chuo. Sato counted: five, four, three—

The cell phone rang.

The voice on the other end said, "You having fun?"

"Sure," Sato said. "How's Miss Romano?"

"You're coming up on Esaka. You'll be there in two minutes."

"I'll bet my sixty-five-year-old boss fucks her better than you do."

"Go out the south exit and find the Budweiser restaurant. Five minutes. Leave the phone on."

"Let me talk to the guy with the beard."

"Put the phone in your pocket and shut up."

"Who is he fucking? Miss Romano or you?"

A pause. "Shut up or your boss loses a finger."

"You don't have the nerve."

Sato heard a rustling in the background, like something being dragged across a cement floor. Then there was a loud ripping sound followed by a gasp, somebody coughing into the mouthpiece of the phone. Sato heard Ozawa say, "What? What?"

"Wait a minute," Sato said, not liking where this was going.

He heard a faint *snap,* Ozawa grunting in what sounded like pain. Then the voice was back on the line.

"Not another word," the voice said.

When the doors opened at Esaka, Sato was ready. He sprinted out the ticket gate and down the stairs. He looked over his shoulder once and didn't see anybody, the rest of the team probably still looking for him in Tennoji, Misato maybe on her way, more likely reading a magazine in a coffee shop.

The Budweiser restaurant. He'd been there once. It was next to the sushi place he liked, past the Mister Donut with the carousel inside. Sato ran around the zombies on their way to work, knocking somebody on the head with his briefcase, hearing the guy apologize for getting in his way.

He was out of breath by the time he got there. Reaching into his jacket pocket, he pulled out the cell phone.

"You there?" the voice on the other end asked.

"Yeah."

"You see the cardboard cutout of the Bud Girl in front of the door?"

Sato looked. "Yeah, I see it."

"Go up there and pat her on the ass."

"What?"

"Go up there and pat her on the ass."

Sato looked around, keeping the phone next to his ear. Somebody was watching this, he was sure of it. Across the street, he saw a foreigner riding a mountain bike on the wrong side of the road, darting around the incoming traffic. A foreigner with a green backpack. Was it the same one from the train? He couldn't be sure. The foreigner turned a corner and disappeared out of sight. Maybe going in circles.

The voice on the line said, "You want me to cut off another finger?"

Cautiously, Sato walked up the stairs to the restaurant door, looking back over his shoulder. The cutout of the Bud Girl was smiling at him. She was wearing a bathing suit with the Budweiser label, her legs longer than his. Sato picked up the cutout and turned it around. Taped to the back were six ATM cards.

"You find them?" the voice on the phone asked.

The way Chris had it figured:

What were they going to do, tell the *yakuza* to put the money in a garbage can on a street corner? Hope that nobody was watching when the three of them came to pick it up?

Japan was a civilized country. Tell the mob to put the money in a bank.

ATMs in Japan accepted deposits from nine to six. The maximum daily withdrawal varied, but was usually in the neighborhood of two million yen. Better to finish everything up in one day, so six hundred million divided by two meant they needed three hundred different accounts. Typing the words *fake account* on a search engine, Chris found a Web site for a guy in Japan who could get accounts under fake names for twenty-five thousand apiece, reducible to twenty thousand for orders of ten or more. So that was, what, about six million. Divided three ways . . .

Taro said (through Jessica), "What do you want to pay six million for? I know some guys, get the accounts for two hundred thousand, tops. That's for all three hundred."

Well, see, that's why they were keeping Taro around, so he could come up with these ideas. New, revised version: Taro's guys get the accounts and two cards per account. The three of them keep one set of cards; the other set would have to be planted around the banks where the *yakuza* could find them. Then, when the day came, it was just a matter of making deposits and collecting them. Taro could steal a scooter or something; they'd each go out in turns and bring the money back to the boathouse.

Jessica said, "Where are we going to keep it?"

What difference did it make? Throw the money in a box.

Jessica said, "And two people stay with it while one goes out? You're going to trust me and Taro not to run off while you're gone?"

All right, Chris wasn't tied to the idea. The next thing he thought, get out of the boathouse altogether, put Ozawa back in Taro's van. Drive to the banks to pick up the money, have the person going inside take the car keys . . .

Jessica said, "You think Taro can't start the van without keys?"

In the end, they decided to buy a safe. For thirty thousand yen it wasn't bad: twenty kilograms, welded steel, impact resistant— the brochure said you could drop it from a ten-story building without it opening. (Jessica: "Who cares what it does when you drop it? What happens when it hits the ground?") It had a combination you could set yourself, with a dial that went from zero to ninety-nine. Each of them chose a number and set it when the other two weren't looking; now the safe could be opened by the three of them together or not at all.

Chris, looking down on it, said, "What if one of us takes it and drops it from an eleven-story building?"

So Taro went back to the place where they had bought the safe and picked up a length of heavy-duty steel chain and a padlock. He wrapped the chain around the safe and around one of the thick water pipes that ran along the south wall of the boathouse. Then he used the padlock to connect the ends of the chain.

The padlock, like the one they had on the door, came with two keys. They threw one of them in the river and decided that the person collecting deposits at any one time would keep the key. That person would also keep the key to the boathouse. While he or she was out, the two remaining would be locked in. To make escape as difficult as possible, the three of them spent one hot afternoon removing anything that could be used to climb up to the windows. They also removed anything that could be used to pry open the padlock or the safe.

When they were finished, Chris said: "Be nicer if we could trust each other."

Jessica looked at him. "You cut off my fucking finger."

Now they were about to find out if everything was going to work. Chris was pacing outside a Sumitomo Quick Lobby when his cell phone rang.

It was Jessica. "All right, it should be done."

Chris said, "Taro told him to make the first six deposits?"

"Yes."

"Two million each?"

"Yeah."

"He gave him all the PIN numbers?"

"Sounded like it."

"He kept him on the phone the whole time?"

"I think so."

"Jesus." Chris tried to picture Sato's reaction. "The guy seemed surprised?"

"What kind of question is that? I don't know. Would you hurry up and find out if the money is there? Taro's already sent him to the next place."

"Okay, I'll call you back."

Five minutes later:

"Jessica?"

"Well?"

"Get ready to be happy."

Jessica couldn't believe how easy it was.

An hour after they started, they had fifty-two million in the boathouse safe. By eleven-thirty, it was one hundred fifty million. At the rate they were going, they would have three hundred seventy million by three in the afternoon and the full six hundred fifteen minutes before the closing time for deposits. Chris seemed to think they wouldn't be able to keep up the pace and would wind up fifty-or-so million short, but Jessica wasn't complaining.

They were looking at—at *least*—the equivalent of 1.5 million dollars each.

As her friend Amber liked to say, un-fucking-believable.

Going to collect her first set of deposits, Jessica had been sure that something was going to go wrong. Before leaving the boathouse, she put on thin gloves to hide the stump where her finger had been, tied a scarf around her head, and put on sunglasses to hide her face. Chris took one look at her and said, "Hey, it's the dye-job Jackie Kennedy," but she was too nervous even to tell him to shut up. It took everything in her to walk into the bank, and when she saw the line for the ATMs, she had to force herself to stay. She waited, legs trembling, sure that the tottering security guard was onto her and the cameras tracking her every move. Feeding the first card into the machine, that was the worst, entering the PIN number and knowing, absolutely positive, what would come next: flashing lights, alarms, a Japanese SWAT team descending from helicopters onto the roof of the bank. But nothing happened. She put in five more cards and walked out three minutes later with twelve million yen stuffed in an envelope in her purse.

She made her fifth set of collections at twelve-ten, speeding off on Taro's stolen scooter to the Bentencho branch of Asahi Bank. It had gotten to be routine by now. Walk in, put the cards in the slot, punch in the codes, and wait for the cash. She loved the sound the machine made when it counted the bills, like a blackjack dealer in a casino shuffling a deck of cards. The sidelong glances she got from customers at neighboring machines weren't bad either. They could hear the sound, too. Jessica would see their eyes opening slightly, little traces of envy on their faces. Who *was* that rich blond bombshell anyway?

She stopped at two Tokyo-Mitsubishi Cash Corners on the way back, picking up another twenty-four million. Then she took a small pair of scissors out of her purse and cut up the eighteen cards she had used in total, threw the pieces in a sidewalk garbage can. She was back at the boathouse at twenty-five to one. Unlocking the door, she threw the keys to Chris.

"Twenty-five minutes," he said. "Not bad."

"Yeah, and I went all the way to Bentencho."

"Get stopped by the cops, it's our ass."

"I'm immune to police."

The chain around the safe was hot to the touch, the temperature in the boathouse easily over a hundred. Jessica held on to the padlock with a handkerchief as she slid the key inside. Taro unwrapped the chain and it was time for the Ritual: Chris, then Jessica, then Taro, spinning the combination dial to open the safe. Jessica put the money inside. Taro closed everything up. It didn't take that long, the Ritual, but it was a pain in the ass. Like Chris had said, nicer if they could trust one another.

Jessica flipped Chris the key to the padlock. He gave her a half salute.

"See ya," he said.

When the door was closed and locked, Jessica walked over to Ozawa, see how the old man was doing. Because of the heat, they had taken him out of the nurse outfit yesterday, but he was still a puddle of sweat sitting there in his underwear, the straw mat beneath him dark and wet. Wringing out a washcloth, she wiped his face and arms. Ozawa groaned, leaning into her. The cut on his head was looking better: a little yellowy around the edges but closing up day by day. She tried not to look at his left hand. She still didn't understand why they had had to *actually* cut off his finger. It wasn't like this Sato guy would have known the difference. But he'd said something to piss Taro off, and now Ozawa had a permanent memento of his summer extortion experience. It was getting a little ridiculous: three of them now with one less digit. Chris had said to Taro this morning, "Hey, we do you and we can form a barbershop quartet. The Missing Fingers, what do you say?" The two of them got into a staring contest until Jessica finally asked if they wanted to concentrate on beating each other's brains out or getting rich. Take your pick.

They were a bad combination, the two of them. Jessica thought it was her fault; she never should have brought them together. Taro was too self-conscious, too full of that macho honor bullshit; and Chris was too much of a smart-ass. Not to mention they had her to fight over. She should have known better than to team up with two guys she was sleeping with.

Look on the bright side: six more hours, eight tops, and she'd be rid of them both.

Once they had the six hundred million, the plan was to take Ozawa to the park surrounding Osaka Castle, find one of the blue canvas tents the homeless used, and dump him in one. Call his gang, tell them where he was, and get out of there. Then the three of them would split up: Jessica to her friend Rebecca's to pick up a few things, Taro to his mom's, Chris to . . . wherever he was going. That would be the last she'd see of him, and thank God for that. The mutilating son of a bitch. Thinking about it made her stump start to itch. She scratched at it, peeling off one of the scabs.

It would be the last time she'd see Taro as well, only Taro didn't know it. She was supposed to meet up with him at Kyoto Station, catch the last train to Yokohama. From Yokohama it was a three-day boat ride to Shanghai, and from Shanghai a week by train and bus to Vietnam and the rest of Southeast Asia. She and Taro, together forever.

Only Jessica had had enough of Taro. He was as much of a psycho as Chris was, but dumber. After leaving Rebecca's, Jessica wasn't going anywhere near Kyoto Station. She was headed for Hiroshima, and from Hiroshima to Shimonoseki and the night ferry to Pusan, South Korea. Move on to Seoul, take care of some investments, and from Seoul . . . wherever her finger landed on the map. She was thinking about Mexico. Maybe the west coast, somewhere north of Acapulco.

She just had to get through the next six hours.

Eight hours, tops.

She felt Taro squat down behind her. He started massaging the back of her neck with his left hand. She let her head go limp, feeling it.

"That feels great," she said.

"It's hard," Taro said. "You got too much high tension."

She laughed. "I'd call this a tense situation, wouldn't you?"

Taro didn't say anything, moving his fingers from her neck to her shoulders, pushing in at the muscles with his thumb. She went with it, not fighting the pressure.

Taro was working down her spine when he said, "You shouldn't worry. I am ready about everything."

Ready? "You mean for the train for Yokohama?"

"No. Ready about today."

She didn't like the tone of his voice, his knuckles digging into the small of her back. "What about today?"

"Better you don't know about all of it. It's set for four o'clock. We can't wait to get all the money, but it's okay."

Jessica felt her bowels tighten. She turned around, feeling her mouth open, tongue suddenly dry. She saw Taro staring at the floor, his face hard, like a mask. "Taro," she said. "Taro, look at me." When he looked up, she asked, "What's set for four o'clock, Taro?"

"Surprise." Then: "Don't worry, I'll take care of you."

Oh Christ. "Taro, what's going on? Taro, goddammit . . ."

But that was all he would say, that something was set for four and she shouldn't worry about it, that he had it all taken care of. She knew what it had to be. If it was planned for four o'clock, anytime before six, it was some sort of double cross. Taro had found a way to cut Chris out.

If this wasn't the last thing she needed. Jessica tried to tell him it was a bad idea. He stood up, shaking his head, trying to walk away from her while she threw every idea at him that she could come up with: that she loved him and not Chris; that he never had to see Chris again after this was over; that he'd already avenged her by cutting off the bastard's finger; that double crosses were why bad guys in movies always ended up dead; that they'd only have four hundred and fifty million, max, by four o'clock; and that four hundred and fifty million split two ways wasn't any better than six hundred million split three. Well, okay, it was a little better, but it wasn't *worth* it.

Shouting at him, Jessica thought of something else.

"Taro, how are you going to do it?"

He didn't say anything.

"It's set for four o'clock," she said. "What do you mean, 'it's set'? Is there somebody else involved?"

He didn't say anything.

It came to her all at once. "Jesus, Taro, not the Iranians."

He didn't say anything.

"Taro, tell me it's not the Iranians. You don't have to tell me who it is, but tell me it's not the Iranians."

He didn't say anything.

"TARO!"

There was a rustling sound from outside, and Jessica heard the padlock over the latch on the front door pop open.

Chris stepped in, sunlight streaming in from behind him.

"Hey, gang," he said. "Miss me?"

When Taro was gone, Jessica looked at her watch. One-fifteen. She had less than three hours to figure out what she was going to do.

"Want some water?" Chris asked. He was sitting on the floor, injured leg sticking out awkwardly, his shirt soaked through with perspiration. He was holding out a big plastic bottle of Evian. "It's cold. I stopped at the 7-Eleven on the way back."

"No, thanks."

He patted the floor next to him. "Sit down."

"I'm all right."

"Come on . . ."

What did *he* want? Jessica pulled over a futon and sat down across from him. Chris said, "Good idea," and moved over next to her. He took a drink from the plastic bottle, letting water spill down the front of him. "It is so fucking hot," he said, leaning back now on his elbows. "You mind if I take my shirt off?"

"Go ahead," she said.

She watched him pull it over his head, the wet fabric cling-ing to his skin. Her heart was jumping in her chest. If Taro had called the Iranians, then Chris was dead. They were going to kill him and Ozawa and leave the two of them in the boathouse to rot. She was dead, too, and so was Taro. Once the Iranians found out how much money was in the safe—if they didn't know al-ready—all of them were dead.

She closed her eyes.

Heard Chris say, "You going to tell me about it?"

It made her flinch, eyes opening, blinking fast.

"What?" she said.

Chris wrung out his shirt, watching the water drip onto the floor. He said, "What Taro has planned for today."

He looked at her, a smile playing at the corners of his mouth.

"I heard some of it before I came in," he said. "Not much, mostly you yelling. I wasn't too surprised—I was expecting him to try something. I think I pushed the little prick too far." When she didn't say anything, he said: "The only question is when. Does he wait till the last minute? Or does he try something early?"

Jessica tried to speak, discovered it was too difficult to move her lips, get any sound to come out.

Chris shrugged. "You don't have to tell me. You want to go with Taro, that's your business. But I'm telling you, you're going to get screwed. Whatever he's got in mind."

He stood up, stretched.

"I'm not saying he'll do it on purpose. I mean, you're right, the guy's nuts about you. But face it, he's a stupid motherfucker. Yeah, I know, I cut off your finger. I'm an asshole. I'm a bastard."

He winked at her. "But you gotta admit it was a good idea. It's not like I wanted to do it. I didn't *enjoy* it. I thought it was the only way to make this work, and, I'm sorry, but I think I was right." He paused, hands on his hips, saying now: "What was I supposed to do? Ask you? 'Jessica, can I slice off your pinkie?' 'Sure, Chris go ahead.' "

"Four," Jessica said, blurting it out.

"Four what?"

Not sure why she was doing it, Jessica told him everything Taro had said to her, and what she was expecting. Chris listened, staring down at her, his chest glistening with sweat in the dim light.

When she was finished, he said: "Good. Be ready for anything after two o'clock."

At two-thirty, Chris went out to make a collection. Turning left out of the gravel road from the boathouse, he rode north, keeping close to the river. He was looking for something. He passed the big cement factory, then the fish market—the place almost deserted now, just a few guys in coveralls outside hosing down the loading ramps.

He turned right onto a small bridge and stopped at the top, looking over the low railing, the river maybe twenty feet below. He sat there, bike idling, for nearly ten minutes, looking at the river, the railing, sometimes turning his head to watch the streets on the either side of the bridge. There weren't many cars this way on a summer afternoon. The only person in sight was a homeless man in a heavy overcoat and sandals, shuffling across the sidewalk at the other end, poking his head into garbage cans.

Chris thought it was perfect.

Gunning the scooter's engine, he rode into the city. He picked up twelve million at a Chuo Bank Quick Lobby, another six at a Mizuho branch, and another six at Citibank. He stuffed the envelopes full of cash down the front of his shorts. They made a crinkling sound when he walked.

On his way back to the wharf, he stopped at a hardware store. He bought two heavy padlocks, a crowbar, and a pair of bolt cutters that was nearly as long as his arm. The clerk put everything in a bag, and Chris put the bag on the running board of the scooter, keeping it in place with his feet as he drove.

When he reached the bridge, it was five after three. He rode across it once, slowly, looking for passersby. He saw two kids playing around an abandoned boat with toy guns; otherwise, the area was deserted.

Chris didn't see any reason to wait. He parked the scooter at the top of the bridge and grabbed the bag from the hardware store. Walking down to the riverbank, his busted knee throbbing, he found a stack of rusted steel pipes overgrown with weeds. He hid the bag behind the pipes and clambered back up. Was at the top of the bridge again before he realized, shit, you could see the top of the bag poking out on the other side. He thought about going back down there, stuff the bag in deeper, but decided nobody was likely to mess with it in the next five or ten minutes.

Sticking the key in the ignition, Chris turned the scooter back on. He waited for a car to pass, then, putting the scooter nearly on its side, rammed it forward into the low railing. The impact jarred his arms; he almost lost control of the bike. Tiny sparks flew near his feet, the scooter's engine scraping against the concrete sidewalk. Grunting, he pulled the bike back and rammed it forward again. Then he shut off the engine.

He was stronger than he thought or the bike was a piece of shit. The paneling had crumpled inward on one side so that it was touching the front tire. The left-side mirror was shattered. The front blinker was cracked, the right-side paneling scraped raw. There were streaks of black paint on the sidewalk. Not bad. Chris looked around, see if anybody had noticed. The boys near the boat were looking over at him, mouths open. He waved. They waved back, hesitantly, jabbering at each other.

Putting the bike back upright, he sat down and turned the engine on. He let it idle for a minute, then rode to the end of the bridge. The scooter made an agreeable scraping sound. Chris parked it at the foot of the bridge and hid the keys under a Styrofoam cup next to the curb.

The sweat was running down his face and under the splint keeping his nose in place. It itched. He tried to ignore it, thinking about what he had to do next. He needed something with a rough surface. There. At the end of the guardrail was a concrete post about a meter high. Chris put his left forearm on top of it, then decided, no, it should be the right.

He closed his eyes, getting ready.

Bearing down, he pulled his forearm across the top of the post.

Managed to scrape off six inches of skin before he had to stop.

Then he bent down and did the same to the right side of his face.

Walking back up the bridge, he felt dizzy, face and arm sting-ing. Small droplets of blood mixed with sweat fell to the side-walk. He decided not to go all the way to the top and stopped about halfway. Reaching into his front pocket, he found the keys to the boathouse and to the safe. He threw them in the greenish-looking water. Up the river the boys near the boat were looking at him again. One of them aimed his gun at Chris and shouted: *"Gaijin-san! Bam! Bam!"*

Chris made a show of clutching at his heart, hearing the boys' laughter across the water. Heard them shout, finally, as he fell down on the railing and pitched forward into the river.

They were going to have a good story to tell their parents tonight.

Taro was saying, "He go somewhere, get a gun."

Jessica said, "Where is he going to get a gun?"

"Some kind weapon. Come back here, take the money."

"Chris wouldn't do that."

Only the thing was, maybe he *would*. Everything had gone so smoothly today that she had forgotten her concerns about him. Now, sitting in the boathouse, wiping the sweat from her forehead, Jessica realized she had no clue what Chris was going to do next. He wasn't the same person she had known in school. Actually, to get right down to it, he wasn't the same person she had known last *month*. This Chris seemed capable of anything.

"Maybe," she said, "he got lost coming back. He got lost before. Remember, he's only been in Japan three months."

That sounded weak even to her. She saw Taro shaking his

head, Taro running his fist against the wall. He looked at his watch. He seemed to think of something, turning to look at her.

"You told him," he said.

"No!"

"You told him. Now he's—" And stopped there, running his tongue along his upper lip, turning it over in his mind.

"Exactly," Jessica said, standing up. She brushed the dirt off the back of her shorts. "He's what? Chris doesn't know anybody here. You think he's rounding up a posse, bring them back here for a rumble with the Iranians? I don't think so." Saw the way Taro was looking at her and said, "I didn't tell him anything, goddammit! Fuck, I don't *know* anything!"

Suddenly, Taro held up his hand, motioning for her to be quiet. Jessica listened. Then she heard it, what sounded like the scooter, coming down the gravel path. The engine didn't sound right, like it was hitching. There was something else, too, a kind of scratching sound.

"Is that him?" Jessica whispered.

Taro put a finger to his lips. Looking around, he found the ceramic bowl they were using to give Ozawa water and handed it to her.

"What I am supposed to do with this?" she asked.

He gestured for her to stand on one side of the door. He stood at the other. Pointing at the bowl, he brought his hand down in a slashing motion.

"You have to be kidding," she said.

He wasn't kidding. Jessica watched him bend down and pull the butterfly knife from his sock and flip it open.

"Taro, for God's sake," she hissed. He wasn't supposed to have a knife. She and Chris had watched him throw the one into the van, but he must have been carrying another.

The scooter's engine cut and died. Jessica heard shoes crunching over gravel, a rattling of metal. Whoever it was stopped in front of the door. Jessica saw Taro tense, bringing the knife up.

"Guys?"

It was Chris.

Jessica let out a deep breath. "Where the fuck have you been?" she asked.

"It's a long story." He didn't sound good. "Listen, I'll tell you about it in a minute, but first, I lost the key to the lock on the front door."

"What?"

"I lost the goddamn key to the front-door lock. I'm going to have to break it open."

"How?" Taro asked.

"I bought some tools. Just give me a sec."

Jessica heard the sound of metal rattling again, then something scraping against the front door. She took a step back. Taro stayed where he was, knife still raised. Jessica heard Chris grunting, then shouting "Fuck!" as something big slammed into the door. "That was me," he said. "That was me. Hold on." He grunted again, and Jessica heard a distinct *pop*. "Little bastard," Chris said. "All right, I'm coming in."

When the door swung open, Taro made his move. Jessica shouted, "Don't!" but Taro raised his right arm, the one in the plaster cast, and shoved it into Chris's neck, forcing him back against the wall. Then with his left he brought the knife up to

Chris's face. Jessica saw a crowbar fall out of Chris's hand. He shouted, "You asshole, what are the fuck are you doing?" but Taro held him there, cast against his throat.

Taro frowned then, looking at him.

"Hey," Taro said. "What happened?"

Chris was soaking wet, some kind of greenish film all over him. He smelled like the inside of a sewer. The right side of his face was scraped raw, as was the length of his right arm.

"Jesus God, Chris," Jessica said.

"I had a fucking accident," Chris said. "Taro, you fuck, would you take that goddamn knife away and let me explain?"

Taro took his arm from against Chris's neck and backed away, keeping the blade extended. Chris stayed where he was, his back to the wall, glaring at him. "You paranoid piece of shit," Chris said. "I thought we said no weapons."

Taro didn't budge. "What happened?"

"I was coming back from the fucking bank," Chris said. "You know that bridge next to the fish market, the one that's not very big?"

Jessica remembered it vaguely. "Yeah, I think so."

"I'm coming across it, got the money in my shorts, not really paying attention. I hear this roar behind me. I look over my shoulder, and there are these two lowriders coming right at me."

"Christ," Jessica said.

"I don't know what they were doing. It was like they were racing or something. I don't have time to do shit. I jerk the scooter over to the right, up onto the sidewalk, but it doesn't help. One of the cars might have sideswiped me, I don't even know. All I know is that I don't have any control, and I'm heading right for the guardrail. I slam into it. The next thing I know I'm in the water."

Jessica put a hand to her mouth. "Did you hit your face on the way down?"

Chris sighed. "Yeah, I think my whole body fell against the side of the bridge. But I couldn't tell you for sure."

Taro said, "How did you get out?"

"What do you mean, how did I get out? I swam over to the flood wall, found a ladder, pulled myself out." He nodded in the direction of the knife. "Are you going to point that at me the rest of the day?"

Taro looked dubious, but he folded up the knife and put it in his pocket. Watching him made Jessica think of something. "Shit, what did you tell the police?"

Chris's laugh ended as a hacking, wet cough. "What police? I got back to the bridge, the two lowriders were gone. Nobody was around but a couple of kids poking at the bike. I just wanted to get out of there. I'm amazed that the scooter still works. Then I realized just before I came back that my pockets were empty. I lost the key to the boathouse lock, the lock on the safe, my room at the *gaijin* house."

"The money?" Taro asked.

"Like I said, that was stuck in my shorts." He pulled out the thick envelopes, water dripping from them onto the floor. He threw them at Taro. "The bills are a little wet, but they're all there if you want to count them."

"We believe you," Jessica said. She put her arms around him, giving him a hug. "Thank God you're not dead." Backed away then, wrinkling her nose. "Though you smell like it."

"Everything must get dumped in these rivers," Chris said. "I hope I don't get sick."

Jessica's eyes drifted to the crowbar on the floor. "You stopped somewhere on your way back, I assume?"

Chris nodded. "There's a hardware store a few blocks away. I picked up the crowbar, there's some other stuff in the bag outside. I didn't know what we would need to open the lock for the chain around the safe."

He glanced over at her then, meeting her eyes, not long enough for Taro to notice but long enough for her to realize that something was up, that it was starting, whatever Chris had planned. Was the accident story bullshit? The wounds on his face and arms were real enough. Jessica started trembling all over, not able to stop, all of the sudden scared to death. Realizing that he had probably scraped the skin off his face himself . . .

"Hey, Jessica." Taro put his arms around her. "Hey, you okay?"

"Yeah." She bit the inside of her lip hard enough to draw blood. It helped her calm down. "Sorry. Scared all of a sudden."

"Just a little while longer," he whispered.

Which gave her the shakes all over again.

Chris had gotten the bag from outside and stepped back in, closing the door. "We're really behind," he said, picking up the crowbar. "We gotta get this safe open right now. Taro, when was the last time you talked to Sato?"

Taro looked at his watch. "Twenty minutes before."

"All right." Chris was in front of the safe. "The bolt cutters, I think. Here, hold this."

He gave Taro the crowbar and pulled out the biggest pair of bolt cutters Jessica had ever seen. He snapped them open and closed, testing them. Fitting the blades around a link of chain, he started to squeeze. Jessica heard him say, "Fuck me." She didn't see him say it; she was looking at Taro now, his hands wrapped around the crowbar, his eyes staring down at it like it was somehow alive. When he lifted it off the ground, she got over there fast, putting her hand on his, shaking her head and mouthing *Later.* Christ, not sure what you were supposed to do in a situation like this.

The chain broke with a sound like a pencil snapping. Chris grinned at them over his shoulder. "Got it," he said, panting.

The Ritual was next. Jessica and Taro turned around, waiting for Chris to spin the dial. When he was finished, it was Jessica's turn. For a second, her mind was blank: all she could think of was that it was almost four o'clock. Whatever Chris was planning, he had to do it fast. Jessica was no longer sure what she wanted. She wanted it over, she supposed, but that was going to happen no matter what.

Finally remembering the number, she spun the dial to the left, then back to zero on the right. When she stood up, Taro handed her the crowbar.

"Hold this," he said.

She turned around, Taro squatting down behind her. She looked over at Chris, who nodded at her. He was mouthing the word *Now.* Now? she wanted to say. Now, what? But then, before she knew what was happening, he had his hands clamped over hers gripping the crowbar, spinning her around. She heard him shout, "Bring it up! Bring it up!" and instinctively she did, raising the hard length of iron, seeing Taro's head tilt up and back, Taro saying something she didn't hear just before she and Chris brought the crowbar down hard on the top of his head.

Taro's head split open with a satisfying *crack!* Chris heard Jessica screaming in his ear, her body twisting out from under him. He let go of her hands and the crowbar clattered to the floor. Taro slumped forward, and Chris saw his body pushing the door of the safe closed. He lunged for it, knocking Taro over on his side and catching the door just in time.

Taro was moaning, blood beginning to pool under his head. Jessica was still screaming, hands up near her mouth, backing away. Chris got over there before she had a chance to bolt, slapping her across the face and telling her to calm down.

"Him or us, Jessica," he said. "Him or us." She screamed again and he slapped her again, her head snapping over and rolling to the side. He shook her. "Are you listening to me?" he shouted. "We've got about ten minutes to get out of here."

That seemed to help her come out of it. She blinked twice, bending her head to look at her watch.

"That's right," he said. "Three-forty-five. We may not have enough time as it is." He saw her eyes drifting and shook her. "Jessica?"

The eyes came back. "What?"

"I bought some more stuff when I was out. It's over next to the scooter outside. Can you go out there and bring it in? I need to start getting the money in one of our bags."

"Is he dead?" she asked, looking over at Taro.

Christ. "Listen to him, for God's sake."

Taro moaned again. Jessica said, "I can hear him."

"See? He's not dead. Come on, hurry up and get the stuff outside."

"Okay."

Chris waited until she had staggered out the door before taking the black Donna Karan skirt out of her bag. Using it to cover his hands, he picked up the crowbar on the floor, careful to hold it close to the middle.

He didn't want to smudge Jessica's fingerprints.

Chris had been thinking about their situation for some time. The problem was, he still could not come up with a good way to get Jessica out of this. Leaving her with Ozawa was out of the question—what if he didn't forgive her? Having her disappear, even if they got Ozawa to somehow think she was dead, wasn't going to work either. Jessica wasn't going to be able to live quietly in some corner of the world. She was the party girl. She needed too much attention. One day she'd slip up, the word would get back to Ozawa, and that would be the beginning of the end. Chris would be looking over his shoulder the rest of his life. No thanks.

Taro's eyes fluttered open as Chris walked over there. Chris said, "What, not dead yet?" and brought the crowbar down on his skull. Not as hard as the first time—it was hard to get enough power, holding the shaft in the middle—but it shut Taro up. Chris brought the crowbar down again, a half-dozen times, watching Taro's scalp turn to jelly. He heard Jessica shouting from outside, "Where is it?"

"Keep looking," he yelled.

Until recently, every foreigner in Japan with a registration card had been fingerprinted. Jessica had; Chris had seen the card. The police would find the crowbar and match the fingerprints against their records and that would be it: Jessica Romano would be charged with the murder of Taro Shimada.

Of course, fingerprints weren't always as clear as they needed to be. And if they ever got Jessica in custody, she'd have an interesting story to tell.

When he was sure the little fucker was dead, Chris reached in Taro's pockets and pulled out the butterfly knife.

Much easier for the police, he thought, to come to the scene and find two bodies: Taro with his head beaten to a pulp, Jessica fatally stabbed . . . where? He'd have to think of someplace believable. He wondered if the police would fall for it, Jessica and Taro killing each other, then realized it didn't matter. Who cared what the police believed? They wouldn't be able to pin anything on him, that was the important thing. They wouldn't be able to *find* him. He was a tourist. There were no records on him anywhere in Japan, except for his disembarkation card at the airport. Officially, he practically didn't exist.

Chris heard Jessica scream outside.

"Oh, man," he said. He looked at his watch. "Taro, you bastard, you didn't really call the Iranians did you?"

Fuck, if he *did* . . .

The door flew open. The first thing Chris saw was Jessica being pushed inside, a hand covering her mouth.

The second thing he saw . . .

They weren't Iranian.

Four years ago, the *oyabun* had told Mutsuo Kawaguchi what to do in the event of a kidnapping: let it play out until the situation was clear, until something happened that left little doubt as to what would happen next. Watching the tall white foreigner Chris Ryan throw himself off the bridge, Kawaguchi figured that was it.

He called Tanaka and told him to move the men forward and have them wait along the wall at the edge of the electrical plant. Then, using his wife's Toyota, Kawaguchi went to the plant himself, to the foreman's office. Inside, he watched the dilapidated boathouse through binoculars, sweating in his gray Hugo Boss suit and wishing he was at the board meeting that he was scheduled to disrupt today. The gun in the waistband of his pants was digging into his hips. When was the last time he had used it? He couldn't remember. Nineteen seventy-something.

Ryan puttered down the gravel road at three-thirty. Kawaguchi saw him park in the weeds and take the white bag over to the door. Watched him standing there, talking, water dripping from his hair, now pulling the black crowbar out of the bag and breaking the cheap padlock on the door.

When he was inside, Kawaguchi called down to Tanaka again and told him to get the men on either side of the boathouse. Quietly, he said. He watched as a few of the younger guys, hair down to their shoulders and wearing wraparound sunglasses, climbed over the wall and moved in. Then Kawaguchi left the office and hurried to get down there himself.

He had known the *oyabun* was in the boathouse since early that morning. It was only through sheer luck and savvy that they had found him at all. The luck: Ozawa getting hold of the cell phone three days earlier. The savvy: the *oyabun* knowing how to use the few moments he had to maximum effect.

He'd said he couldn't talk very well. That his throat was sore and he needed his lozenges. Miss Romano was with him. She'd said they were in some sort of old building, maybe on Port Island in Kobe. Wherever it was, they were right next to the water; Ozawa said he could smell herring and other fish. The Romano woman claimed it was Sato behind the kidnapping. Watch him, Ozawa said, but keep it quiet. Pay the ransom, and when everything was done, then he and Kawaguchi could clean things up. He asked Kawaguchi to tell his wife and two boys that he was all right. Then he hung up.

It was a masterpiece. Long ago they'd worked out code words

for just such an event, but Ozawa had incorporated them so seamlessly into the conversation that Kawaguchi was still marveling. "I can't talk very well." That one was obvious. He suspected something. A trick, or someone listening in. "I need my lozenges." *Nodo ame. Ame* also meant "rain." It was raining where he was. And he did not want to say so directly, which meant it was somehow something his captors had overlooked. "I can smell herring and other fish." *Nishin* and other *sakana*. *Nishin* meant "herring," but *nishi* meant "west." *Sakana* was their code word for "Osaka." So Ozawa thought he was in West Osaka, not Port Island. Which also meant the Romano woman was wrong at best, lying at worst. "Tell my wife and two boys that I'm all right." He had identified a woman and two men. Romano was the woman. Who were the men? In any case, there were only three people involved that Ozawa was sure of.

As soon as the *oyabun* was off the line, Kawaguchi checked the weather in Port Island. It wasn't raining. Kawaguchi wasn't sure how Ozawa had known that, but there it was. He was definitely not in Port Island, nor anywhere in Kobe. However, it *was* raining in West Osaka. And "right next to the water" plus the "smell" of fish couldn't be far from the central port.

After that it was easy. True, there had been a few territorial issues to resolve with the other gangs—a little tricky, with the *oyabun*'s kidnapping still a secret—but by and large the Ono-*gumi* controlled the waterfront. Finding the boathouse was just a matter of manpower and gradual elimination.

Interestingly, the place was owned by a Japanese woman known to be associated with a gang of Iranians. Kawaguchi hated Iranians. Dirty, violent, unpredictable—they weren't as bad as the Chinese, but bad enough. He'd sent a group over to the tenements where they lived to see if they were involved. Two hours later, he was talking to their leader, Khatani, over the phone. The man sounded broken, saying over and over again in a raspy voice that it wasn't his fault, that the Filipino had broken into the boathouse and he had known nothing about it. Kawaguchi said, what do you mean, "had known"? That was how he learned about Taro Shimada's plan to double-cross Ryan.

The Iranians were dead thirty minutes later. Right now they were in black plastic bags on a garbage scow headed for Hase Island in the Inland Sea.

Tanaka wanted to move on the boathouse immediately. Kawaguchi said no. First, there was the Sato problem. Ozawa had indicated that Romano was wrong or lying about their location, but not about Sato. Which meant the *oyabun* didn't know. Kawaguchi had placed Sato had under immediate surveillance. He had yet to go to the boathouse or meet with Romano, Shimada, or Ryan; but that was hardly conclusive evidence. It seemed inconceivable to Kawaguchi for Sato to be involved with the three of them; still, these days you never could tell. Sato was a throwback. Not a psychopath like some of the new kids, but a genuine throwback to an older type of *yakuza*. Sato wanted the tattoos and the gang wars and the old codes of the underworld. But those days were gone, and as far as Kawaguchi was concerned, good riddance.

It was the eighties that had changed things, the speculative boom that had made the whole of Tokyo more expensive on paper than the entire United States. The banks were throwing money at everyone, and Ozawa *oyabun* and the other bosses had taken the opportunity to move their business interests aboveground. When the bubble collapsed, the gangs were worth trillions of yen and had stakes in some of the biggest companies in the country. Kawaguchi now sat on the boards of a dozen legit companies and was a silent partner in a hundred more. Why waste time collecting hundred-thousand-yen loans from deadbeat individuals when you could steal billions from deadbeat corporations? But Sato still didn't see the beauty of it.

Then there was the *oyabun* himself; that was the other reason Kawaguchi told Tanaka to stay put. Years ago, when the Zeniya opportunity had presented itself, the *oyabun* had sat Kawaguchi down and told him what he was going to do and where it might lead. Kawaguchi had begged him not to, but the *oyabun* was adamant. "Remember," he said, "what I always used to say? When we were starting to move into the straight industries? That we were going to make so much money we'd regret it? Well, I do. What's the point of being *yakuza* if you have to sit through meetings with accountants like anybody else?" The *oyabun* was a bit of a throwback himself.

Now, moving in toward the boathouse, Kawaguchi wondered if the *oyabun* still felt the same way. Forgot it then, hearing the Romano woman scream. He drew his gun, watched the other men do the same. He saw Tanaka wave them to the side, where they crouched down and waited. Peeking from around a corner, Kawaguchi saw the Romano woman stumble outside, looking like she was in shock. He watched her run to the scooter, head down, searching for something. Heard her shout "Where is it?" Kawaguchi thought there wouldn't be a better time. He nodded at Tanaka and whispered "Go" into his lapel.

She heard them first, head popping up like a frightened rabbit. Then she saw them, twelve men in black suits and sunglasses surrounding her, and she screamed again, the woman with a good set of lungs. Kawaguchi told Mori to shut her up, and the burly ex-wrestler butted her in the mouth with his gun, knocking her to the ground. She whimpered, and he grabbed her arms, pulling her up and putting his hand over her mouth. Kawaguchi motioned for them to go in, use the woman as a shield.

Mori put her in front of him and kicked the door in. Six of the younger men moved inside almost at once. Kawaguchi heard the sound of guns being cocked. He shouted for them not to fire. He heard the sound of something cracking and a garbled cry that could not have been from the woman. Then it was Mori, yelling that the building was secure.

Kawaguchi stepped inside, trying not to brush against anything with his suit. He had to stop almost immediately, recoiling from the wave of heat and body odor. Taking off his sunglasses, he pinched his nose, squinting in the dim light.

Mori had the Romano woman on her knees, sobbing quietly in what looked like a pool of blood. The blood seemed to be from a prone figure about a meter away. It was the Filipino. His head looked misshapen; it took Kawaguchi a minute to realize that it had been bludgeoned. Next to the body was a crowbar, perhaps the same one Ryan had used to open the lock on the boathouse door.

Ryan himself was slumped against the far wall, next to an open safe with packets of bills inside. He appeared to be unconscious, blood dribbling down his face from the most broken nose Kawaguchi had ever seen.

"Did you . . . ?" he asked, gesturing at Kanno, who was standing next to Ryan. Kanno was flexing his right hand. The hand was bloody.

"It was mostly like that already," Kanno said.

"Mostly?"

Kanno shrugged.

The *oyabun* was in a corner, tied up in his underwear on a filthy *tatami* mat. He looked like death, head wrapped in bandages, gauze mask over his mouth. His arms and legs were black with dirt. Tanaka was hovering over him, using a skeleton key to open the cuffs around the *oyabun*'s ankles and hands. Kawaguchi moved to help him.

"He's alive," Tanaka said. "His pulse is strong."

"Take the mask and bandages off, but be careful."

In the oppressive heat of the boathouse, the bandages clung to the *oyabun*'s skin. He moaned as Tanaka gingerly tried to pull them off. Kawaguchi told him to do it all at once, get it over with. Tanaka jerked his hand back, and there was a loud ripping sound as the bandages came off, some of the *oyabun*'s facial hair and skin coming off with them. His eyes opened and he blinked rapidly, pupils coming into focus and resting on Kawaguchi. The *oyabun*'s head jerked back.

"Just another minute," Kawaguchi said gently.

But the *oyabun*'s hands—the left one bandaged—were already coming up and pushing him away. Kawaguchi stepped back as the *oyabun* ripped the gauze mask off his face and pulled the tape away from his mouth. He spat out a small plastic ball.

"Water," he rasped.

Tanaka snapped his fingers, looking back at the men. "Bring him something."

Kawaguchi saw them look at one another. Nobody had thought to bring water. One of them, Suzuki, small and wiry with a shaved head, picked up a bottle from a bag near his feet and looked at it, lips pursed.

"What is it?" Kawaguchi asked.

"I'm not sure," Suzuki said.

"Taste it!"

Suzuki opened the cap and took a drink. Nodded then, wiping his lips and passing the bottle to Kawaguchi. Kawaguchi gave it to the *oyabun,* watched him close his eyes and put the bottle to his lips. He gasped once, drank some more. Then he let the bottle fall to floor and gestured to Kawaguchi and Tanaka.

"Help me up," he said.

Jessica did not feel afraid.

She didn't feel much of anything, except for a throbbing pain in her jaw where the big guy in the black suit had hit her. She supposed she was in shock. Sensory overload. There were tears streaming down the sides of her face, but she hardly noticed them. Taro was dead on the floor next to her, his skull caved in. Chris was out cold against the wall. And now Ozawa was getting to his feet. He staggered forward a few steps. Turned around. One of his men, in his fifties maybe, with short-cropped silver hair, offered him a jacket. Ozawa shrugged him off.

He turned, saw her.

Shuffled over to her, pain making the lines in his face stretch and deepen. Jessica saw him wave his hand slightly, and the big guy behind her pulled her to her feet.

Ozawa reached out, took her face in his hands.

Smiled.

"Beautiful," he said in English.

Somehow Chris had the presence of mind not to open his eyes when he came to. He didn't see the hurry. He doubted there was anything around him he really wanted to see.

These guys weren't Iranians. They were *yakuza;* Chris was sure. He could hear them now, barking at each other in Japanese. How had they found them? The fact that they had shown up right at four led Chris to suspect that Taro had called them, Taro maybe a gangster from the very beginning. Except that didn't make sense. Chris moaned involuntarily. It was so hard to think. It felt like what was left of his nose had been driven up into his brain.

He noticed then that everything had gotten very quiet. It made him wonder if the *yakuza* had left. Maybe they thought he was dead and had gone home. That was a nice idea; he held on to it for as long as he could. Then thought maybe there was blood in his ears, and that was why he didn't hear anything. No, wait. He did hear something. Footsteps, maybe. Somebody walking across the room. Not moving very well, whoever it was. Chris heard something else then that he couldn't make out at all. Maybe there *was* blood in his ears.

Somebody said, "Beautiful."

He heard that. *Beautiful.* That was English. English, and it was a *man's* voice. The first thing Chris thought was that he had said the word himself somehow without thinking. The state he was in, he couldn't discount it. But why would he have said the word *beautiful*?

The next thing he thought was that Taro had said it. Only Taro was dead. Chris thought he was dead. Suddenly he wasn't sure. Maybe that's why the room had gone silent, everybody watching Taro get to his feet, nobody believing it. That was why the footsteps were so weak, Taro having a hard time staying on his feet. Jesus, like something out of Stephen King. How many times had Chris hit him? Half a dozen? He had seen the guy's *brain*.

Chris didn't think there was any choice now. He had to open his eyes. If Taro was alive, he had to see it. If *Taro* was alive, shit, maybe there was some hope for him, too.

Jessica heard Chris say, "Taro?" She looked over at him, saw him blinking, not sure where he was. Saw his eyes focus on Ozawa then and watched him flinch. The *yakuza* standing next to Chris pressed down on his shoulder to keep him from standing up. Chris groaned and threw up on the man's shoes. The *yakuza* jumped back in disgust. There was a murmuring in Japanese; Jessica thought she heard a gun being cocked. Ozawa said something, loud. Everybody shut up at once. She turned to look at him.

The silver-haired one was handing Ozawa a gun. Jessica felt

herself shaking; the numbness was starting to wear off. Ozawa ejected the clip and looked inside. He said something in Japanese to the silver-haired man and laughed at the response. Then he put the clip back in the gun; Jessica heard it click home. Holding the gun at his side, Ozawa walked over to the safe and sat down on top of it. He looked at Jessica, holding up his bandaged left hand.

"Who cut my finger?" he asked. Keeping his eyes on her, he raised the gun and pointed it at Chris. "Him?"

Jessica shook her head. She was trembling all over now.

"Who?" Ozawa asked.

"Taro," Jessica whispered.

"Taro?"

Jessica pointed at Taro's body on the floor. Seeing him lying there, face-down in his own blood, she retched.

Ozawa stood up, shuffled over to the body. He aimed the gun at Taro's lower body and shot him. Taro twitched like a rag doll. Jessica shrieked. Ozawa looked at her. "Why did he cut my finger?" he asked.

Jessica was crying and screaming at the same time. The big guy holding her up hit her on the back of the head. Ozawa yelled something at him, pointing the gun at him over Jessica's shoulder. She felt the guy stiffen and she bit her tongue. Heaving, she spit blood on the floor.

Ozawa stood in front of her. Raising her chin with his forefinger he said gently, "Why did Taro cut my finger?"

"I don't know," Jessica said between sobs. "Sato said something."

"Sato?"

"Something on the phone this morning. Taro got mad. Took out the knife."

Ozawa barked something in Japanese, and two of the men left the boathouse. He sat back down on the safe, looking pensive. He asked the silver-haired man a question. The silver-haired man bowed stiffly and said *"Hai."* Ozawa barked something else, and two more men left.

He didn't say anything after that. He held up his hands to his face, turned them front to back. Unwrapped the bandage around what was left of his little finger and looked at the stump. Finally he said, "Do you know how old am I?"

He glanced over at Jessica.

"No?" he asked. "Sixty-five years old. I am *yakuza* all my life and never lose any finger." He spat on the floor. "Sato. *Aho ka kora.* Idiot. You want to watch me kill him?"

Jessica was crying softly now, body limp. She shook her head.

"Yes," Chris said from the corner.

Ozawa looked over at him.

"Boyfriend?" he asked Jessica.

Jessica shook her head again. She didn't feel capable of doing anything else.

"Jessica-*chan.*" Ozawa sighed. Smiled lightly. "You know, I'm impressed. I felt not sure you could do it."

The *yakuza* around her were murmuring. It was probably the first time most of them had heard Ozawa speak English. Jessica was too exhausted to ask him what he was talking about.

"Take me, how do you say? Kidnap?" Ozawa asked. "Then try to say it's Sato's plan? That was very clever." He beamed. "And the finger! Wonderful!" He gestured to the man holding her up and Jessica felt her left hand come up. Watched Ozawa squint in the direction of the stump, marveling. He asked:

"It's your idea?"

Jessica didn't know what to say. She opened her mouth, closed it again.

Heard Chris against the wall say, "Why?"

Ozawa looked over his shoulder at him. He seemed amused. "You mean Zeniya?" he asked.

"Who is he?"

"This one, it's funny. *Omoshiroi,*" Ozawa said. "There is real Zeniya. President of Daijo, one company. My group owns stock there. He didn't know it. One day, he understand, be angry. He went to police." Ozawa chuckled at that, the guy getting caught up in his own story. He said something to the *yakuza* standing next to him. The *yakuza* pulled out a pack of Lucky Sevens and handed it to him. Ozawa tapped out a cigarette. Looking at the box, he said to Jessica: " 'Lucky Seven.' You know that song? PAP?" When Jessica looked at him blankly, he said, "I like it, that song."

The silver-haired man lighted Ozawa's cigarette. He drew on it sharply, then exhaled a puff of smoke. "The police tell me about this guy. I think somebody have to talk to him. Always, another person does that kind of thing these days, not me. But I felt, how can I say? Boring? All day, meetings, meetings, meetings. So I did it myself. I went to his house, talk to him. You saw his house. It's nice, don't you think?" Looked for a reaction. "No? *Tonikaku,* anyway, I see him for the first time," Ozawa said, drawing on the cigarette again, "and it was strange. He looks like me. Same old, same tall. He has house, nice family, good company. I thought, how different, his life?"

Ozawa glanced at Jessica, grinning, showing her his teeth.

"Suddenly I had one interesting idea," Ozawa said. "You can guess. Ozawa is *yakuza oyabun*. He can't do anything. Sit in front of bodyguards, go to meetings, meetings, meetings."

Against the far wall, Chris started laughing. He choked, spitting up blood. "That's it?" he asked. "You pretended to be Zeniya, using his business card, getting a driver's license in his name, bringing chicks to his house, because you were *bored*?" He laughed again.

Ozawa laughed, too. "Why not?" Then his face turned serious. "It is difficult to be *yakuza* these days. No challenge. Always *yakuza* say, 'We are weak, we are not strong,' but"—he shrugged—"now we have too much money. Go to meetings all the time, talk to politicians. It's not so interesting."

"Zeniya's life?" Chris asked.

Ozawa laughed again. "To tell the truth, more boring. I start to think, how can his life be interesting?"

"And here we are," Chris said.

"Yes," Ozawa said. "Much more interesting." He turned around on the safe, facing Chris for the first time. "How did you do it?"

"Kidnap you?" Chris asked. "You really want to know?"

Jessica felt her mouth opening, sound coming out. "Chris, don't."

"Why not?" Chris said. He coughed, blood spraying out of his nose. Groaned. "My very own James Bond talking villain scene, only in reverse."

Ozawa perked up. "Zero zero seven?"

"Listen," Chris said, and told Ozawa what happened, not

from the beginning but from the love hotel: the video they made for the wife, the drive to the Zeniyas', the escape to the boathouse, Taro's attempted double cross. Jessica watched Ozawa listening, head cocked, smile playing on his lips. When Chris was finished, Ozawa turned and asked the silver-haired man a question in Japanese. Then he shook his head.

"One week," Ozawa said in English. "One week *more*." He looked up at Jessica. "You know real Zeniya never say anything to my *saiko komon* about your video?"

"Imagine that," Chris said. "You think maybe he doesn't like you?"

"Maybe not," Ozawa said. He was still looking at Jessica. "What should I do about that, do you think?"

Bringing down the gun, Ozawa shot Taro in the head. Blood spattered up onto the safe and onto Jessica's legs. She screamed, a hand clamping over her mouth. "You know," Ozawa said, "I have a interesting idea." He shot Taro again, this time between the shoulder blades. Taro was starting to deflate like a punctured tire. Ozawa didn't seem to notice. He hopped off the safe and peered inside, fingering the packets of bills. "How much money did you get?" he asked.

Jessica was blubbering again. She had wet herself, a warm trickle running down the side of her leg.

Ozawa looked over his shoulder at her. "How much?"

"Three hundred," she said, the words coming out in bubbles, "Three hundred and forty, three hundred and fifty."

"Three hundred and fifty million," Ozawa said. He looked at the ceiling, scratching his head with the butt of the gun. Then he looked at her again, eyes bright. "I'll give you," he said.

Jessica heard Chris say, "What?"

"Not all," Ozawa said. "One hundred twenty. In dollars, same as I promise you before."

Ozawa held the gun out in front of her.

"If," he said, "you kill your friend."

The *yakuza* were murmuring again, looking at the gun. Chris was saying something else, louder now. Jessica didn't hear him. Ozawa said something to the man holding her up, then said it again, shouting. He let her go. She swayed slightly but stayed on her feet.

"What?" she asked, staring dumbly at the gun.

"Kill him," Ozawa said, gesturing at Chris.

Jessica looked over at Chris, struggling to get up. The *yakuza* next to him was holding him down.

Looked back at Ozawa.

"Kill Chris?" Jessica asked dully.

"Yes," Ozawa said. Then: "No! Wait! More interesting!" He clapped his hands together. "Kill your friend, and take the money. Or, *leave* the money and both of you are free."

He was grinning like a madman, chapped lips cracked and oozing blood. He thrust the gun into Jessica's hands. She let it rest on her palms. It was hot.

Against the far wall, Chris had stopped struggling. "You'll let us both go?" he asked.

"Sure," Ozawa said.

"If Jessica leaves the money."

"Yes."

"Well," Chris said, "that's an obvious choice."

Jessica stared at the gun for a long time, Ozawa standing in front of her. She had stopped shaking. Looking up, she suddenly realized how ridiculous Ozawa looked, a little old man in his dirty underwear. She laughed. "What if I just kill *you*?" she asked.

He nodded, considering it. "You could," he said. "Of course, then both of you will die."

"We're both going to die anyway."

"No no," he said. "Didn't you listen to my talking?"

"I don't believe your talking," she said.

"About what?" he asked.

"All of it. You're not going to let me go no matter what I do." The grin was back. "Maybe I will. Who can know?"

Chris was saying, somewhere far away, "Why are you debating this with him? Jessica?"

Ozawa said, "You see? It's interesting, don't you think?"

Putting her right hand around the grip, Jessica held the gun, feeling its heft. She had never held a pistol before. She had fired a rifle once, at her uncle's farm in Maine. This gun felt heavier. In the background, Chris was shouting at her; she no longer heard him. She put her finger on the trigger. She felt absolutely calm.

Chris was right.

It *was* an obvious choice.